HER HUSBAND

Verity Stratton was forced by the demands of her family and the pressures of society to wed the Marquess of Unger, a husband whom she alone among all the young ladies of London's marriage mart did not wish to have.

AND HER HERO

It was worship at first sight when Verity met Alan Parry, the author whose romances had intoxicated her imagination, and whose dark good looks and dazzling intellect completed his conquest of her awestruck admiration.

One man held title to Verity's hand. The other held sway over her mind. And now she had to choose which one should have her heart. . . .

A Novel Alliance

Delightful Regency Romances from SIGNET

A
Novel Alliance

Ellen Fitzgerald

A SIGNET BOOK

NEW AMERICAN LIBRARY

Copyright © 1984 by Ellen Fitzgerald

SIGNET, SIGNET CLASSIC, MENTOR, PLUME, MERIDIAN AND
NAL BOOKS are published by New American Library,
1633 Broadway, New York, New York 10019

First Printing, December, 1984

1   2   3   4   5   6   7   8   9

PRINTED IN THE UNITED STATES OF AMERICA

Part One

One

Lady Verity Stratton, blue eyes wrathful, stood on a small platform in the middle of the sewing room at Harcliffe Manor, wondering if the dressmaker would ever finish pinning up her hem. It seemed to her that Miss Micklestane was sticking the pins in slowly and viciously as if she were torturing the cloth. Of course, it was not the material that was proving so irksome, it was the fact that the woman had been hired only to make the costume Verity would wear while traveling to London.

The wardrobe for her first London season would be designed by her grandmother's favorite mantua maker. Fortunately, the offended Miss Micklestane would not be wanting for work. As usual, she would be sewing for Lady Caroline and Lady Eva Stratton, who, much to their combined ire, would not be joining their elder sister in London.

" 'Tis as much as I can do to have one of you on my hands," Lady Harcliffe had said coldly. "I'll not be saddled with three females. I've not the place to put you."

That, of course, was a gross exaggeration. Her grandmother's townhouse was immense. There was a family legend to the effect that some of its rooms had never been opened. The Dowager Countess of Harcliffe's chief pleasures were faro and piquet. She resented every moment spent away from the card table, especially on what she crossly characterized as "my late son's brood of wenches."

Verity grimaced. She wished her sisters rather than she might have the dubious pleasure of being their grandmother's guest. The excitement of going to London was mitigated by fears that the purpose behind the visit might spell the end of her flourishing literary life. Unknown to her grandmother or her sisters, she was a published authoress. She had written her first novel at thirteen, her second at fourteen, and her third at sixteen. While these effusions had entertained Caroline and Eva, they had not been told that the third, entitled *The Scandal*, and loosely based on gossip concerning a noble family in the district, had been purchased by the Minerva Press.

"Pray do not fidget," snapped Miss Micklestane.

"I am sorry." Verity stood still, thinking indignantly that the dressmaker was deliberately prolonging her ordeal. Generally, she worked hastily, but now, sensing Verity's impatience, she was being contrary as if to pay her back for all the fashionable ensembles she would not be creating. Of course, that might not be what was motivating her, but it was an intriguing notion. It might serve for a character inhabiting some future novel, an envious dressmaker who deliberately makes the heroine's gown too tight. When she wears it to the Assembly Rooms, it tears and she must dash to a chair and sit out all the dances!

"Ah!" Verity exclaimed, hoping she could remember this idea until she escaped to the library and her notebook.

"Did I stick you?" Miss Micklestane inquired.

"No, I was just thinking."

"Of London, no doubt," the dressmaker commented acidly. "Well, I pray you'll not be disappointed. To my mind it's an ugly crowded city, and so noisy! A body can't hear herself think what with all the peddlers screaming their wares on every corner and the jumble of traffic in the streets and people hurrying every which way and the dust in the air from the sea coal they burn, enough to choke one. However, the young never mind that sort of thing, and, of course, you'll be dwelling near the Park, where it's pleasant. There, I'm done!" She rose stiffly. "I'll be finishing the hem shortly, and if you'll send your abigail to me an hour hence, she'll be able to iron it." She looked out the window. "I hope you'll have a fair day for your journey. Last September was, as I recall, a very rainy month. There are quite a few clouds in the sky at present."

"They were there yesterday, as well, but it didn't rain," Verity said cheerfully.

"We can but hope for the best," Miss Micklestane replied

in the gloomy accents of one who expects the worst. "It's a great shame your poor dear mama cannot see you, and your papa, too."

"Yes." Verity mentally added to the characterization of her fictitious dressmaker. In common with Miss Micklestane, she would be wanting to ruin the heroine's pleasure at her forthcoming visit to the city.

In her own character, she longed to tell the woman that her late parents would probably have been in agreement that the launching of their eldest daughter in society would be a dead bore. Arabella Stratton, a beauty, would have loathed the idea of being known as the mother of an eighteen-year-old daughter. Verity's father, Lord Harcliffe, would have been profoundly indifferent. If Miss Micklestane had hoped to fill her with retrospective sorrow for the curricle accident which her father could have avoided had he driven down an unfamiliar road at a sensible speed, she was unsuccessful.

With considerable relief, she divested herself of the new traveling ensemble and slipped into the old blue round gown she wore at home. After an exchange of farewells, insincerely lachrymose on the part of the dressmaker, Verity hurried down the stairs to the library.

She was inscribing her notions of the last hour in her notebook when there was a tap on the door. She looked up in annoyance, knowing that her visitor must be either Caroline or Eva. "Yes?" she called reluctantly.

"I looked for you in the sewing room." Caroline bounced into the library and sank down in a chair near the desk. "Miss Micklestane was more prune-faced than ever. Oh, she is so angry at Grandmother for not letting her have the fashioning of your new gowns. I am angry at Grandmother, too. I should have been allowed to come with you. I'm nearly seventeen. I don't see why I have to remain in the schoolroom. I'm not learning anything. Miss Marshall thinks the only one of us who has any intelligence is you. She has made that very clear!"

"I believe Miss Marshall said that if you'd study, you'd do very well, and Eva, also."

"Ugh." Caroline screwed her pretty features into a most fearsome frown. "I don't want to study. I want to dance and

meet handsome bucks and Corinthians. Do you suppose you'll
be married by the end of the Season?''

Verity winced and stared down at her notebook. Her possible marriage was a favorite topic with her sisters. They were
sure that once she arrived in London, she would be snatched
up willy-nilly whether she liked it or not. She could not like it.
She did not want to marry. Though she could not hope to
achieve such eminence, her favorite novelist was Jane Austen,
and that lady lived unwed while happily writing her wonderful novels. She said defiantly, ''I have no intention of marry-
ing at all.''

''We'll see what Grandmama says to that,'' Caroline laughed.

''She cannot force me to it,'' Verity cried.

''Can she not? From all accounts, Mama did not want to
marry Papa, but she did. The matter was arranged between
their parents. They had met but once. That's the way it
always is with us, Verity. You know that. I'd not repine, if I
were you. Afterwards, when you are a married lady, you'll
be able to have lovers. Mama did.''

''Lady Caroline! You are not to repeat such ugly slander!''
exclaimed a deep voice behind her.

Caroline looked over her shoulder and paled. ''Miss
Marshall,'' she yelped, staring in horror at the lady who
stood just inside the door she had heedlessly left ajar.

Verity, on the other hand, smiled warmly at the governess,
whom she had been expecting. In her late thirties or early
forties, Miss Marshall was tall and thin to the point of
gauntness. Her mousy brown hair was neatly braided and half
hidden under a plain lawn cap. Though her forehead was too
high, her nose too prominent, and her mouth too wide, her
eyes, dark brown and deep-set under winged brows, were so
bright and so intelligent that they more than made up for her
lack of beauty. Generally, they were alight with humor and
compassion, but at present, her gaze was glacial. ''You are
speaking of your mother,'' she continued. ''And certainly she
deserves your respect.''

''Everyone knows . . .'' Caroline began sulkily.

''Everyone knows nothing,'' snapped the governess.
''You've been listening to gossip, which is bad enough—but
to repeat it is . . . well, it leaves me without words. You will

please go directly to the schoolroom and write 'I will honor my mother and father' twenty-five times on the blackboard.''

"But that will take forever, and it's Verity's last day!" wailed Caroline, her gray-blue eyes filled with fury.

"Twenty-five times in readable handwriting, Lady Caroline."

"You . . . have no right," Caroline burst out. She jumped out of the chair. "I am not a child . . . I am nearly seventeen!"

"And in consequence should not act like a hoyden and repeat gossip learned, no doubt, from servants."

" 'Twas not from the servants." Caroline drew herself up. "It was from Cassie Dilhorne, so there."

"Lady Cassandra is well known for her loose tongue," Miss Marshall said. "Now I charge you, Lady Caroline, go to the schoolroom and do as I said—else I will increase the number to thirty."

Caroline glared at her. Then, holding her head high, she stalked out.

Verity arose and shut the library door after her sister. "I agree she should not have said it. But everyone talks about Mama, you know," she commented uncomfortably.

"Then 'tis high time the chatter ceased," Miss Marshall reproved. "And certainly your sister should not be advising you to emulate such practices. Marriage is a sacrament, and it's a wife's duty to . . ." The governess flushed. "Mind you, I am not casting aspersions on . . ."

"Darling Miss Marshall," Verity cried warmly, "I understand exactly what you are saying. But . . ." She looked at her unhappily. "I do not want to be a wife. Oh, dear, I wish I were not beautiful and an heiress. It's the very worst possible combination for my purposes. In fact, it's absolutely calamitous!"

Miss Marshall's lips twitched. "My love, your appearance and your wealth can hardly be termed a calamitous condition."

"If I were in modest circumstances like Miss Austen, no one would be forcing me to marry."

"No one is forcing you to marry anyone, as yet, my love." Miss Marshall put her arm around Verity.

"They are!" Verity whirled away from her and came back to face her. "Why am I being sent to London tomorrow? So that I may be given a ball and exhibited like a prize sow at a county fair!"

"Do not borrow trouble, my dear," the governess advised. "Think of *all* that does await you in London."

"Ah!" Verity's frown vanished. "The Minerva Press," she whispered. "And Mr. Newman. We will be able to meet him, will we not?"

"Of course."

"But if grandmother knew . . ."

"She'll not know," Miss Marshall said firmly. "It's not my practice to deceive my employers—but in this circumstance . . ."

"You will! And do you think Mr. Newman will like *Elvira* as much as *The Scandal*?"

"I am sure he will agree with me that it is even better, more mature in its perceptions, my love. Though I cannot take much away from *The Scandal*, particularly when one remembers that you were not yet seventeen when you wrote it."

"You helped me with it," Verity reminded her. "You also wrote to Mr. Newman at the Minerva Press and sent him the manuscript."

"I am fortunate enough to have a slight acquaintance with him," Miss Marshall temporized. "As far as helping you with it, I gave you only a few suggestions. I do not deserve a smidgin of your glory. I only wish it need not be kept secret. You deserve recognition."

"I do not think anyone writes for the Minerva Press except under a pseudonym," Verity said seriously. "And I dare not. Grandmother would be furious. You know what she thinks about bluestockings, and as the daughter of an earl, I am supposed to be nothing but a lady of fashion, a wife, and a mother. Oh, dear, it all sounds terribly tedious. I do hope that nothing but fortune hunters offer for me. I am sure Grandmother will be able to tell the wheat from the chaff."

"I am sure she will, but you might enjoy yourself more than you imagine, my dear."

"Only because you'll be with me, Miss Marshall. And promise, promise that the moment we have the opportunity, you'll take me to Leadenhall Street and Mr. Newman."

"On my honor, I promise that, my dear," the governess said gently.

Thanks to the workings of the capricious fates, it was not

until a chill day in early October that Verity was able to realize the hope she had entertained since the publication of *The Scandal*, a year and three months earlier. During the twenty-one days that had passed since her arrival in London, she and Miss Marshall had been sightseeing, but never in the direction of Leadenhall Street. At the request of the dowager countess, Miss Marshall took Verity to the British Museum, the Tower of London, St. Paul's Cathedral, and Westminster Abbey. They had gone forth upon these visits in the countess's coach, driven by Lawrence, her elderly and extremely cantankerous coachman, who, it seemed to Verity, watched them, especially herself, with a definitely suspicious eye. Were he asked to drive them into the Mercantile City where the Minerva Press was located, he would have undoubtedly relayed the whole matter to her grandmother, adding to that lady's already considerable disapproval of herself.

That had been apparent to Verity within a day of her arrival. She had been found wanting in all respects. The countess had despaired of her wardrobe, not excluding the gown Miss Micklestane had made for her entry into the city, which she pronounced "unspeakably dowdy." She had also criticized the unfashionable length of Verity's golden curls, and upon closer scrutiny of her granddaughter's deportment, she had not found that to her liking, either.

"You are too impulsive," she asserted. "You giggle like a serving wench. You move too quickly. You are not to run down the stairs. You must walk down them. Poise, my girl, poise is what you lack." She had turned a cold eye upon Miss Marshall, uncomfortably present at this diatribe. "I look to you to see to your charge. You are a lady. You come from an excellent family. I find no fault with Verity's speech or her ready intelligence, but she needs polish—town polish. I am sure you understand me."

"Yes, milady." Miss Marshall had turned an imperturbable face toward the countess. "I shall do my best."

Verity had listened to her grandmother's words with an indignation spiced with amazement. It was true she had been a little giddy upon arriving in London. It was exciting to see streets and streets lined with houses—and such grand houses, too. Some of them would have swallowed Harcliffe Manor whole—and it was very large, or so it had always seemed to

her. And she had never seen so many fashionable people all
in one place—but to accuse her of not being poised and of
lacking polish was outside of enough! Miss Marshall had
always praised her on her quiet manners and held her up as an
example to her more boisterous sisters. Her indignation was
not so much for herself but for her grandmother's implied
criticism of her governess. Consequently, she had burst out
angrily, " 'Tis not Miss Marshall's fault. She has done her
very best to instill decorum in the three of us . . . we've just
not heeded her!''

An ominous pause had followed this rash defense. "I
see," Lady Harcliffe replied heavily. "Then, I shall not
blame Miss Marshall, but I charge you to please listen—else I
think I will have to wait another year before presenting you to
the *ton*.''

This awful threat would have sent her into raptures were it
not for the stricken look she read on her governess's face.
Belatedly Verity remembered that she was the mainstay of an
elderly aunt and a brother who had not been right in the head
since being invalided home from the Peninsula. Undoubtedly,
she feared that she had been wanting in the eyes of the
formidable countess. Consequently, Verity, with lowered eyes
and voice, said, "I shall do my very best to make you
approve of me, Grandmother.''

"See that you do," snapped Lady Harcliffe. "I am far too
old to deal with unruly children.''

Her cruel set-down had infuriated Verity more than it had
humbled her, but nothing in her manner indicated that she
was other than eager to earn her grandmother's good opinion.
In the following days she did her best to curb any excitement
she might feel on her forays through London, and she followed all Miss Marshall's old dictums on poise and posture.
She knew that she had made definite progress when, on her
seventh morning at the home of her grandmother, she came
down the long curving staircase to the first floor and found
that lady nodding her approval.

"That is much better, my dear. Your posture has improved.
You did not skip. You may tell your governess that I am
extremely pleased with your progress.''

Verity was glad that when this information was dutifully
relayed to Miss Marshall, the countess could not hear the

governess say caustically, "It is a shame that you should be scolded. I have never found you hoydenish. I think your grandmother might have made allowances for the excitement any traveler feels on seeing London for the first time."

"Oh, I do not mind what she says, as long as you are not taken to task, but I do wish we might go to the Minerva Press."

"As soon as the occasion presents itself, we will," the governess promised.

Unfortunately, Lady Harcliffe having decided that Verity could be introduced to the *ton* without any embarrassment to herself, the following fortnight was devoted to fittings at various mantua makers, to visits at the bootmakers and to the Pantheon Bazaar. Her grandmother even took her to the jeweler's, buying her a set of cameos and a simple gold necklace. "Your mother, as you know, had some exquisite jewelry, my child. However, none of it, except for the pearls, is suitable for a young girl." She had added ominously, "You will be given it upon your marriage."

Verity opened her mouth and closed it on an observation that must have struck her grandmother as both impulsive and foolish.

She was thinking about the trials of the past three weeks as she and Miss Marshall walked decorously down the street seemingly bound for an equally decorous stroll through Hyde Park. Lady Harcliffe had enjoyed a winning streak at the faro bank in a small, select private club. She had stayed late and was still abed. She had, however, given her permission to Miss Marshall and Verity to remain in the Park, even though she could not understand why they should want to stroll there when it was already so cool. She did approve Verity's desire to look at the fall colors.

"As long as you don't choose to sketch 'em," she had complained. "I do not hold with this great craze for sketching. It's not useful to a female. Nor is composing poetry and singing. Leave painting, music, and wit to the Fashionable Impures. Your duty's to comfort a man, bear his children, and manage his household. 'Tis common sense will serve for all three."

A passing man of fashion smiled at the ladies and received

a fierce look from Verity. "Oh, I do hate it when they stare at me so," she hissed to Miss Marshall.

"They cannot help staring at you, my dear. You are so beautiful, and that new blue challis is just the color of your eyes."

"I hate it," Verity muttered. "I hate everything I have in my wardrobe. Lures to attract the male. I do not want to attract the male. I want to go home and write!"

"Even if you were to marry, child, you'd not need to give up your writing, you know."

"I pray that you'll not talk of marriage, also," Verity begged.

"My apologies, love," the governess said, as she hailed a passing hackney. "Come," she added as the driver obligingly stopped for them.

Verity, settled in the hackney next to Miss Marshall, said excitedly, "I cannot believe we are truly going there. You do have the manuscript, do you not?"

Miss Marshall pointed to a capacious pocket in the inside of her dark cloak. "It is here," she murmured with a conspiratorial smile. Leaning forward, she gave the direction to the driver.

The man repeated the address in some surprise. "Yer sure you wants to go down there, ladies?"

"Quite sure," Miss Marshall told him composedly. To Verity's surprised glance, she explained, "It's not often ladies of quality venture there. In fact, few who reside in this area of town are willing to make such a journey."

"How strange. Were I to remain in London, I should want to know every inch of it!"

"But you are an authoress, Verity. The world of fashion has smaller boundaries."

"I beg you'll not mention them to me now." Verity pulled a long face. "I want to enjoy myself."

The so-called Mercantile City of London was confusing and amazing to Verity. Leadenhall Street, she learned, was in the south part of London near the river. Getting there was difficult and time-consuming but also interesting. The streets were dreadfully crowded. Stagecoaches, their roofs crowded with baggage and also with outside passengers, lumbered along, taking most of the street, an imminent danger to smaller vehicles. Drivers of drays forced their way through masses of hackneys and private post chaises and even a curricle or two. Horses whinnied loudly and occasionally reared, adding another touch of peril to the thoroughfares. Pedestrians thronged the walks, and moving among them were the ubiquitous peddlers calling out their wares. Milk vendors, water carriers, piemen, scissors grinders, and old-clothes men blended together in a cacophonous chorus in which each attempted to out scream the other. These eager entrepreneurs were often jostled by boys in aprons, who were probably apprenticed to a nearby shopkeeper. This sometimes resulted in a fight, happily viewed by other apprentices, clerks, and a stray gentleman or two urging one or another contestant to do " 'is worst."

Certainly, the streets here were a contrast to the relatively ordered byways of Mayfair. A memory of Miss Micklestane's plaint came to Verity's mind and as swiftly left it as the hackney stopped in the front of a neat store topped by the sign "Lane's Lending Library," which, Verity knew from her governess's description, adjoined the offices of the Minerva Press, which, along with a whole network of circulating libraries, had been once owned by the late William Lane. The circulating library's shelves, she further noted, were stacked with books. Inside were a number of people, some fashionably dressed, and as the driver assisted her to the street, Verity saw a lady and her abigail carrying between them some twelve volumes. For a second, she entertained the happy thought that among these books were the three volumes of *The Scandal*, but, she remembered, it had come out the previous year and was probably long forgotten.

"Come, dear," Miss Marshall urged. "We go in here." She pointed to an arched doorway a few feet away, situated under a gilded statue of the goddess Minerva.

Verity nodded. Excitement had momentarily robbed her of speech. She followed Miss Marshall into a small anteroom where a clerk was perched on a high stool bending over a desk and inscribing something in what appeared to be a ledger. However, as Miss Marshall closed the door behind them, he turned to stare at them over spectacles perched on a thin nose. His small blue eyes were both inquisitive and admiring. "What might I do for you, ladies? You'll find the circulating library next door."

"We are in hopes of seeing Mr. Newman," Miss Marshall said.

"Oh, dear, oh, dear, that may not be done without an appointment." The clerk shook his head so emphatically that his rather lank brown hair swirled about his narrow face. "Mr. Newman is closeted with an author. He—"

"We were unable to make an appointment," Miss Marshall interrupted. "But this young lady is also an author. Her *nom de plume* is Mrs. Maiden, and her book is called *The Scandal*."

The change in the clerk's attitude was as pleasing as it was rapid. "*You* are Mrs. Maiden?" he inquired, staring at Verity in respectful surprise.

"Yes, I am," she responded shyly, delighted at being addressed by her pen name for the very first time.

"Well, now that was a book, a very fine book, but I did not think its author would be such a very young lady."

"I am not so young, sir, I am turned eighteen."

"Eighteen, gracious me! If you will excuse me . . ." He was about to clamber down from his stool when a door located a few feet behind his desk opened and a tall, pleasant man in his late thirties, conservatively but well dressed, came out with a slightly shorter and much younger man, who, Verity guessed, must be the author, for in addition to his youth, he was shabbily garbed. Time had added a shine to his well-fitting coat. His stockingette trousers were well enough, but his Hessian boots, though highly polished, were cracked and their gold tassels tarnished. His shirt was of pristine whiteness, his collar starched, and his cravat beautifully tied, but, again, the shirt was mended just below the collar. Her observing eye had taken in all these details quickly, but she forgot them as quickly when she met dark gleaming eyes set in an undeniably handsome contenance. She looked down quickly, but not before she had noted his dark wavy hair and the warm olive of his skin, a shade hinting at Italian or possibly Spanish ancestry. However, he could also be Cornish or Irish.

Her speculations were interrupted by the tall man's saying, "Miss Marshall, I received your note. I expected to see you a

good deal sooner.'' His eyes shifted to Verity's face and
widened in surprise. Without giving Miss Marshall a chance
to reply, he continued, ''You'll never be telling me that this
child is Mrs. Maiden?''

''I am not a child,'' Verity said with a hint of indignation.

''Of course she is not,'' the younger man agreed. ''But I'm
thinking that she is a maiden.''

He had a beautiful speaking voice, and the accent was
similar to those she had heard all her life. Obviously, he
came from a good family, but why was he so poorly dressed?
Reverses in fortune? Gambling? He could have been disinher-
ited, too. Her second set of speculations was also interrupted
as Miss Marshall said, ''My dear, I fear I am remiss. This is
Mr. Newman.''

Verity put out her hand. ''I am delighted, sir. Also grateful.''

''I, too, am delighted, and I should like to know why you
are grateful, my dear little Mrs. Maiden.'' He bowed over her
hand.

''You published my book.''

''You must never be grateful for that, my dear. Rather I
am grateful that I was given that privilege.'' He turned to his
companion. ''This young lady penned *The Scandal*.''

The dark eyes widened. ''Really, at eighteen. I must congratulate you, Mrs. Maiden. I found it a delightful book.''

''She had not yet celebrated her seventeenth birthday when
she finished *The Scandal*,'' Mr. Newman said. ''And now I
have been remiss. Miss Marshall, Mrs. Maiden, may I present Mr. Alan Parry, who, under the name of Anthony Hunter,
is one of our more prolific authors.''

''Anthony Hunter!'' Verity said excitedly. ''But I have
read your books—several of them.''

''Have you indeed?'' He smiled. ''I am complimented. If
you'd said you'd read one, I should have been gratified—but
more than one proves you liked them.''

''Oh, I did,'' she cried. ''*The Greek Slave* was so authentic
. . . I felt as if I were actually in Athens. And *The Egyptian
Princess*—I cried and cried when they buried her alive in that
horrid way.''

''You liked that, did you?'' His smile broadened. ''Mr.
Newman, here, tells me that he is still receiving letters from
readers who wrote in to complain of her demise.''

"Oh, no, it was exactly the way it should have been. Not everything in life can end happily."

There was an unexpectedly somber look in his brilliant eyes. "You are very wise for one so young, my dear Mrs. Maiden."

"I do not feel young," Verity said, and flushed as they all laughed at her. "Well, I do not," she insisted.

"Do not denigrate your youth, Mrs. Maiden," Mr. Parry advised. "Particularly so beautiful a youth as you possess. It will not last forever, you know." Turning to the publisher, he said almost abruptly, "Well, I must go, Tony. I am in the midst of a rather trying section of my book."

"Are you writing another, now?" Verity demanded.

"Yes, and it is overdue."

"Indeed it is, Alan, and I give you leave to quit our presence," Mr. Newman said sternly.

"Where does this tale take place?" Verity questioned, finding herself very reluctant to see him go.

"In Rome during the time of the Borgias." He grinned. "As you can see, I follow that old axiom about writing on subjects with which you are familiar."

"Oh, I do not think the place or the period matters," Verity said. "People are the same everywhere, do you not agree?"

"Dearest," Miss Marshall murmured. "Mr. Parry has told us that he must get back to work. We should not detain him any longer."

Verity blushed. "Oh, dear, I am sorry. I did not mean to . . ." she began.

"Please," he protested. "I pray you'll not apologize for a detention I have found most delightful." Taking Verity's hand, he lifted it to his lips. "I shall look forward to a second novel from your pen, Mrs. Maiden."

"And I to your Romans, sir," she replied, wishing that she had not been wearing a blue kid glove—for then she might have felt his lips against her hand. Conversely, she was glad that once he released her hand, he strode from the office hastily. Otherwise, he might have seen what she was sure was a flush on her cheeks. She was equally sure that Miss Marshall would give her a set-down for her boldness in speaking to a strange gentleman, but she did not care.

"And now, my dear," the publisher said. "What about your second novel? I am told you have written one."

"My second novel . . ." Verity spoke vaguely.

"Indeed, there is a second." Miss Marshall reached into the pocket of her cape and brought out the manuscript. "And here it is."

"Good heavens, has that been weighing you down all this time?" Mr. Newman raised his eyebrows, "You should have mentioned it before."

Verity had a remorseful look for the governess. "I fear I did not give her the opportunity."

"No matter," Miss Marshall assured her. "I think it most instructive to meet other authors."

"Yes," Verity agreed eagerly. "I did find it so."

"I shouldn't be surprised if Mr. Parry felt much the same way." Mr. Newman smiled. "Now let us talk about your novel. Its name?"

"*Elvira*," Verity said. "I have written it in an epistolary style."

"Ah, I like those novels," Mr. Newman approved. "And may I know what it is about?"

"Elivira is. . . . well, she . . ." Verity hesitated and looked appealingly at Miss Marshall. "I pray you, please tell him. I become so involved when I try."

"That does not surprise me," Mr. Newman commented. "All authors do. Well, Miss Marshall and Mrs. Maiden, I think we'll go into my office—and there you'll have all my attention. Come."

An hour later, emerging from the Minerva Press, Verity sent a quick look around the street, wishing she might glimpse Alan Parry, but, of course, she knew that to be futile. He was in his lodgings writing. She wished that she had been able to find out more about him. Thoughts of him had been plaguing her all through their conference with the publisher. Though she had been looking forward to meeting Mr. Newman for two whole years, she didn't even have a very clear image of the man in her mind. Superimposed over it were the darkly handsome features of Mr. Parry. And in her mind were Olivia's lines from *Twelfth Night*, a play she had recently seen at the Haymarket: "How now? E'en so quickly may one

catch the plague/Methinks, I feel this youth's perfections with
an invisible and subtle stealth to creep in at mine eyes.''

She had not quite understood that speech at the time. She
understood it now, and it took all her large supply of common
sense to tell herself, ''Don't be a fool. You'll probably never
see him again.'' She would never have believed that such a
thought could make her so profoundly unhappy.

Two

It had been six years since the ballroom at Harcliffe House had been opened. Lady Harcliffe stood with Verity near the door of the huge room, overseeing the maids and the footmen. The former were hard at work polishing the mirrors, and the latter were waxing the floors.

Verity was staring into the mirrors watching herself and her grandmother reflected into infinity and wishing that she had Lady Harcliffe's height. She was at least five feet eight and had not lost any of her inches. She was really a handsome and regal woman, with her crown of iron-gray hair, her wide blue eyes, and her fine-boned face. Verity recalled that her father had had much the look of her, and so did Caroline. She and Eva took after their mother, who had been small and dainty.

"One day, Verity, you will be standing in your own ballroom watching the preparations for a ball, possibly that of your eldest daughter. Are you attending?"

"Yes, Grandmother."

"Your housekeeper will be in attendance, of course, as is Mrs. Bellmore," she said as she nodded toward a small woman in a neat gray gown standing across the room. "She is very capable, but I have found it expedient to watch her, as well."

"I see," Verity said, feeling some comment was expected. She wished her grandmother were not constantly regarding her future. In the last fortnight, she had mentioned marriage far too often for her own peace of mind. She, herself, had refrained from commenting on a subject that depressed her even more than formerly . . . formerly being before she had

23

encountered Mr. Alan Parry. Try as she did, she could not get him out of her mind. His face appeared in her dreams with depressing regularity, depressing because upon awakening, she missed him, and because she was all too conscious of the impossibility of ever seeing him again. She was beginning to fear she would never see Mr. Newman, either. There had not been a minute of free time. Last week, she had been presented at court, and this week there would be the ball—and between these two events were fittings, fittings, fittings!

Also, after her presentation, less intimidating than she had feared, there had been appointments with the dancing master, for, of course, her grandmother had found fault with Verity's waltzing, witnessed at a small select dance given by one of Lady Harcliffe's old friends.

In addition to that dance, she had been bidden to several dinners and a rout, where she had met quite a few gentleman, all very attentive and obviously taken with her. Thinking about them afterwards, she found she could not remember one—only *his* face remained in her thoughts.

She was seeing it now, his dark brows, large dark eyes, high cheekbones, firm mouth, and cleft chin. His nose had been beautifully shaped, too. If only he could have partnered her through all her waltzes—but since that could not be, it was very difficult for her to produce the correct amount of enthusiasm for the pleasures in store for her this evening. Her mind was divided in thirds—one for him, one for news of the publisher's reaction to *Elvira*, and one for the ball, a smaller third or no more than a fourth.

"You'd better rest now," the countess advised. "Lord, all this makes me think of my first ball. Over half a century ago, it was, though it does not seem nearly that long—or perhaps it seems much longer, I am not sure. It was in '64 and I wore a most cumbersome gown, all frilled about the skirt and with huge paniers. My hair was powdered and dressed high over a wire cage with plumes on top. Had we waltzed I should have fainted, I am sure, but we danced the minuet.

"It was during a minuet that I met your grandfather. He was in white brocade, and his hair was powdered, too. We took to each other immediately, and what was our surprise and delight to learn that our parents had already arranged our marriage!"

"Without even consulting you?" Verity demanded in surprise.

"Of course we were not consulted. We were but eighteen and nineteen. The young do not know their own minds. We suited each other very well." The countess's eyes were misty. "We loved each other devotedly all the years of our marriage."

Seeing tears in her faded eyes, Verity felt sorry for her grandmother, and for the first time she also experienced some measure of empathy for the irascible old woman. She had loved her husband deeply—and he had been dead for nearly thirty years. It must have been very hard for her to exist without him. Of course, their situations were scarcely comparable—but it had been proving very difficult for her to exist without even a glimpse of the man to whom she had given her heart in what seemed now to be no more than the twinkling of an eye. It was really stupid to think of herself and her grandmother in the same context. Still, Lady Harcliffe had spoken about falling in love at first sight, and that, Verity now knew to her sorrow, did not happen only in novels.

It was nearly time for Verity to desert her chamber for the ballroom. Regarding herself in her mirror, she thought she looked tolerably well. She was wearing a round gown of white crepe over white satin. Its bodice, cut just above the swell of her bosom, was lavishly trimmed with exquisite lace, which also bordered her skirt. For the occasion, she was wearing her mother's pearl necklace, bracelet, and earrings. Her hair, newly coiffed, curled charmingly around her face, but her eyes, she noted, reflected her nervousness.

"Oh, milady!" Kitty, the abigail she had brought with her from the country, regarded her with wide-eyed admiration. "You do look a picture."

"Thank you, Kitty," Verity said edgily. She had not anticipated the variety of emotions she was experiencing at this moment. Excitement warred with anxiety. She wanted to be as successful as her grandmother insisted she must be, but she had discovered within herself a new shyness. In spite of being presented at court and meeting select members of the *ton*, she quailed at the thought of the ball where her grandmother and a great many more ladies and gentlemen would be scrutinizing and criticizing her, not only in her own person but as a representative of her family.

"I have not always been in sympathy with poor dear Arabella," the countess had said, referring to Verity's late mother, "but she was an excellent hostess. You are her child. Also, you are named for my mother, Verity Cullinger, whom everyone remembers as an exemplary woman. I hope you will match her in graciousness and poise."

"My dear, how lovely you do look!" Miss Marshall, clad in cranberry satin, stood in the doorway.

"Do I?" Verity regarded her dubiously.

"Sure you can entertain no doubts as to that, my love."

"On the contrary, I am beset with them," Verity moaned. "I have not only myself to think about this night—but the family on both sides all the way back!"

"Surely not to the time of Harold, last of the Saxons!" Miss Marshall teased.

"You know what I mean . . . *Grandmother*."

The governess firmed her lips. "I cannot think she will be displeased with either your person or your deportment."

"But my dancing . . ."

". . . is as graceful as anyone could wish. Think no more about it, just enjoy yourself, my dear."

"Enjoy myself?" Verity echoed in hollow tones. "I cannot see how that is possible."

" 'Twill be ever so pleasant to dance, milady," Kitty said.

"I am sure you will find it so," agreed Miss Marshall.

"But grandmother will want . . ."

". . .you to enjoy yourself," Miss Marshall said firmly.

Verity weathered the rigors of the receiving line with an ease that amazed her. Later, waltzing in the arms of one of the many young men who had bespoken dances, she *was* enjoying herself. It was impossible not to be excited by all the compliments she received, by the gentlemen who crowded around her besieging her with their eager requests. The ballroom, itself, pleased her. Baskets of hothouse roses were set at intervals along the walls. The floor glistened with newly applied wax, and the great chandelier with its hanging crystal drops blazed with the light from at least a hundred candles. They were further reflected in two large mirrors facing each other from across the room. Whirling past one of these, Verity laughed delightedly as she saw the multiple images of herself and her partner seemingly waltzing down countless corridors.

Thanks to the efforts of her dancing master, she felt much more confident, easily suiting her steps to her various partners. Her feet were a trifle sore, but it had been pleasing to have every dance promised, and each to a different gentleman! She smiled up at the man who was expertly guiding her through a difficult twirl. His name, she recalled, was Derek Vane, Marquess of Unger. He was, she had to admit, extremely handsome, even if his coloring was as fair as her own. She had learned from her grandmother that he was the son of her parents' good friends. It had seemed to her that Lady Harcliffe demonstrated a decided partiality for him and his mother, Lady Unger, who was also present.

She, herself, had not really liked the marchioness. She was a tall imperious woman with an air of great consequence and cold eyes which did not reflect her smile. Derek Vane resembled his mother, but his smile was in his eyes as he looked down at her from his considerable height, saying now as the music was drawing to a close, "I wish all your other dances were not promised, Lady Verity."

"I wish they were not, myself," she replied, thinking more of her feet than the implications of her response.

"Ah." His smile broadened. "I am indeed complimented, Lady Verity."

She was momentarily surprised at that, but guessed that he had misunderstood her. It would not be polite to correct that impression. She merely smiled at him as he led her from the floor and into the arms of another eager partner.

By the time the evening was at an end, it was morning, and Verity, falling into bed, could not help but be pleased. Not only had she enjoyed herself, her grandmother had praised her poise and her dancing as well. "You were quite unexceptionable, my dear," she said in the tone of one delivering a final judgment.

Verity fell asleep immediately and dreamed of dancing, but not with any of the gentlemen present. It was Alan Parry who held her in his arms—Alan Parry with whom she waltzed to infinity in the mirrors of the ballroom.

*   *   *

Lying in her bed, Verity had wept until she could weep no more. Her eyes ached and her throat throbbed. Her grandmother's words still resounded in her ears. "You seemed to like him well enough at the ball, and you accepted his invitation to go riding in the Park and driving with him in his curricle."

"You said I should," Verity had reminded her.

"I do not deny it. Can you think what an honor it is to be courted by the Marquess of Unger, the scion of one of our oldest and most distinguished families? Derek Vane is the most eligible young man in London."

"I . . . I have seen him no more than three t-times and you tell me he has offered for me!"

"You have found favor in his eyes."

"He has not found favor in mine. I do not love him."

"Love," sniffed her grandmother. "Love is an illusion and very often a delusion. You will suit each other admirably. You are both of excellent families. He is not a fortune hunter. He is wealthy in his own right. His lineage is impeccable. Furthermore, he is extremely fastidious in his tastes. He has never indulged in the vices so unfortunately prevalent among scions of the nobility. He does not drink, wench, or gamble. He is clean-living and high-thinking. He has vast estates in the North and he oversees the tenantry himself. You could not find a better match in all England! I pray you will not put on this missish air with me. Have you no idea of the honor he has done you—to offer for you within two weeks of your first meeting?"

"How could he have formed a . . . a partiality for me so quickly?" Verity had cried.

"Partiality be damned! You are a Stratton from a family as old as his own—the bloodlines are excellent."

"You speak as if I were a brood mare!"

"Do not be impudent, girl. The bloodlines *are* excellent. You are beautiful, young, wealthy—wealthier than either of your sisters, since your mother's late brother saw fit to leave you an extra ten thousand pounds."

"Uncle James . . ." Verity sobbed, thinking of him with love and regret. She had been terribly cast down when he had been drowned after his yacht was capsized in a storm. She still missed him, but at this moment she wished she had not been his favorite niece. "Could . . . could I not sign over my money to Caroline . . ."

"What is the child saying?" Lady Harcliffe addressed the air.

"If . . . as you say, the bloodlines are excellent. Caroline is nearly seventeen, and . . ."

"It is not Caroline with whom he has fallen in love. It is you!"

"You said he . . . he did not love me. You said it was the bloodlines."

"I said nothing of the sort. Young Vane is very much smitten with you. I have never seen him in such a taking as when he offered for you."

"He might have said something to me first!" Verity burst out.

"On the contrary. He acted with the greatest propriety, applying to me as your guardian. He could do nothing without my consent."

"And . . . and you have given it?"

"I have given it," Lady Harcliffe said coldly. "And I must say that I hardly expected such a reaction from you. Lord, one would think you doomed to perdition rather than being the promised bride of the Marquess of Unger."

"Could . . . could we not know each other a little longer?" Verity asked and swallowed a lump in her throat. Implicit in that request was capitulation. She had not meant to sound as if she were agreeing to this preposterous proposal.

"You will have a lifetime in which to know each other. And you will see. Once you have entered the married state, you'll find that your ridiculous objections will be quite forgotten."

"I do not want to marry him! I do not want to marry anyone!"

"Nonsense. Would you be a spinster like Miss Marshall?"

"Yes, that is exactly what I wish to be."

"You are talking foolishness, and let me tell you, my girl, that you owe a creditable marriage to your family, and certainly to your sisters, who, since they do not have such sizable portions, can only be aided by your bridegroom's eminence and wealth. I might add that this marriage was discussed while you were yet in leading strings. It wanted only young Unger's sanction. He has given it. I have accepted for you and that is all there is to it!"

"And have I no sanction?"

"None at all. You'll do as you're told, my girl. You have a name to uphold and a duty to fulfill. As I have explained, I married your grandfather at the behest of my family."

"But you loved him, you said."

"If I had not, I still would have been governed by my duty to my family. It is a great shame your parents were killed before they could instill in you what is expected of those in our circumstances. We are not ordinary people. We have to think not only of ourselves but of the generations that have gone before us and of those that will follow us. The banns are going to be posted this Sunday at St. Martin-in-the-Fields. They will be posted the next two Sundays, and you will be wed on December tenth."

"That's scarce a month away!"

" 'Twill be time enough to sew upon your brideclothes. After your marriage, you will spend your honeymoon at Castle Unger in Northumberland. My felicitations, Verity. My dearest wish has been fulfilled, and I trust that by this time a year hence, you will not only be contented with your lot, but on the way to producing an heir. That is very important, since the marquess is an only child with only a second cousin to inherit. Yet, for all that, he has never sought another young woman in marriage." The countess's eyes gleamed. "I suppose it can mean very little to you, my dear, but you have enjoyed a triumph such as is accorded to very few females. You will have married into one of the most prestigious families in England—and within a month of your first ball! There are few who can match that!"

It did mean very little to her, that empty triumph, spelling the end of a hope which had been, she knew, quite vain, but to which she had stubbornly clung. But what was a mere interested look in a gentleman's eyes?—a gentleman whose shabby garments proclaimed a poverty she would gladly have shared had he followed it with a word. He had not, could not have followed it with a word. They had met only once for no more than ten minutes, and probably much less than that estimate. Probably he had forgotten her the minute he was out of the building. Certainly he would have forgotten her by now, and if he had not, what could that matter? Once she had been badgered and bullied into accepting Derek Vane's offer of marriage, Leadenhall Street became as remote as a castle on the moon!

Fittings once more became the order of the day, and between them Verity was introduced to more of her grandmother's friends, elderly ladies who gushingly congratulated her upon her "triumph." She was bidden to routs, to tea parties, to the opera and the theater. Oddly enough, however, beyond the initial interview when Verity, painfully aware of her grandmother's presence, dutifully accepted Derek Vane's offer, she saw very little of him. He had posted back to prepare Unger Castle for the reception of his bride. His departure was a surprise but it was also a relief.

In his absence, she was not constantly confronted with his warm smiles and unabashedly loving looks, the which she felt it incumbent upon herself to return. Over and over he had pronounced himself the happiest, the most fortunate of men. He had also relayed to her his friends' encomiums on the subject of his amazing good luck in wedding one whom they did not hesitate to describe as the most beautiful heiress in the world!

Verity's light remark that this rather put a girdle around the compliment had not amused him and, she feared, was not understood. Derek did not have much of a sense of humor. However, she did have to admit that he was pleasant and certainly very handsome. Even though she preferred dark hair and dark eyes to his golden beauty, she found him similar in appearance to a statue of Apollo in the British Museum. She was quite sure that there were many who would prefer the Apollo to the bust of a Roman general which, she thought, much resembled Alan Parry. Yet it was the memory of that particular sculpture that brought tears to her eyes when she retired at night and instilled within her a fugitive hope on the day she finally concocted an excuse that must give her enough time to visit Leadenhall Street.

It concerned the unexpected arrival of Lady Julia Ardmore, who had been her very dearest friend at home and who was now wed to Sir Arthur Ardmore, who was in the diplomatic service and bound for a post in Milan, Italy. Lady Julia had been devastated to learn that Verity would be wed at a time

when she was out of the country and had bidden her to tea at
Fenton's, the hotel where they were residing. Since she would
be accompanied by Miss Marshall and since the hotel was
located on St. James's Street, not too great a distance from
Harcliffe House, Lady Harcliffe graciously gave her consent.
Fortunately, since she herself was due in at the mantua
maker's, she did not offer Verity the use of her coach, a
contingency that Verity had belatedly anticipated and desperately feared.

"It does seem an age since we visited Mr. Newman," she
remarked as the governess took her seat beside her in the
hackney. "I do wonder what he thinks of *Elvira*. 'Tis a pity
he could not write to us, but, as you have said, my grandmother would have wondered, seeing the direction on the
envelope."

"We shall soon know, my dear. I sent him a note saying we
would be there today."

"Oh, did you. I am glad. I do hope he approves the
manuscript, for it is unlikely that I shall be writing any
more." Verity tried to speak lightly as she added, "Before I
left the manor, my sisters quizzed me upon my marriage,
which they thought must happen immediately . . . and it
has."

"Yes, it has happened very quickly."

It seemed to Verity that there was a pitying note in Miss
Marshall's voice. Impulsively, she leaned forward and said,
"Oh, if only I were like you and could go out to be a
governess."

"I do not think the life would suit you, my love. You've
been born to wealth. You'd find it very difficult to do without
it."

"I would gladly do without it if . . ." Verity wrung her
hands. "I do not want to be married. I want to write. I know
I am not a Walter Scott or a Byron, but there is that within
me that demands expression, even in my poor way, and now
Grandmother talks about the duties of a wife. . . ." Verity
brought her hands up to her face. "If only I could have stood
against her—but there's my duty to my f-family and my
s-sisters, and I do not believe *he* will contenance his wife
being a . . . a bluestocking."

"Child, I cannot think he will. But you have your notebook,

and there's nothing to keep you from jotting down your thoughts. I have not seen much of the young man, but he does not strike me as a tyrant. He does seem very fond of you. And certainly he is well connected, wealthy. I know 'twas not what you wished, but once you are wed, perhaps you will find your new life more to your liking than you anticipate.''

"You sound just like Grandmother," Verity said wearily. "And you know what writing means to me . . . or do you? Have you only been humoring me—until such time as I would wed and put it away from me as I did my old dolls?"

"Verity!" the governess exclaimed indignantly. "Have I ever not encouraged you with your writing? It was I who sent your first book to—"

"Oh, I know." Verity seized Miss Marshall's hand and held it to her cheek. "It is only that I am so miserable. I had hoped . . . oh, why did *he* find me to his liking so quickly?"

"That is the way it is with love, my dear. It has been compared to lightning—so fast does it strike."

"I should know that," Verity murmured.

"You should know it?" Miss Marshall looked at her narrowly. "But did you not just tell me . . ."

"I . . . was not thinking of *him*. I was thinking of *him*!" Verity looked down at her hands, at the heavy gold betrothal ring on her finger.

"You are not making sense, my love."

"I will make sense if you'll promise you'll never betray me." Verity fixed her eyes on Miss Marshall's face.

"Need I make such a promise?"

"No, no, no, you should not . . . of course, you should not, I trust you more than anyone in this world!" Verity flung her arms around the governess. "I . . . I was much taken with Mr. Parry."

"Mr. Parry!" Miss Marshall stared at her in amazement. "But you've scarce exchanged a word with him."

"There were . . . several words," Verity contradicted. "And I did find him so much to my liking."

"He is an attractive man, of course, but . . . my child . . ."

"I know . . . I know all that you will tell me. And undoubtedly I am being very foolish."

"Very romantic, my dear. You are a romantic, as witness your novels . . . but life is a very different matter."

"I know that, too."

"And yet," Miss Marshall mused, "what could be more romantic than Lord Unger's hasty proposal?"

"It had been decided years and years ago. I told you that."

"Yes, but no one could have forced him to it, had he not seen you and loved you."

"At first sight," Verity agreed ruefully.

"Definitely at first sight . . . and, my dear, you were never cut out to be the wife of an impoverished young writer. You have your position . . . "

"I did not think that you would prate to me of position, Miss Marshall!"

" 'Tis only common sense, Verity."

"Oh, I know, and I have been horrid again, but I am so confused and so . . . oh, why could I not have had this one Season to myself without being bespoken so soon?"

"Because your fiancé is eager and does not want to wait lest he lose you."

"How might he lose me with grandmother so adamant? Ah, well, perhaps 'tis better to wed him now . . . since there's nothing will prevent it."

"I pray you'll not be so prosaic on your wedding day," Miss Marshall said wryly.

"You disappoint me. I thought you'd be in my corner." Verity frowned.

"I only want what is best for you. Love in a cottage is a popular theme among dramatists, but poverty is never pleasant. To watch every coin that you spend, to eat frugally, to deal with harsh landladies who threaten you with eviction if the payment for your lodgings is even a day late, to have bailiffs sitting in your hallway waiting to drag you off to a sponging house or a debtor's prison . . . those are some of the lesser joys of cottage romance." The governess spoke with unaccustomed bitterness, her eyes grown grim.

Verity shivered. It occurred to her that she knew very few of the particulars concerning Miss Marshall's past life. She hoped her mentor was not speaking out of her own unhappy experience. She refrained from pursuing the subject further out of a fear that she might be. Yet, if one were wed to a man like Alan Parry . . .

She uttered a little cry of excitement as the hackney drew to a stop and a glance out of the window showed her the facade of the circulating library.

At that welcome sight, excitement replaced the welter of assumptions and confusions currently plaguing her—and the beleaguered *Elvira* reigned in solitary splendor. Would Mr. Newman like it? Would it be published in three volumes, the way *The Scandal* had been? Or had he not liked it and was her manuscript to be no more than a mass of paper to be pushed into the back of some drawer and forgotten?

She could hardly wait for the steps to be put up to the cab door, and when they were, she hopped down at great peril to her skirts. Her lessons in deportment were seemingly forgotten as she dashed toward the entrance to the publisher's offices. However, a glimpse through the window gave her pause—the clerk was not alone. There was another man with him. She slowed to a walk and waited for Miss Marshall to join her.

"There is someone ahead of us, I believe," she muttered, half expecting a set-down from Miss Marshall, for her untoward behavior in leaping from the coach.

"That will not matter. He is expecting us," the governess said composedly. She opened the door, and Verity, impulsive once more, hurried inside, coming to a dead stop as the man who had been talking with the clerk turned and smiled, his dark eyes bright with pleasure.

"Lady Verity, well met by sunlight!"

"Mr. Parry," she whispered, shocked by this granting of a wish she had hardly dared entertain, shocked, too, by his use of her real name. She guessed that the publisher must have revealed her identity. It did not matter. She put out her hand, and he bowed over it, his gaze then shifting to her companion.

"Miss Marshall," he said as he released Verity's hand.

"Good afternoon, Mr. Parry," she responded, favoring him with a pleasant smile.

"I had wanted to see you"—he was looking at Verity again—"that I might congratulate you."

"Congratulate me?" Verity repeated in a small voice, her heart plummeting.

"Indeed, yes. I hope you'll not think it wrong of Tony, but knowing my interest in your work, he was kind enough to let me read *Elvira*. It is not out of the way, I assure you. He often seeks my opinion on a novel, and I found this one extraordinary."

"Extraordinary?" she echoed.

"Indeed, yes. The other one was very good, but this is a definite improvement, and the epistolary style is very difficult to handle effectively—but you have managed it splendidly."

"I am so pleased to have my opinion corroborated," Miss Marshall said.

"I am glad you found it to your taste," Verity murmured.

"I, too. I wanted to like it."

"Did you?" Her heart was beating somewhere near her throat as she tried to guess his exact meaning.

He nodded. "So many young writers have but a single book in their—er, quivers. But you, I am happy to note, are a real authoress. I only hope . . ." Some of the light left his eyes.

"What do you hope?" she prompted.

"I should like to see you grow in your craft, but I understand you are affianced to . . . Unger."

She bit down a cry of surprise. "How did you know?"

"I, too, read the *Morning Post*, and I should have offered my felicitations immediately. Pray accept them now."

She looked up at him. He did not tower over her as her fiancé did—and was it possible that she read regret in his eyes? Something else occurred to her. "Are you acquainted with Lord Unger?"

He shook his head. "We do not move in the same circles."

It seemed to her that there was a trace of sarcasm in his tone, but that hardly mattered—what mattered was that he knew she was about to be married and he had just congratulated her upon her forthcoming nuptials, something she had failed to acknowledge. However, also replete in his preceding remarks was an implication she was in haste to refute. "I have every intention of continuing my writing," she said firmly.

"Good!" he exclaimed. "You must. You have originality and a lively turn of phrase—both very important in this frivolous art of novel-fashioning."

"Frivolous, sir?"

"So it is thought to be by some. Do you not agree, Miss Marshall?"

"You are quite right, Mr. Parry," the governess said equably.

"Ah, good afternoon." Mr. Newman came quickly into the room and joining them said, "My congratulations, my dear. I am happy to add your *Elvira* to my list, and with Alan, I can only hope that you will produce another."

"I shall make every effort to do so, sir," she said, reading doubt in his eyes. "Despite any . . . changes that must necessarily occur in my life, I could not forsake my pen."

"Changes often bring with them new insights, Lady Verity," Mr. Parry said.

"Yes, I expect they do." Under the curtain of her lengthy lashes, she scanned his face, hoping to find . . . she was not sure. No, that wasn't true. She wanted to see if the regret she had fancied she saw a minute ago still remained. However, there was no hint of it in his pleasant smile. Yet, he had come to see her—but as one author to another, no more. And why should there be more from a man she had met only once?

"Well," he said. "I must go. I will be seeing you, Tony."

"Only after you've written *finis* to your final chapter," the publisher said firmly.

"That will be soon, I promise. Lady Verity, my wishes for your happiness and your continued industry."

"I thank you, sir," she said steadily. "And you have mine as well."

" 'Tis my turn to thank you." He brought her hand to his lips again, pressing a light kiss upon it. Releasing it, he bowed to the governess. "Miss Marshall, good day."

"Good day, sir," she murmured, adding as he left. "A very well-spoken young man."

"Yes, indeed," the publisher agreed. "Well, ladies, please come in and let us discuss *Elvira*. I would like to bring it out as soon as possible."

"That is most gratifying to hear, is it not, Verity?" prompted Miss Marshall.

"Indeed it is, sir," she said brightly, her gaze shifting to the front window—in the vain hope of catching one more glimpse of him. Unexpectedly, she found him standing outside staring back at her, a moody look written large upon his countenance. Just for a second, their glances locked. Then, with a brief nod, he wheeled and strode away.

She had the impression he had taken her heart with him—and had he left a little piece of his with her? She dared not dwell on that. Her course was clearly marked and she could only follow it.

Part Two

ঝ ঝ

One

The Marquess and Marchioness of Unger left the Haymarket Theater in the interval between the fourth and fifth acts of Mr. Edmund Kean's highly acclaimed *Richard III*. Not only would they miss his famed soliloquies, they would also miss the farce that must lighten hearts after the carnage of Bosworth Field.

Verity, who had not been attending to the actor's histrionics, did not care. During the fourth act, she had been concentrating on the scene that must surely take place once she and her husband were in their chamber and their respective servants dismissed.

Sitting in her corner, clutching the strap and bracing herself against the jolts that one must suffer even in so well sprung a post chaise, she thought of Cassie Dilhorne and her brother Rob with something less than affection. Actually, she knew she was being unfair to them. It was not their fault that fate had placed them in a box directly across from the one occupied by her and her husband. Nor was there any reason why they should not wave and smile at her.

She had not seen Rob since he had entered Oxford in 1814, and the last time she had met Cassie had been over two years ago, in that same September she had come to London. Though Cassie was more Caroline's friend than her own, they had known each other since they were in leading strings. Cassie's presence, she reflected, would make life more pleasant for Caroline, who had only just arrived in the city—a year later than anticipated because of their grandmother's unexpected bout with a quinsy that had weakened her greatly, making it impossible for her to launch Caroline during the winter of

1817 as promised. Her mind sped back to Cassie, or rather
Rob, who had smiled at her with an appreciation that had
made her cringe.

She wished his attitude had not changed so drastically.
Years ago, he had teased her and made horrid faces at her.
Even up to the time he left for Oxford he had made a dreadful
pest of himself. If only he had not coupled his appreciative
gazing with a smile that could be termed ardent and compounded the whole by visiting their box to speak to her with
the familiarity of an old friend! Of course, Cassie had been
equally friendly, but her smiles did not matter. Verity glanced
at her husband, sitting so stiffly in his corner, staring out at
the gaslit thoroughfare. She bit her lip and mentally prepared
herself for the storm that was to come.

At this moment, she almost wished herself back in the chill
old castle which had been in Derek's family for six hundred
years. During the winter and a half she had spent behind its
weathered walls, there had been days when she thought she
must go mad listening to the mournful howling of the wild
snow-bearing winds above and the lashing of the icy waves
upon the rocks below. However, her initial pleasure at being
in London for the season was now dimmed by the thought of
other chance meetings with old friends at her grandmother's
house or at the routs and balls to which they would undoubtedly be bidden now that Derek had opened Vane, his beautiful house in Great Jermyn Street.

They turned into the driveway, and the footman hastened
to place the steps at the carriage door. Verity emerged,
followed by her husband, who silently tendered his arm,
escorting her up the steps between the Corinthian pillars into
the circular hallway and thence up the sweep of staircase to the
second floor, where he said coldly, "I will attend you shortly,
my dear."

Verity caught a look of surprise on the face of Kitty, who
was waiting for her in the hall beyond her chamber. "Did
you enjoy the theater, milady?" the girl inquired a few
minutes later as she unclasped Verity's diamond necklace and
received the matching earrings from her. These she placed in
the large leather jewel box on the dressing table.

"It was pleasant, Kitty, but his lordship was unexpectedly
fatigued."

"I see, milady." Kitty made no further comment, but Verity, gazing into her mirror, saw the abigail's eyes harden and was sure she had guessed the reason behind their early departure. Servants always knew and Kitty was bright, but, at another glance in the mirror, Verity realized regretfully that her anxiety was easily discernible in distressed eyes, the flush on her cheeks, and the tautness of her body. She forced a smile but could not maintain it. The gossips belowstairs would have much to discuss over their morning tea. She could not dwell on that. Kitty was waiting to disrobe her. She rose and the girl began to unfasten her gown.

A short time later, clad in her nightgown and lacy peignoir, she was once more at her dressing table while Kitty brushed her hair. Verity drew several long breaths in and released them slowly. Soon he would come in and the interview, or rather the interrogation, would begin. She prayed that she could soothe him quickly. Though she deplored the cause, she had not regretted leaving the theater so soon. She was still weary from their long journey to London, now two days behind her, but they had been badly shaken in going over some parts of roads pitted by spring rains. Nor had all the inns where they passed the nights been comfortable. She craved sleep, for tomorrow would be another difficult day. She and her lord would be visiting her grandmother and Caroline, neither of whom had she seen since her marriage. And under Derek's eagle eye, she would have to present the picture of happily wedded bliss. However, she was not thinking about that alone—she wanted to see Miss Marshall, wanted to have a short time alone with her, something that might be very difficult to arrange unless she could placate her husband this night.

Just as Kitty put the brush down, Derek's peremptory knock was heard on the door to her chamber. Verity tensed and once more meeting the abigail's eyes in the looking glass, read commiseration in them. She glanced down quickly, saying coolly, "Admit his lordhsip, please, Kitty. And you may go."

"Yes, milady." Kitty bobbed a curtsy.

Rising as he entered, Verity had a lightning memory of the first time she had encountered his jealousy. They had been on their honeymoon journey to Northumberland and his castle.

Arriving at an inn, they were mounting the stairs toward the suite he had bespoken when a man descending those same stairs had smiled at her. She had smiled back. Subsequently, listening to an angry diatribe from her husband, she had actually giggled at the idea of his believing she would flirt with a stranger. His baseless suspicions no longer aroused her risibilities. They angered and wearied her.

Facing her now, his blue eyes hot with accusation, he said, "Are we always to be confronted with your cast-off lovers here in London, madame?"

"My—what?" She stared at him incredulously. "Sure you cannot be serious!"

"I am perfectly serious, madame. The way he looked at you . . . the familiarity with which he spoke to you—and you, smiling at him as if . . . as if I were not present."

Had she smiled at Rob? Possibly. It had been nearly two years since she had seen anyone she had known before her marriage. A tart response rose to her lips, but she swallowed it. She had to keep her temper in check, else they would be quarreling all the night. She said calmly, evenly, "Robert Dilhorne is Cassie's brother. Cassie is Caroline's best friend, but I have known them both since I was very little.

"Was he often at Harcliffe Manor?"

"I expect he was, but he was such a dreadful tease . . . I never liked him."

"Did you not?" Derek's blue eyes glittered icily. "It seemed to me that you displayed a singular preference for him tonight."

She said patiently, "I have no preference for Rob Dilhorne. I have not seen him in at least four years."

"Really?" He continued to regard her suspiciously. "Then it seems to me that your reception of him was overly friendly and definitely—"

"Derek!" Verity interrupted. "You do weary me with this ridiculous questioning and probing every time I address a word to any single gentleman. Have I ever given you cause to believe me . . . unfaithful?"

"I could not approve the familiar way in which you addressed him," he said insistently. "How often have I tried to impress upon you that . . ."

". . . looks can be misconstrued and smiles are dangerous?" she inquired caustically. "I have lost count, my lord."

"You do not care for him?"

"No, no, no, I care only for you. Have I not given you proof enough of that?" she cried.

He moved to her and caught her in his arms, caressing her and murmuring between passionate kisses, "I am sorry, my dearest. I expect I am unreasonable, but I do love you so entirely . . . and there are times when I fear you have ceased to love me."

"Oh, Derek," she sighed. "How can you be so foolish?"

"Am I?" He still sounded uncertain as he stared down at her.

"Utterly," she chided. Standing on tiptoe, she smoothed back his hair and kissed his ear. "Utterly, utterly foolish my darling," she whispered. Fortunately, he was in a mood to be mollified, and gathering her into his arms, he carried her into his bedchamber.

Later, sitting up beside her sleeping husband, Verity, clasping her knees, stared into the darkness wondering, as she had so often wondered during the nineteen months of their marriage, how she could cope with a jealousy that allowed her no friendships with men or women either and that, in effect, kept her a virtual prisoner in the country and bid fair to do the same in the city. His attitude toward Rob Dilhorne was typical. He could not bear that she should smile on anyone.

The reasons behind their hasty marriage had long been apparent to her. Not only had he fallen in love with her at first sight, he was determined to possess her as soon as possible because of his all-abiding fear that she might find someone else more appealing to her than himself. Her ball had been an agony for him because he, who wanted every dance, could claim only one. Since their marriage, he had forbidden her to join in cotillions or country dances—only waltzes were allowed because he, alone, would partner her. Furthermore, he did not like to accept invitations, mainly because he must needs be separated from her after dinner.

Even if she had been madly in love with him, this intense concentration on herself might have palled, she thought. As it was, it wearied and annoyed her. Aside from his unreasonable jealousy, he was a pleasant companion, and when they

were alone together, matters went smoothly enough. They
had a great deal in common. They both enjoyed riding and
music. Surprisingly enough, he was a fine musician. He
played the violin beautifully, and several evenings a week
were spent with her at the pianoforte accompanying him. He
also enjoyed reading poetry aloud and had a flair for the dra-
matic which was particularly apparent in poems by Walter
Scott and Robert Burns. Fortunately, he also proved to be a
considerate lover, and once she recovered from the surprise
and embarrassment of the wedding night, she found it easy
enough to respond to his ardor. She even missed him during
the weeks he was away from her overseeing his other properties.
Still, she wondered if she would have missed him quite so
much if she had not been left alone with his mother. The
dowager marchioness felt it incumbent upon herself to instruct Verity in every facet of managing the great house. She
did it grudgingly, obviously having no desire to surrender
reins she had held since the death of her husband, three years
after the birth of her only child.

Verity longed to inform the elder Lady Unger that she was
as reluctant to assume those responsibilities as the dowager
was to relinquish them. Unfortunately, this confidence would
only have won Verity the deep displeasure of her mother-in-
law. It had been she who had instilled in Derek the strong
sense of obligation that resulted in absences of a fortnight to a
month while he dutifully consulted with estate managers and
overseers, with tenant farmers and cottagers. It was during
these periods that his mother also pointedly decried the fact
that Verity had not yet conceived the heir she and her son
both desired.

To do Derek justice, he had never reproached her, though
she was sure his disappointment equaled and might even
surpass that of his mother. She could match those feelings. If
she bore his child, his *son* or a daughter, perhaps he would be
more at ease, less possessive of her, and some of that passionate adoration would be transferred to the baby. She loved
children. She would not have minded four or five. It seemed
amazing to her that in the time they had been wed, she had
not conceived. Her own mother, much to her loudly voiced
regret, had borne Verity within nine months of her marriage.
Caroline had arrived nine months later, and Eva ten months

after that. If Lady Harcliffe had not injured herself riding and miscarried, she might have had a round dozen, she had once said in Verity's hearing.

"Verity . . ."

She turned. Derek was awake and reaching for her. Obediently, she snuggled down beside him.

"What were you thinking about?" he asked.

Since the truth must have pained him, she said merely, "You."

"Love." His lips grazed her cheek and then he fell asleep again.

She did not. Her thoughts had shifted to the notebook where she had set down an outline and three chapters from the novel she had managed to transcribe from notes scribbled at odd hours when she was not learning the essentials of household management from her mother-in-law.

It had not been easy for her to pursue her writing—for it had to be done in secret and the notebook carefully hidden, not only because Derek, cannily questioned, had revealed a chill disdain for books from the Minerva Press, but because it was based on an episode concerning a member of his family.

Probably he would never have mentioned his Aunt Cicely had she not seen her portrait in the Long Gallery at Unger Castle. Lady Cicely had been his father's younger sister, and she had eloped with a footman, committing the crowning indiscretion of not coming to grief. The erring couple had fled to Canada, where he had sold her jewels and purchased an inn, which was flourishing! According to all reports, his aunt and her lowborn husband were both wealthy and unrepentant. Of course, she had not based her novel on the story alone. It merely formed the basis of a romance she was tentatively calling *The Canadian Cousin*.

If Derek were to come upon it, she shuddered to contemplate the repercussions arising from his perusal of what he must easily recognize as the tale of his Aunt Cicely. She wondered if many of the *ton* were acquainted with this particular scandal. She intended to have Miss Marshall make some discreet inquiries, if that was possible. Even though Derek did not read circulating-library fiction, her novel might prove familiar to those members of the *ton* who did not hold the Minerva Press in such odium. In those circumstances, word of its publication might reach Derek. She did hope that Aunt Cicely *was* forgotten. She really itched to finish her book. In her estimation, her beginning chapters, again in the epistolary style, were among the best she had ever written. And how could she pass them to Miss Marshall on the morrow? Undoubtedly, the governess would not be present at the reunion of herself and her family. She would be either in her room or in the library. She would think of some excuse. . . . In the midst of these plans, she, too, fell asleep.

"I would not have known you!" Caroline said, regarding Verity with an amazement not entirely free from envy, her gaze ranging from Verity's high-crowned hat to her little white kid shoes. "That is a love of a gown, and as usual, blue is your best color. Do you like the fuller bodies? I wish we still might wear those clinging Grecian costumes with practically nothing underneath! You could carry them off—you're so slim. And let me see those pearls! Oh, they are lovely. Oh, Verity, I have missed you."

"I have missed you, too, Caroline," Verity said warmly. "And you are looking charming, too."

Caroline grimaced. "I am getting so old."

"Old?" Verity laughed. "You are not yet nineteen."

"I am within four months of my nineteenth birthday," Caroline complained. "And Grandmother has not extended herself for me as she did for you. But, of course, I did not have the Marquess of Unger dangling after me since babyhood."

"Come." Verity put her arm around her sister's waist and gave her a loving little squeeze. "I am sure you'll not want for a husband."

"I expect I will not—but I cannot hope for a marquess." Her eyes glinted, and lowering her voice, she added, "Rob Dilhorne's in town."

"I know." Verity winced. "I saw him at the theater last night with Cassie. Have you still a penchant for him?"

"Oh, yes, though . . ." She glanced across the drawing room to where Derek sat talking to Lady Harcliffe. "He is not nearly so handsome as your husband."

Verity longed to say, "Handsome is as handsome does," but loyalty forbade such confidences, and truthfully, he was handsome, especially with the sun lighting his golden locks. Pierre, his valet, had turned him out with especial care. His starched shirt collar touched his cheeks, his cravat was an admirable creation, and his blue coat, just a few shades darker than his eyes, was a miracle of the tailor's art. His trousers were gray, and rather than fitting into Hessians, they were loose around his ankle boots. Though he was garbed in the very latest style, he could never be called a dandy, for there was a certain carelessness in his dress, and he seemed utterly unaware of the attractive figure he cut. As if he were conscious of her eyes on him, he turned and smiled at her.

There was so much affection in his gaze that Verity swallowed a lump in her throat, wishing it were not necessary to deceive him, as she was just about to do. She wished, too, that she could care for him as much as he cared for her. If only he were not so jealous and possessive. It did seem a curious characteristic in a man as fine-looking as her husband, but she could not dwell on that now. She must act while he was still deep in conversation with Lady Harcliffe.

"Caroline," she said urgently, "might I know where Miss Marshall is?"

Caroline looked surprised. "I expect she's in her chamber. She would have come down, but Grandmother thought she could see you on another day."

Though she had expected as much, Verity said, "I do think she should have let her come, especially if she made the request. Grandmother knows the esteem in which I hold her."

"Yes," Caroline agreed, "but she is a servant."

"I do not consider her in that light, and nor should you, Caroline. She has been our mentor and she is my friend."

"More yours than mine," Caroline responded. "I never could understand your affection for her . . . well, I suppose I could. She encouraged your writing. Of course, I do not blame her for that. I miss your stories. I think they are as good as anything published in the Minerva Press. Do you still write?"

"No, I do not. But I should like to see her." Verity edged nearer to the door of the drawing room. "If Grandmother or Derek should ask, tell them I will be back in minutes." Without waiting for her sister's reply, she opened the door and hurried into the hall. She was starting up the stairs to the third floor when she heard an exclamation and glancing upwards saw Miss Marshall. Picking up her skirts, she dashed up the rest of the way and flung her arms around the governess. "Oh, what exceedingly good luck! I was about to search for you and I was no longer sure which room you occupied—but let's go to it. I have so much to tell you."

"My dearest!" Miss Marshall's eyes were very bright. "I was thinking that you looked very different, but I see you are just the same—only more beautiful."

"And you are just the same, too." Verity's own eyes were blurred with tears. She added urgently, "Please let us go where we can talk and they'll not be able to interrupt us."

"Come." Miss Marshall led her down the hall and opened the door to a narrow little room furnished only with a bed, a night table, a chair, and an armoire. A vase of flowers stood on the table, and a tall window faced the Park.

"Oh, you should have more space!" Verity exclaimed indignantly.

"I would not exchange it for my view of the Park," the governess said lightly, her eyes, appraising now, resting on Verity's face. "Pray sit down, my love."

"No, I shall have to leave shortly. Derek will be wondering where I've gone. But no matter." Verity opened her reticule and brought out the crumpled sheets of paper from her notebook. "I am sorry that these are in such a condition, but they are the first chapters of a novel. I should like you to read them if you will and tell me what you think. Also I have much else I wish to discuss with you, and I should like to see Mr. Newman. I am sure that Derek will be called away sooner or later. I pray it will be soon . . . for I do long to hear what you will say about my work."

"I'll read it at once and send you a note, or better yet, call on you."

"No." Verity shook her head. "You must not do either. It's not that I do not want to receive you, dear Miss Marshall, but we'll not have an opportunity to speak privately—not if Derek knows you are coming, and he will know. You see, he's not aware that I have written anything, and he'd be furious if he found out. He loathes the Minerva Press and he has the utmost contempt for all those who write for it. I have inserted a note explaining about his Aunt Cicely, and I do hope you'll be able to discover something about her—perhaps Grandmother will know, but you mustn't say that I have asked, and I do not know quite how you will be able to ask, either, and I am sure Derek must leave town soon . . ."

"My dear," Miss Marshall said as Verity paused for breath, "such alarums and excursions! And why is all this secrecy necessary?"

"I will explain it all, but not now. I must go." Verity hurried to the door, pausing a second to add, "I pray you will like it." Blowing a kiss at her, she hurried into the hall and ran down the stairs. She was not surprised to find Derek standing with one hand on the newel post, gazing upwards, frowning. "I went to see my old governess," she explained hurriedly.

"You might have told me that was what you intended," he said heavily.

"I left word with Caroline. You were quite occupied with Grandmother and I didn't think you would mind."

"And what had you to say to her all this time?" he demanded.

"Was it such a long time?" She gazed at him wide-eyed. "I was not aware of it."

"No, I presume you were not. I have never known you to be purposely discourteous."

"Discourteous?" she echoed.

"To your grandmother—who also wondered where you had disappeared."

"Gracious, such a pother . . . when all I wished to do was visit Miss Marshall. Did not my sister explain to her, as well?"

"She did, but Lady Harcliffe, in common with myself, could not understand why you'd not make your own excuses."

"I have already told you . . ." she began, but looking at his set face, she knew that explanations would never suffice. She was glad she had impressed Miss Marshall with the need for remaining silent, and she stifled a sigh. On seeing her, she had briefly felt like her old self again—rather than the staid and watchful matron she had become—but as her husband offered his arm, she realized the dangers inherent in gazing backwards into a past she had never appreciated enough.

Probably she should not have tempted fate by beginning the novel. She almost hoped it was not as good as she thought it might be. If it was, she would be led into further deceptions, and she was not at all sure she wanted to chance them. She had come to appreciate tranquillity.

Unfortunately for Verity's peace of mind, the fortnight following her reunion with Miss Marshall was very busy. In addition to accompanying her husband to the British Museum and other similarly educational exhibits, she was sitting for the portrait that would eventually hang in the Long Gallery at Unger Castle. There was no opportunity to visit her grand-mother, and consequently her frustration soon outweighed her discretion. Derek showed no disposition to leave town, and a delicate question as to whether he would be visiting any of his estates was ill received.

"Do you wish to be relieved of my presence?" he had asked.

It had taken at least a quarter of an hour combined with fervent denials and kisses to soothe his ruffled feelings. Meanwhile, the sittings were scheduled for twice a week. Any hope that she might be able to cut one of these short and visit Miss Marshall on the sly was quickly squelched by Derek's presence in the studio. Knowing him as well as she did, Verity was sure he distrusted the artist.

That Mr. Tavener was a gentle and benign man of sixty-odd did not allay Derek's suspicions. A noble lady of his mother's acquaintance had eloped with the young man who had come to paint her portrait, and this scandal had given him a horror of the entire breed. Verity was sure that even without that episode, Mr. Tavener would have been suspect.

Since it was impossible to use her sittings as a ploy, she had to fall back on Caroline, telling Derek that her sister wanted her to approve a new gown she would be wearing to an important ball, important mainly because a young gentle-man who had showed a distinct partiality for her would be present. Her sister, Verity explained, was uncertain of both the color and the cut. Fortunately, he raised no cavils concern-ing this visit; he, himself, was bound to Tattersall's for an auction of thoroughbreds, and there was one he particularly wanted to purchase—so Verity finally had her excuse.

The meeting was highly gratifying. Verity listened to Miss Marshall's glowing praise and also learned that she had made discreet inquiries among the servants. "For they always know family histories, my dear. And none of them has ever heard of this erring lady."

There was an even more exciting message for Verity. Miss Marshall had dispatched the material, carefully recopied on clean sheets of foolscap, to Mr. Newman, who had expressed a definite interest in it. However, he had some suggestions, and rather than relaying them through the governess, he wanted to meet with the author. That, of course, presented another problem compounded by the usual complications. Though she made a notable effort not to criticize her husband, Verity was so used to confiding in Miss Marshall that finally and reluctantly, she told her about his strictures.

"But the man must be a veritable monster!" Miss Marshall exclaimed angrily.

"He's not really monstrous," Verity said. "But he does seem to feel I am not trustworthy. Consequently, I do not see when I will be able to get away—unless he leaves the city."

"Such a handsome young man. I do not understand it."

"No more do I. It is very difficult not to be able to . . . to even have someone look at me without . . ." To her surprise and embarrassment, Verity found herself blinking away tears. "And of course he holds the books from the Minerva Press in such anathema, which I s-suppose is no more than r-right, but . . ."

"They are not all of the same caliber," Miss Marshall responded hotly. "If you continue to improve as you have been doing, I've no doubt that one day you'll find a much more prestigious house."

"Oh, do you think so?"

"I do."

"Oh, dear, if I could only tell him about it . . . 'twould make it so much easier to continue."

"Perhaps I might drop a word to him."

"No, I pray you will not. Besides, it would make no difference. He is very set in his opinions, and he would be furious that I had not told him about my writing. I shall have to continue as I have been doing . . . and he is away quite often."

"My poor girl."

"Oh, please." Verity wiped her eyes. "I am very well. He can be kind, you know."

"Still . . . " Miss Marshall frowned and shook her head. " 'Tis wrong that the honesty that is such an integral part of your nature should be doubted."

"I wish you might persuade him of that, and his mother, also, for she seems to distrust me as much as he does. But no matter, I must go. I have given my sister Caroline quite enough advice upon her gown." Verity winked at Miss Marshall, kissed her, and hurried down the stairs. It occurred to her that she ought to have informed Caroline of her ploy, but her sister was not home, and besides she was not sure Caroline could be counted on to keep a still tongue in her head concerning her unfortunate situation. She might tell Cassie Dilhorne, and Cassie would spread it all over town!

It was most unfortunate that within two days of her visit to Miss Marshall, her grandmother should invite Verity and her husband to dine with her. Though Derek often found reasons to refuse such invitations, this time he accepted with alacrity. Any hope that she might have a moment to be private with Caroline was flouted by her grandmother's engaging herself and Derek in a long conversation concerning the Prince Regent's growing *embonpoint* and her fear that his highness was far from well, which meant that one of his brothers might succeed to the title and to the throne, and she could not imagine which one of them could reign creditably.

Fortunately, it was a topic that merited further discussion over the dinner table, and Verity was breathing easier when Derek suddenly looked interrogatively at Caroline and jocularly asked if she was pleased with her new ballgown.

"My ballgown?" Caroline regarded him in surprise.

"You remember." Verity managed to speak lightly. "The one you're wearing to the Drummond ball. You were concerned about the color."

"Oh, yes, of course," Caroline said quickly. "Yes, I am most pleased with it. I did think the pink too insipid, but now I must agree with you."

Verity could have kissed her for that speedy recovery and inspired invention, especially when Derek, obviously unaware of Caroline's hesitation, said, "I often rely on my wife's suggestions for my own wardrobe. She has a highly developed sense of color.''

"Indeed, she has." Caroline sent a swift glance in Verity's direction.

Fastening what she prayed was a speaking look upon her sister's face, together with a tiny nod, Verity hoped she had assured Caroline that an explanation would be provided later. She dared to visit a second look upon her husband and found him totally absorbed in his portion of the well-cooked neat's tongue they had just been served. It was only then that she released the breath she had been holding. For once, he had not noticed!

Three days later, it seemed as if all her connivances had been unnecessary. Derek was called away! Told about the summons, Verity's nineteen months of marriage stood her in good stead. She managed to suppress the wild joy she experienced upon hearing news that would allow her to visit the Minerva Press without resorting to further stratagems. In fact, she was even able to simulate distress and produce a tear or two at the thought of being separated yet again from her husband.

Though he appeared extremely gratified in this display, Derek adjured her to accept invitations from no one save her grandmother. "For to go about without me would give rise to talk, my love," he said more than once. "I could wish that my mother's letter had not come so soon after our arrival in the city. If we had had the opportunity to go about more . . . but we have not, so I pray you'll find ways to occupy yourself at home, or possibly you might ride in the Park with your sister if she is so inclined."

"I will do my best to give you no anxiety, my lord," Verity assured him. "I do hope you'll not be gone overlong."

"I cannot say. I expect it will not be much longer than a fortnight."

It was not until his post chaise had rounded the bend in the street that Verity, watching and waving at the wrought-iron gates in front of the mansion, dared to breathe easier. She could hardly believe her good fortune, and at the same time she felt sorry that there was so little she could share with her husband. She still needed to be careful. The servants, Mrs. Browne, the housekeeper, Crane, the butler, and the rather faceless collection of footmen and maids, grooms and stableboys, went about their duties with an eye to the house-keeper rather than herself.

Her husband's insistence that she remain with him most of the time during this first month had kept her from exercising the vigilance demanded by her mother-in-law. She had made tentative mention of this to Derek only to be told crisply, "Nonsense. Mrs. Browne will see to all that. You need only order up the meals."

That did not mean she was entirely aloof from the household. Kitty, who had as interested an ear to the ground as any red savage in distant America, brought her bits of gossip concerning people she knew and those she did not know in Great Jermyn Street and beyond. This information suggested the existence of a grapevine belowstairs that tentacled into every noble house in London. It was the existence of this gossip mill that was responsible, she was positive, for many of the items that found their way into the *Morning Post* and other similar newspapers, as well as for the lampoons and cartoons which were to be seen in many a printer's shop window. They caused considerable trouble, not excluding duels, separations, and, on occasion, even divorce.

Thus primed, she would have to be exceptionally cautious. Only Kitty could be taken into her confidence—that was necessary, for there might be times when she would need a companion. And, of course, it must be Kitty who would convey the glad tidings to Miss Marshall. With that in mind, Verity sped inside the house. Reaching her apartments, she was actually inclined to do a little dance. She felt really exultant! In the country, she had found herself missing Derek—but this was London, and located on one special street was the Minerva Press, no longer a tantalizing chimera, but a reality which could be visited as soon as tomorrow!

Two

Once more, Verity, seated in a hackney coach beside Miss Marshall, was driving in the direction of Leadenhall Street. The feeling of the past was strong in her mind, and that was hardly surprising. Once again, she was betraying a trust, only this time a husband, not a grandmother, was to be cozened. In her mind, she challenged the word as soon as she employed it. Her husband was unreasonable, and his sense of his own consequence was almost as strong as that of her grandmother. It was he who was forcing her to act in a way much at variance with her desires. As Miss Marshall said, by nature she *was* open and honest. Circumstances were forcing her to be closed and dishonest. She wished once more that she were as talented as the late Miss Austen. No one had ever looked down on her because she wrote novels. She doubted that Jane Austen had ever been required to work in *secrecy*.

Granted, her own outpourings were the stuff of romance rather than witty exposures of society's foibles. Still, young women of her class with a bent towards self-expression were encouraged to draw and paint. Insipid delineations of flowers, barely recognizable sketches of ruined churches or Roman pillars, *were* acceptable, but writing was not—unless one penned immensely clever letters! Society did approve these.

It occurred to Verity that she really did not give a fig for society with its conventions and its gossip. It was a strange world where empty chatter and the artful dissection of character were permissible and romances were not. If she wanted to write, she must continue to cloak her efforts in secrecy—and she would never, never be free from the fear that her husband would ferret out the truth. She declined to consider what would happen then. Resolutely, she put Derek out of her mind. For the nonce, she was free and on her way to see Mr. Newman!

It surprised Verity to find, once she set foot in the publisher's anteroom, that everything was the same, with the same clerk perched on his high stool, bending over his ledger. The windows with their small square panes were still slightly grimy, and glancing down, she found that the carpet was still a little frayed. So much had changed in her life that she had expected that everything must keep pace with it, which, of course, was utterly ridiculous!

The clerk smiled at her. He was more obsequious in his manner. He clambered off of his stool immediately. She received a low bow in deference to her change in circumstances, but as before he said, if more deferentially than in the past, "Mr. Newman is closeted with an author, but I will tell him you have arrived, milady."

An author.

Verity remembered that these had been the clerk's words when first she had come here—and the author who emerged had been Alan Parry, whose visage had haunted her dreams in the days before she was wed.

It had been ages since she had thought about him. What a child she had been. Life and love had been closed volumes to her then. In those days, everything she had read and written ended with a chaste kiss, preferably on the cheek. She had heard that kisses on the lips were dangerous because that was how babies were conceived. Had she really credited such fables? She had. She smiled derisively. She might as easily have believed one of Perrault's fairy tales! She felt a hundred years older than the Verity Stratton of those years and also a hundred miles removed from this world of struggling authors, whose livelihood depended on their output—as must have been the case with poor Mr. Parry of the shabby garments and the proud carriage.

Had he held himself proudly? She rather thought he had. He had been nice-looking, too. Dark? Yes, he had been dark and not as tall as Derek. Odd to have forgotten him so completely until this moment, especially since she vaguely remembered having wept over the fact that they would never meet again. She laughed and turned to Miss Marshall. "I was really a ninny, when I first came here. In fact, I might have stepped from the pages of one of my own novels."

"Why do you say that, my dear?" The governess looked surprised. "I never remember you being a ninny."

"Perhaps I never told you, but . . ." She paused as the door to the inner office opened, and arrested by a voice she seemed to know, she turned to find Mr. Parry coming toward her, followed by the publisher. He was carrying two books, and he looked more prosperous than she remembered. She knew a great deal more about the masculine wardrobe now and guessed that his garments had been cut by a good tailor. In common with Derek, he wore trousers and ankle boots, and the hat he had just doffed was wide at the crown. His dark hair was cut relatively short and curled about his face, and she was reminded of the bust of the Roman emperor she had seen in the British museum. She remembered, too, that the same analogy had occured to her once before.

"My dear Lady Unger." The publisher bowed over her hand.

"Mr. Newman, how very pleasant to see you again," she said composedly. "And Mr. Parry, is it not?"

"It is, Lady Unger." He took her hand but did not kiss it, and looking in the governess's direction, he added, "Miss Marshall." He bowed.

"Mr. Parry," she said, smiling at him, "I think I must offer you my congratulations. Mr. Newman has told me how well your book on travel in the Levant and Greece is doing, and I am delighted."

"I thank you, Miss Marshall." He favored her with a warm smile.

"Oh, have you been traveling, then?" Verity asked.

He nodded. "It was my good fortune to be the courier for a young couple who were much enamored of Lord Byron's poems and wished to visit some of the sites that inspired him."

"Ah." Verity smiled at him, and declaimed, " 'He left a Corsair's name to other times, link'd with one virtue and a thousand crimes!' "

Mr. Parry's dark eyes glinted appreciatively. "I see you have conned your Byron well, Lady Unger."

"How could I not? It is the very essence of romance. Did you have many adventures in Greece and Turkey?"

"Some, but alas, I was forced by the limits of my inspiration to turn them into prose, not poesy." He touched one of the volumes he was carrying.

"Is that your book?" she asked.

" 'Tis the sequel, a few extra adventures, only enough to fill a single volume."

"The other has sold out," Mr. Newman said with considerable pleasure.

"Oh, how lovely!" she exclaimed. She added impulsively, "Might I see it?"

"You may more than see it . . . might I make you a present of it?"

"Oh, but I couldn't take it," she protested. "Those must be advance copies."

"You couldn't take it—because you have it, already." He held the volume toward her.

She flushed. "I do thank you, but if you are making me a gift, you must sign it, please."

"I'd be delighted." He looked up at the clerk. "Aloysius, might I have the loan of your quill?"

"Of a certainty, Mr. Parry." The clerk handed him the pen.

Leaning the book against his high desk, Mr. Parry wrote what appeared to be more than his name before handing the book to her.

"I do thank you," she said gratefully. "I . . ." She paused, startled, as the front door swung open and a small gentleman came inside, looking around him vaguely. "I say," he said aggrievedly. " 'Tis not the tobbaconist's 'ere at all."

"No, my good man, I fear you've been misdirected," the publisher said.

"I'll say I 'ave," responded the interloper, glaring at them. He left hastily, slamming the door behind him with a force that rattled the windowpanes.

"Gracious," Miss Marshall commented. "He must have been sorely in need of a smoke."

"May he choke on it for his rudeness," Mr. Parry said. He turned back to Verity. "I pray you'll let me have a copy of *The Canadian Cousin,* when it's printed."

"It's not even fully written yet, sir."

"But it must be, and soon," Mr. Parry said enthusiastically. "I'll not rest until I'm granted a look at the final chapters."

"Oh, you have read this one, too," she said, remembering that Mr. Newman had given him *Elvira*.

"I have," he said and nodded.

"Alan agrees with me that it is nearly ready for publication— that which you have written down, save for a few minor changes which I propose to discuss with you now," Mr. Newman told her.

"Oh, I am so pleased that you both like it!" she exclaimed. She turned to the publisher. "And Miss Marshall has told me that I will not be treading on anyone's toes by mingling a few facts with my fiction."

"Not at all. I have my spies, and all tell me that there have been so many scandals in the last twenty years that Lady Cicely's elopement is long forgotten," Mr. Newman assured her.

"And everyone who writes is inclined to mingle even more than just a few facts with their fiction," Mr. Parry affirmed with a roguish wink.

"I fear that is entirely true," Miss Marshall commented.

"You should not fear that, Miss Marshall," he admonished. "If we authors didn't keep our ears and eyes open, we should surely run out of inspiration. Do you not agree, Lady Unger?"

"I have no choice but to agree, Mr. Parry. And I must look and see what you've inscribed in this book." She opened the flyleaf and giggled as she read out loud, " 'From one to another with sincere appreciation.' I vow, sir, that could mean anything!"

"Should I add the word 'author'?" he smilingly demanded.

"No, there's no need for a further translation. I do understand it," she said lightly, thinking at the same time that she must be careful to put the volume where Derek would not find it. At the thought of her husband, she had a deep sense of regret for those baseless suspicions that took so much joy out of their lives. It was well that it had not been he who had blundered into the office; she could guess what he would have imagined seeing her speaking with such familiarity to another gentleman. Nothing she could have said would have prevented him from deciding that there was an illicit intrigue

afoot. It was particularly annoying to her that he should
believe her so lacking in moral fiber. Even if she had not
wanted to marry him, at least not so hastily, she did have
respect for him, and affection, too. Certainly she would never
bring shame to him through some hole-in-the-corner intrigue!

With that in mind, she was actually pleased when Mr.
Parry said to the publisher, "You'll be wanting to speak with
Lady Unger, Tony, and I must go." This time, he bowed
over her hand. "Your servant, my lady. 'Twas a pleasure to
see you again."

"It was my pleasure, too, Mr. Parry, and my best wishes
for your continued success."

"I thank you." He kissed Miss Marshall's hand and with
the publisher's handshake and farewell he was gone.

"Such a nice young man," Miss Marshall said appreciatively.

"Very," Mr. Newman agreed. "I'm thinking that we may
lose him soon."

"Lose him?" Verity repeated, experiencing a queer little
pang. "Why?"

"I feel that he is moving away from the circulating libraries and into a more serious vein of literary endeavor, not that
I am decrying my field—but of late, he has shown a disposition to abandon the romantic for the picaresque. Or he might
even concentrate on nonfiction. You will see what I mean
when you read the book he has presented to you."

"I am looking forward to it," Verity said, wondering why
she was so relieved by this confidence. She had feared . . .
but she was not sure what she had feared, she decided, as she
and Miss Marshall went into the publisher's inner office.

Verity was in the library working on her novel when the
curious communication from Cassie Dilhorne was brought to
her by the butler. She was extremely annoyed at the
interruption. In the last two days, her book had been progressing very well; her pen had literally sped over the paper that
morning, and she was looking forward to an equally produc-
tive afternoon. She needed to work quickly, for it was impossible to guess when Derek would be returning. Consequently,
Cassie's missive, delivered by a footman who had informed
Crane that he must wait for an answer, was in definite danger

of being crumpled and tossed into the wastebasket. Of course, Verity changed her mind. Lady Cassandra was not in the habit of dispatching such urgent summonses to her. In fact, this was the first note she had ever received from the young lady, who was really Caroline's friend.

She was surprised to read that Lady Cassandra begged that she be allowed to see her that afternoon at two upon a matter of the utmost importance, that sentence emphasized by no less than three dark strokes of the pen under each word.

Verity was minded to send back a note saying that it was impossible to grant this favor. She had never been particularly fond of Cassie, less so now because of Derek's reaction to Rob's attentions at the theater. Her sense of fairness intervened to remind her that that had not been the fault of the Dilhornes. And, of course, she was curious to know why Cassie was so anxious to communicate with her. Accordingly, she sent back a note saying she would be pleased to receive Lady Cassandra at the requested hour.

Lady Cassandra arrived a few minutes before two, and Verity, summoned to the drawing room, found her standing in front of the sculptured marble fireplace gazing up at an equestrian portrait of Derek's late father and wringing her hands.

"Cassie, dear," Verity said with more warmth than usual. "What's amiss?"

Cassie whirled, and Verity was amazed to see that her large green eyes, usually sparkling with laughter and often with mischief, were red-rimmed and tearful. Reaching out her small-mitted hands she grasped Verity's wrists and said imploringly, "I wonder if you can help us."

"Us . . . you and Rob?" Verity questioned in some surprise.

"No, not Rob." Cassie gave her a fierce look which, Verity guessed, was really directed at her brother. "Do you remember Reggie Delaville?" Without giving Verity a chance to reply, she continued hastily, "He's being sent to Jamaica, and the Lord knows when he'll return—if—if ever." Cassie's tears overflowed and ran down her cheeks.

"Reggie Delaville." Verity did remember him, remembered, too, that he had been known as a loose-screw, always into mischief but charming, and, also, a particular friend of Rob Dilhorne's and his sister's as well, obviously. "I did have a slight acquaintance with him, but why is he being sent to Jamaica?"

"Because his miserable uncle has a sugar plantation and his family is insisting he join him. Poor Reggie's been in so many scrapes, and he's in debt, too. I hold no b-brief for him, but he—he is leaving tomorrow and I—I must see him." Cassie held a handkerchief to her streaming eyes. "We . . . have arranged to meet at Vauxhall Gardens at seven tonight. Of course, no one must know. Rob is ever so stiffnecked when it comes to Reggie, especially now that I am engaged to Lord Ormond. It just happened—the engagement, I mean; it will be announced at a b-ball—but I must see Reggie. I . . . I could not let him go off into the . . . the wilds without a final farewell. I do love him, you know. And he loves me—but it is all impossible. And I must see him.

"Fortunately, Mama is ill with the toothache and Rob is out this evening—so it will be easy enough for me to get away. I have hired a closed carriage, but Verity, I . . . I dare not go to the Gardens alone. I need to have a chaperon, and since you are married . . . I know your husband does not approve of us, but Caroline has told me he is away."

"He is, but it's not true that he doesn't approve," Verity began kindly.

"No matter," Cassie interrupted impatiently. "I do not care what he thinks. Will you come to the Gardens with me? I'll only be there for a half hour and then I shall leave immediately, with no one the wiser save that I will tell Rob that I came to visit you."

"Vauxhall Gardens . . ." Verity regarded her in amazement. "But I shouldn't be there without a male escort."

"Verity, as a married woman, you can be my chaperon," Cassie insisted. "I would ask Caroline—but she *couldn't* go. And we will not be without a male escort, because Reggie will meet us there and he'll bring us both home, but he cannot call for me. I shudder to think what would happen if anyone in the family saw him!" Again, Cassie made use of her handkerchief. "Oh, Verity, I do not see how I can bear it . . . a half hour to see him and then a *lifetime* without him!" Putting both hands over her face, Cassie began to weep in earnest. "Please, please," she sobbed. "Say you will help me."

It was impossible for Verity not to sympathize with Cassie, impossible for her not to remember how she had been rushed into marriage at a moment when she had been close to falling in love with someone else, or thought she had been. Of course, she could not compare her situation to that of Cassie, who had known Reggie nearly all of her life, but it was tragic that they were being separated. Still, it was a very risky thing to do—for her as well as for Cassie. "I . . . would have to take my maid," she began.

"Oh, no." Cassie stared at her in horror. "You must not dream of such a thing. Servants gossip so dreadfully. It would be all over London within six hours. 'Twould be best for you to leave by a side door—you must have a side door. Then you could meet me. Reggie and I will bring you back and no one the wiser. You can return the way you came. Just leave the door on the latch."

"I suppose that would be better," Verity agreed, knowing full well that the whole scheme was preposterous—but at the same time she did want to help Cassie, and she had always wanted to visit Vauxhall Gardens, something she would never be able to do when Derek was in town. He did not approve of pleasure gardens. "Too many cits" had been his dictum. His decision had been extremely disappointing, especially since she had hoped to use Vauxhall in *The Canadian Cousin*. Her eyes brightened. Actually, the opportunity was too good to miss!

"Very well," she capitulated. "I will go with you."

"Oh, ooooh, Verity!" Cassie squeaked, throwing her arms around her. "I will be in your debt for ever and ever—ask of me what you will and you shall have it! I swear it to you on my mother's head!"

It occurred to Verity that she had never cared for Cassie's excessive behavior. It also occurred to her that she would have been far wiser not to have acquiesced to this scheme, but on viewing Cassie's radiant face, she did not have the heart to offer any further objections.

Getting away from the house without alerting any of the servants to her intentions was not as complicated as Verity had feared. Kitty, she recalled, had often complained that when the master was absent, the staff served dinner and then, one and all, retired to their quarters and could not be raised. Her contention was that the footmen and butler should at least remain in the hall for fear of thieves—not that they would have been much use, since all were elderly and most had been hired by his lordship's father. Consequently, Verity ordered an early supper and told Kitty that as she intended to write far into the night, she would give her the evening off and not require her services until morning.

Unfortunately, this meant that she had to dress herself, something she had rarely done. She chose what she hoped was a chaperonish gown, being a pale gray muslin with very little trimming and with long sleeves and a high neck. While she had no trouble getting into it, the buttons at the wrists and the back of the neck proved extremely difficult. They were so small and pesky, and besides, her fingers were shaking. She had not expected to feel so nervous, but by the time she had slipped into her shoes and swathed herself in a light hooded cloak, she longed to send a message to Cassie explaining that she had been stricken with a blinding headache. Of course, she could not do anything so craven, could not back out of a promise—that would not be honorable.

She went down the stairs very quietly, but, actually, Kitty had not erred in her description of the servants' habits. Verity might easily have left the house by the front rather than the alternate entrance, but just to be on the safe side, she kept to her original plan, going along a passageway to the door that opened on the garden and also on a path leading to the front of the house.

Once she reached the sidewalk, Verity realized that this was the first time she had ever been abroad without a companion. She had not expected to feel so intimidated. Glancing swiftly around her, she saw that Cassie's post chaise was standing at the end of the street, a yellow ribbon dangling from one window to identify it.

Verity found it surprisingly daunting to walk even that short way to the vehicle. There were not many people on the street, but she had the uncomfortable feeling that those who passed her looked upon her with surprise and even suspicion. She was considerably relieved when she reached the post chaise but experienced another jolt of nervousness when she saw that its shades were drawn, giving it, she thought, an oddly sinister aspect.

The door opened at once to her tap, and Verity felt much easier in her mind, seeing Cassie sitting there smiling at her. "You are right on time, my dear. I was so worried. I really feared you might not be able to get away." She called to the driver, and a second later, a postboy had placed steps in front of the carriage door.

Cassie did not look worried, Verity decided as she sat down beside her. In fact, she seemed amazingly calm, much calmer than she herself felt. However, she soon divined that her companion was nervous. She talked incessantly, thanking Verity for coming with her and the extolling the virtues of Reggie—poor Reggie, so unjustly treated and sent abroad like a criminal. Verity listened with half an ear. It seemed to her that it was taking a very long time to reach their destination. They had traversed so many streets and made so many turns, and now there was an odor in her nostrils that she recognized. They were nearing the river! And then she remembered something she had forgotten until this moment. "The Vauxhall Gardens are in Lambeth!" she exclaimed.

"Yes, of course, dear," Cassie affirmed. "And we're approaching the bridge now. I am glad we did not have to go by boat. Years ago they used to go by boat, and I become ill when I so much look at one of them!"

"I'd forgotten that it was so very far," Verity said nervously.

"It is quite a distance," Cassie admitted. "But we will be back in good time, I promise you that."

"You'll not be spending more than a half hour with him, you said."

"I said it and I meant it. I dare not remain away very long, myself, so I beg you, dear, trust me."

The horses' hooves made a hollow echoing sound on the bridge. Listening to it, Verity, sitting with clenched hands, was more and more convinced that she had made a grievous error in consenting to come with Cassie. If Derek were ever to find out . . . but he would not, because he was in the country and she would return by the same door through which she had left. She did not think any of the servants would discover that she had left it on the latch, and she must comfort herself with the fact that Cassie did not dare remain in the

gardens above a half hour. She did wish that she had known
it would take such an unconscionably long time to reach their
destination.

Verity's qualms, at their zenith when the hackney stopped
at the entrance to the Gardens, were replaced by excitement
as she stepped out to find herself in a veritable fairyland.
Though many of the trees that had once stood on that vast
acreage had been chopped down, many remained, and threaded
through their branches were tiny, glimmering bulbs, some
red, some blue, some green, and some white. Each encased a
tiny gas flame. It was an amazing and beautiful sight and
would become even more beautiful, she knew, as twilight
faded into dusk. Her excitement increased as Cassie paid the
four shillings that would grant them access to this wonderland.
And there were more wonders to come. She could see a huge
tower glittering through the trees—that, too, was a lovely
sight. She wanted to stand and look at it, so that she might
impress it on her mind and describe it when she got home,
but Cassie plucked impatiently at her arm.

"Come, we must go to the dance platform, which is near
the orchestra pavilion. It's not far—you can see it through
the trees." She pointed in the direction of the tower.

"Oh, I do want to see that," Verity said excitedly.

"Well, come, then. That's where Reggie said he'd meet
us—though I must say we'll be lucky if we find him in this
crush."

It was crowded. Verity was glad of the hood that shaded
her face. Many gentlemen looked at them and some tried to
talk to them, only to be rudely dismissed by Cassie, quite as
if she were the chaperon, rather than the other way around.
"Come, Verity," she urged again. "You mustn't stop and
stare at everything you see. You'll have a chance to do your
fill of gazing once we are in our box."

They had reached the tall building that housed the orchestra,
and on viewing it close up, Verity found it even more fascinating than she had imagined it would be. It was fancifully
shaped, rather like an Oriental palace. Its domed roof was
topped by a bright globe. Beneath the dome there was an
immense balcony, and beneath that was the level containing
the orchestra. At the base of the edifice were doors leading to

he stairs by which the musicians ascended to their alcove.
However, it was not its construction that caught and dazzled
he eye, it was the myriads of lights decorating it from dome
o base. Thousands of little glass bulbs were arranged in an
infinity of different patterns—blinding in their varicolored
radiance. A dance platform stretched in front of the pavilion,
and there were so many people dancing or merely watching
that Verity was confounded. She did not see how Reggie
would ever be able to find them. She was about to say as
much to Cassie when a tall, dark, and dissipated-looking
young man came over to them and dared to tap Cassie on the
shoulder. Verity was expecting her to give him the angry
set-down he deserved, but instead she shrieked and cast
herself into his arms, crying, "Reggie, oh, darling, Reggie."

"Cassie, my dear." Reggie kissed her with a passion that
surprised and shocked Verity. The pair appeared totally oblivi-
ous of more than a few interested observers among the crowds.
Finally, reluctantly, they separated, and positioning himself
between herself and Cassie, Reggie hurried them along to the
box he had bespoken.

There were rows of these boxes. They were draped in
scarlet velvet, and their front panels bore paintings of sylvan
scenes replete with nymphs and shepherds. There was room
enough inside for small tables and chairs and for the waiter to
serve light refreshments. Reggie had chosen one at the far
end. "We'll sit here until the wine comes," he said as he led
Cassie and Verity up a small pair of stairs into the box.
"Then, Verity, my dear, Cassie and I will desert you briefly."

"You are leaving me?" Verity questioned on a note of
panic.

"Briefly, my dear," Cassie emphasized. "But not yet.
We're here to toast each other and to gobble a few cakes and
. . ." Just for a moment her voice quavered. "To wish you
Godspeed, Reggie."

"Better spend those wishes on the Jamaicans," Reggie
responded with an attempt of lightness that was not entirely
successful. "My father and my noble brother will, I assure
you."

"I cannot believe that," Verity said quickly.

"You may believe it, Verity. A black sheep amid the
lambs."

"Oh, fortunate lambs," Cassie murmured.

Looking from one to the other, Verity was very sorry for them. They were very much in love, that was evident. It was also evident, alas, that Cassie's family was right in its contention that Reggie was no husband for her. Certainly he had been doing it too brown of late. Though he was still in his early twenties, there were dark pouches under his eyes, and the lines across his forehead were surprisingly deep. In repose, his mouth was too slack, and his color even in this uncertain light was not healthy. She guessed that his father and brother hoped that once removed from the temptations of the city, his health must improve.

"And so you, Verity, my child, are the Marchioness of Unger," Reggie drawled. "But you do not look like a marchioness, does she, Cassie?"

Verity started and flushed. She had been so absorbed in observing Reggie that she had been unaware that he might have been engaged in that same occupation. "What must a marchioness look like?" she asked.

"Not as if she had just been let out of the schoolroom." He smiled. "I vow I was surprised when I heard Unger was dangling after you."

"You were?" Verity questioned. "Why?"

"Well, let us say that I am surprised you accepted. I should think you'd have preferred a bit more bend to the bow."

"My husband's quite well enough," Verity said loyally.

"Is he?" Reggie shrugged. "It's a pity his father died so young. Merry old soul, so I've heard. Would have given your marquess some honey with the physick."

"I expect you mean my mother-in-law." Verity meant to speak haughtily. She had certainly not intended to giggle. Unfortunately, she did.

"Ah." Reggie placed a long finger under her chin and tilted her face up. "Not quite gone. Glad to see it."

"Gone? What can you mean?" Verity demanded.

"You . . . the way you used to be. I don't like to see you looking as stiff and solemn as a nun on her knees."

"I should think a nun would look stiffer if she were standing," Verity observed.

"Now that's more like it," Reggie approved.

"Do stop teasing her!" Cassie chided.

"I think she could do with a bit of teasing." Reggie pulled a horrendous face at Verity. "I'll wager she doesn't get much of it from the Hermit of Unger."

"The . . . Hermit of Unger?" Verity repeated.

"That is how he was known at Harrow, I understand from Clive Chalfant, who was at school with him."

"Why did they call him a hermit?" Cassie demanded.

"Because he was so damned unfriendly . . . so full of his own consequence."

Verity was about to defend Derek, but a waiter brought the wine and the cakes. Reggie poured three glasses, and they toasted him. Three more, and he toasted them. Then he ordered another bottle and they toasted the natives in Jamaica, Reggie's father and brother, and Verity's mother-in-law.

She was feeling pleasantly mellow, and she did not remember laughing so much in ages. Consequently, when Cassie and Reggie rose, albeit somewhat tipsily, Verity said, "Hurry back," but quite without her earlier feelings of panic.

Cassie bent and kissed her on the cheek. "On the wings of the wind, love," she murmured and was gone.

Verity was glad to be alone; it gave her a chance to observe the crowds and to watch the dancers on the platform. She wanted to inscribe the scene in her mind so that she might produce it as she had produced so many other pictures when she started writing. She wasn't quite sure where she wanted to insert this section—but she would find a place. It was difficult to concentrate on the trials of her heroine. Her head felt light, or did it feel heavy? She was not quite sure. Probably she should not have had so much to drink. Derek frowned on her taking more than a glass of punch or champagne. He frowned on so much. He would certainly frown if he were here tonight—but he was not, and she must take full advantage of the fact that she was here. She would not have a second chance to come to Vauxhall. Of that, she was gloomily positive.

The Hermit of Unger . . . that was a good description of Derek. He really didn't like other people very much. And actually, they had been living like hermits—well, not entirely, but the castle had been like a huge cell, lonely, forsaken, cold.

She did not want to think of him, not in the midst of all this merriment. All around her, young couples were enjoying themselves. She and Derek were both young—why couldn't they be like other people? She sighed and pushed back her hood. It was uncomfortably hot. A warm breeze had risen. She lifted her face to it and then rested her chin on her cupped hands. The music was so pleasant, so hummable, and all the colored lights were so pretty, though rather hazy and inclined to blur together. Her eyelids felt heavy—but that would wear off. She did wish she had not taken so much wine. She also wondered where Cassie and Reggie had gone. She hoped they would not remain away long. How long had they been gone, she wondered, and stopped wondering as her eyelids grew heavier. She could hardly keep them open. She decided to close them, because the lights were so bright and they hurt her eyes. She closed them and leaned back in her chair.

"Well, Sleeping Beauty, as I live and breathe. Shall I wake her with a kiss?"

Verity, opening her eyes, felt an arm heavy on her shoulders and a horrid sucking pressure on her lips. A scream rose in her throat, and bringing up both hands, she thrust them against the shoulders of the man who was embracing her, the while she struggled to turn her head away. She was unsuccessful in both counts. He continued to embrace her and then, laughing loudly, rose and stood grinning down at her. "That's no way to greet your Prince Charming, little love," he chortled.

She brought her hand to her assaulted lips. "How dare you!" she cried. "Leave this box at once. My . . . my friends will return at any moment, and I warn you . . ."

"Warn away, my pretty little ladybird. I've been watching you for quite some time, and by my guess they've been gone at least an hour. I'm not sure. I did not consult my watch . . . not when I could look at you slumbering so sweetly." He sat down in the chair that Reggie had vacated and ran his hand down her bare arm. " 'Tis my guess they'll make a night of it out there on the grounds, and shouldn't you like to do the same?"

She regarded him in horror. He was a big man. She judged him to be somewhere in his late twenties. He had a coarse face, a loose mouth. She had an inward shudder, remembering that he had dared to kiss her—and was he speaking the truth? Had they been gone so long? She could not be sure—could not be sure how long she had slept. He had said an hour . . . an hour? He still had his hand on her arm. She had to get away from him. She said icily, "Please remove your hand, sir. And also your person. I have not given you leave to sit at my table."

"But I want to talk to you," he said in a low voice. He did remove his arm, only to slip it around her shoulders. "Look about you, my lovely. Everyone here is two by two, just like in old Noah's ark. Now it don't seem right to me that we should be one and one . . . doesn't seem like a proper equation at all, especially when you're such a pretty little ladybird and I'm not so bad-looking, myself."

Her head was clearing with amazing rapidity. She had to get away from this lout—but she mustn't panic. She must be clever. With a great effort, she made herself smile. "I think you're right, sir. It does seem a great shame that I've been left alone here, especially when I am longing to dance. I hope you dance. I do love a waltz."

"Well, now," he said approvingly. "That's more like it. So you love a waltz, do you? I love a waltz, myself . . . especially when I can lead a lovely little ladybird like yourself around the floor. Come then."

He was a very big man. That was impessed upon her anew as he rose and without further ado, pulled her from her chair. His breath reeked of liquor, and he was holding her arm so tightly! She let him lead her out of the box—any hope that she could jump down the steps and dash away was flouted by the fact that he waited for her at the bottom of them, his arms held out. If she could call for help . . . but who would heed her? Laughter rose on all sides of her, and some women were screaming, but only in fun, she was sure. And where were Cassie and Reggie? Had they really been gone as long as he said? She had a terrible feeling he had not lied about that. She heard giggles. Could that be Cassie returning? She peered through the darkness but saw nothing. Still, that sound had given her an idea.

"Oh," she cried. "There you are, my dear. Whatever kept you both so long?"

As she had hoped, his attention was diverted. She leaped

from the steps and sidling around him began to run through the crowds. With an angry roar, he was after her. She ran faster, dodging around couples, around trees, and all the time he was yelling at her—and then suddenly, she ran against someone who with an exclamation, caught and held her. She looked up into the surprised face of another man.

"Oh, please, please, let me go . . . he . . . he . . ." she sobbed. "Please . . . I must get away from . . ."

"But what is the trouble? Am I to understand that someone is pursuing you?" The man spoke in a soft and cultivated tone of voice.

"Oh, yes, I . . . I came with friends and they left me and he . . . oh, please, sir, let me go." She struggled against his firm grasp, and in that moment her pursuer came lumbering up.

"Here you, what're you doin' with my woman?" he growled.

"He's not . . . I am not," Verity panted. "Oh, why did you stop me?"

"Because he knows how it is when true lovers quarrel," boomed the large man. He lowered his voice, saying coaxingly, "Come on, love. I'll make it up to you . . . just come nice and peaceful. I'll buy you another glass of the Blue Ruin and we'll go home."

"I do not know you," Verity cried. "Go away."

"The lady does not seem to long for your company, sir," commented the other man.

"She's foxed, that's all. Now you wouldn't want to inter-fere between a pair of lovers, would you? Wouldn't want my fives in your face, eh?"

"No, I do not believe I should like that," came the low response.

"Then let her go, damn you!"

"I do not think I should do that, either. I am not really inclined to abandon a lady in such obvious distress."

"Blast you, I'll have . . ." He broke off suddenly as the man struck him a powerful blow to the chin, felling him. With a curse, he leaped up, only to be knocked down a second time. "Come, my dear," her champion said coolly. "Before our Hercules regains his feet." He escorted her

swiftly toward the entrance of the Gardens. "I have my
curricle here—where can I take you?"

"Home, please," she cried unthinkingly. "I live in Great
Jermyn Street. My husband's the Marquess of Unger—" She
came to a sudden stop, realizing that she never should have
revealed her identity. "I mean . . . oh, please, I shouldn't
have said . . . you mustn't tell . . . My husband mustn't
know . . ."

"Of course, I shall say nothing. Now come." Before she
knew what he was about, he had effortlessly lifted her in his
arms. "I think we will make better time with only my legs,"
he said gently, as he continued toward the entrance to the
gardens.

In the light from the little lamps, Verity saw that he was a
well-built man with strong and not unhandsome features. His
eyes were large and heavy-lidded, his mouth full but well-
shaped. She guessed that he must be in his late twenties or
early thirties. His hair was dark brown and well-cut. She was
sure that a valet must have arranged his complicated cravat
and that his suit had come from a Bond Street tailor—perhaps
even the miraculous Stutts. Probably, in common with Derek,
he boxed at Cribb's Parlor. With a little shudder, she wondered if he knew Derek, and thought that he very well might,
for he was obviously a member of the *ton*. If only she had not
blurted out her husband's name! Gentlemen gossiped, too,
and if Derek were ever to learn of this night's adventure . . .
She shuddered again.

"You must not be frightened. You'll not be troubled by
that swine again, I promise you," he assured her.

"I do thank you, sir," she murmured.

"My pleasure." He smiled. Moving through the gates, he
walked down the road a few yards and set her down near a
curricle drawn by a pair of matched grays which must have
set their owner back a pretty penny, she guessed. In the light
from the carriage lamps, she saw a small boy in green-and-
white livery perched on the driver's seat. He regarded her out
of big round surprised eyes as her rescuer said, "This urchin,
my lady, is Jonah, my tiger, who has yet to see the inside
of a whale—but who is excellent with horses. And this,
Jonah, is the fair unknown."

Verity was grateful to her rescuer for that introduction. She was sure that he was telling her in an elliptical way that he did not mean to betray her confidence.

The boy did not acknowledge his master's words; he merely grunted, hopped down from the seat, hurried to the back of the curricle, and took his accustomed place on the boot.

Lifting Verity to the seat beside him, the gentleman took the reins and clucked to the horses. He handled the ribbands well, Verity thought, as the horses plunged forward. However, she must not think of that—she must not let him take her to her door, but what could she say? Her thoughts were in chaos, but at least she was no longer quite so frightened. They were going away from Vauxhall Gardens, and as they rounded a bend in the road, she looked back only to find she could no longer see them. She was pleased. She never wanted to see them again!

In a relatively short time they were over the bridge and into London proper. Verity wondered what time it was—it must be very late, and they still had a great distance to go.

"I wonder, sir, would you know the time?" she asked.

"I should think it was past eleven."

"So late?" she breathed.

"Your husband will be worried, I fear."

"He is not in town."

"I see."

"I never should have gone to the Gardens," she sighed.

"Possibly not."

"I do not know what possessed me to agree to such a thing!"

"It might have been rather unwise." He was silent, concentrating on his horses, as they swept around a corner and around another corner.

Verity began to recognize the devious route by which she and Cassie had come. She had not been able to see any of the landmarks because of the drawn shades, but she remembered the twists and turns. She expelled a long breath. Soon she would be home. She was glad it was so late. No one would be up and she would be able to creep into the house unseen. They turned another corner, and he brought his horses to a halt, whistling softly to his tiger.

The boy came hurrying around to the front of the curricle to hold the horses as his master lifted Verity from her seat.

He did not put her down. Instead, he strode toward a wrought-iron gate, opened it, and carried her quickly up a flagstoned path to a door flanked by two Corinthian pillars, setting her down gently as, fumbling in his pocket, he produced a key.

She regarded him in surprise. "This is not where I live." She remembered that she had not told him her direction. She had only mentioned Great Jermyn Street. "Where are we?" she asked.

"This is where I live." He opened the door and pushed her gently into a hall lighted by a large crystal chandelier. "I thought you must want some refreshment after your experience, and perhaps 'twould be best to comb your hair and put your clothing in order. Your husband must appreciate that, I think."

"That is thoughtful of you, sir, but he is not at home."

"Yes, I do remember, but sure a glass of wine before I bring you to your door."

He had been so kind that her rising fear was swiftly assuaged. "Perhaps I should tidy myself up a bit," she said. "But I do think I have had enough wine tonight."

"I will show you where you may go." Taking a candle from a table in the hall, he lighted her up the stairs and up yet another flight of stairs. Stopping in front of a paneled door, he said, "I pray you wait out here in the hall while I light the candles."

"Thank you, sir," she said shyly. Standing alone as he went into the champer, her nervousness returned and then retreated. If she could trust anyone, she could trust this man—who was obviously a gentleman and wealthy, she guessed. She wondered who he was and why he had not introduced himself, but forgot about that as the door opened again and her host returned to the hall.

"You may go in," he said, and started for the stairs.

"I do thank you, sir."

Coming into the room, she blinked against the brightness of a pair of candelabra standing on a marble mantelshelf, their flames reflected in a large oval mirror. The furniture was graceful and intricately carved. The bed, she noted, hearkened back to 1807 or thereabouts when Egyptian furniture had been all the rage. The headboard was decorated with double sphinxes and the base was finished in clawed feet. The chairs also ran to sphinxes and crocodiles, but what inter-

ested her most of all was a dressing table with a mirror over it
and a washstand on which stood a pitcher and basin which,
upon closer examination, proved to be full of water. There
were fine linen towels hanging on the stand and also a small
washcloth. She dipped it into the water and held it against her
face, grateful for its coolness.

She was almost afraid to look in the mirror—and when she
did, she was even more grateful to her host for giving her an
opportunity to adjust her garments. Her dress, she noticed,
was torn at the collar. She did not remember how or when
that had happened. Probably it had occurred while she was
struggling with her captor. Her hair was much tangled. She
had a comb in the reticule that hung almost forgotten on her
arm. She dragged the comb through her curls, and when she
had done as much as she could to her person she came out of
the chamber to find that he had not gone down the stairs after
all—but was waiting in the hall.

"The wine is in the library," he said. "I will lead the
way."

"I thank you, sir, but I do not want any wine," she said
firmly.

"Might I offer you water?"

"I would much prefer that, thank you."

"Then, water it will be."

The library was large—though not as large as the one at
home. It was dimly lighted by another pair of candelabra, one
set on a table and another on the mantelshelf. The light from
the candles illumined a fine hunting scene.

"Oh," she said appreciatively. "That is a splendid painting."

"I thank you. It was commissioned by my father, who was
much enamored of the sport."

"And you are not?" she asked, having caught a slightly
derisive note in his speech.

"Oh, I am fond of hunting, but I prefer game other than
the fox or the deer."

"Oh. Birds?"

"No." He smiled at her. "Will you not sit down?"

Her eye had been caught by a volume that lay open on the
desk. Bending over it, she found that it was *Childe Harold*.
"Byron," she said. "He is such a fine poet."

"I agree. He is also a friend. You are fond of poetry, then?"

"Oh, indeed I am. Are you acquainted with many poets, sir?"

"Yes, I often go to their readings. Last week, I was fortunate enough to meet Coleridge. His literary output is finished, I fear, but to hear him speak . . . But come, sit down, my dear, and let me bring you some water." He indicated a wide, almost thronelike chair.

"You are very kind," Verity said gratefully, sinking down amid soft down-filled cushions.

"It is not difficult to be kind to such a one as yourself, my dear." Going to a crystal pitcher, he picked it up and brought it to the table beside her chair. Moving back across the room, he returned with a fine crystal goblet, poured out the water, and handed the goblet to her. "You are really a most beautiful little creature."

Verity set the glass down hastily. There had been something in his tone she had not liked. Raising her eyes, she found him smiling derisively. She said quickly, "I really do think I must be leaving, sir."

"Do you think so?" He moved to her, and standing very near her chair, he said softly, "You really interest me. I thought I knew all the tricks that Cyprians are wont to employ, but yours are different. I must commend you on your ingenuity. You are an exceptionally talented young woman."

"Tricks?" she repeated angrily, trying to rise, but he was blocking her way. "You think I am a . . . a . . ."

"Cyprian," he finished. "Come, you cannot be afraid to speak it aloud, and believe me, I am not insulting you. I am all admiration. If you had not prated of your connection with Unger, I vow I might have believed your tale." His voice hardened. "But you see, my dear, I am acquainted with the noble marquess. And you, for all your loveliness, your excellent manners, your cultivated speech, are still not the sort of bird with whom he flies. He has, to my certain knowledge, never kept a mistress. His mother has seen to that! And I know for a fact that he is wed to a damsel of impeccable antecedents, selected for him while he was yet in his cradle and from a family with a pedigree as noble as his own. This lady would never be seen alone in so dubious a spot as the

Vauxhall Gardens. However, I do commend you for using a most unusual ploy with which to entrap me.''

"Entrap . . .'' she whispered. "You believe . . .''

"In everything except the pretty prevarications of lovely women. How much did you pay that rogue to chase you into my arms? I do compliment you on your theatrical ability. Are you from the stage? No matter, you need not give me your life history. You know, you are even more beautiful than I thought at first glance. Furthermore, my sweetest frailty, I am not encumbered with a wife.'' Leaning forward, he kissed her fully, suffocatingly upon the lips.

Held powerless against the chair, Verity was aghast. This terrible change in the man she had so foolishly trusted was so terrifying that for the moment she could not even struggle against his odious embrace. Finally, he drew back and she was able to move. "P-please, sir. I am not . . . I mean, I pray you . . .''

"I pray you, my lovely child, no more fairy tales,'' he murmured. "I have been kind, I think, and I can be so much kinder. What would you say to a snug little house, to your own coach and four, to the services of the best mantua makers in London, to jewels and furs and all the trifles that delight the feminine soul?'' As Reggie had done earlier that evening, he put a finger under her chin, tilting her face toward him. "No need to tease me longer with your simulated fears, my adorable little love. I'll not eat you, though I am sure you'd be a most dainty morsel to set before a king. I'd never waste you on the Regent, though. You are far too delectable . . . and besides, he has the most regrettable taste for older women.''

As he spoke, her fear had given way to determination. She had to escape from this man—but how? He was so near to her, and no doubt when he finished speaking, gloating, rather, he would be nearer yet. She needed a weapon, and of a sudden she remembered the pitcher of water beside her on the table. The thought being father to the action, she grabbed it and without further ado, she flung the contents full in his face. He sprang back, and Verity, rushing out of the library, sped down the stairs and to the front door. Fortunately it was on the latch. She pulled it open and a second later was at the gate, which was still slightly ajar. She was out onto the sidewalk in a trice running, running, not knowing where she was going, knowing only that she must get away.

It was growing light. Verity, huddled in the hackney, stared out of the window with lackluster eyes. Her feet were sore. Her whole body ached, and in addition, there was fear. Contrary to her expectations, her erstwhile rescuer had not pursued her. Possibly her swift action had convinced him that she had spoken the truth, or possibly he saw little sport in pursuing so contrary a female.

She could not dwell on that, not with the ordeal facing her. How might she provide the servants with reasons for her arrival in the early-morning hours when they had believed her long abed? How could she tell them about the terrors of walking through territory totally unfamiliar to her—and in darkness? Finally, she had arrived at a huge building, and standing before it, bathed in the waning moonlight, was a statue which, to her horror, she recognized immediately. It was the famous Grinling Gibbons sculpture of Charles II, and it rose in front of the hospital he himself had endowed. Derek had brought her to see it, and it was located in the village of Chelsea, far, far from home! After what seemed hours more, she found a hackney.

The man pulled his horse to a stop. "That'll be three shillin's," he growled.

Verity reached for her reticule—but it was not on her wrist, and she remembered now that she had taken it off to comb her hair. She must have left it in the bedchamber. Any hope that she might be able to steal back into the house without the servants' witnessing her return was flouted. "I have not the fare, but my butler will pay you," she said in a small voice.

"Yer butler," he rasped, turning a doubtful eye on her. "A likely story! I'm takin' you to Bow Street."

"No, please," she protested. "Come with me to my door, I pray you."

"Very well, but don't try to make a dash for it."

Anger welled within her—but she was in no position to give him the set-down he so richly deserved. She climbed wearily out of the hackney, and followed by the grumbling and suspicious old coachman, she walked slowly to her door, and picking up the knocker, she let it fall against the plate.

There was a brief wait during which time the coachman continued to mutter to himself, and then the door was opened wide—and on the threshold, eyes blazing, stood Derek!

The shock, coming on top of all the other shocks she had sustained in the last few hours, was too much for Verity. Staring into her husband's furious contenance, she began to shake with laughter, to shake and howl with it until a sharp slap across her face silenced her.

After paying an astounded coachman, Derek slammed the door, and grasping Verity's limp wrist, he pushed her toward the stairs. It was then and only then that she noticed the butler, several footmen, and the housekeeper watching her in open-mouthed amazement. To her horror, laughter threatened again, but her cheek stung and throbbed where he had struck her, and she managed to quell it as, at his curt command, she proceeded him up the stairs.

Three

On the way home, it had been very difficult for Verity to keep her eyes open; she had dozed part of the way. It was not until the coachman threatened her with arrest that she had been shocked into wakefulness. Now, sitting in the library facing Derek, who was ensconced behind the desk, looking for all the world like a judge ready to pronounce sentence upon a thief or even a murderer, she had never felt more alert.

She had just concluded her halting recital of the night's mishaps, carefully glossing over her foolish acceptance of her rescuer's so-called hospitality, telling Derek that he had assaulted her in his post chaise and giving a colorful but fictional account of her escape from him. Staring into Derek stern contenance, she was almost tempted to say, "The defense rests, my lord."

She resisted that temptation. It would have seemed as if she were mocking him, and she was far from that. She was half frightened, half defiant, or perhaps it was the other way around. She was having great difficulty in sorting out her emotions and trying, at the same time, to ascertain his. She had anticipated anger, but it seemed to her that he was looking at her with actual hatred. She said nervously, "That's the way of it."

"I see," he responded coldly. "An interesting fabrication."

She regarded him in utter amazement. "You believe it to be . . . to be a fabrication?" she demanded in ascending accents.

"Yes, madame." He rose from the desk and came around to

stare down at her. "I believe it to be a fabrication—a tissue of lies from beginning to end!"

She sprang from her chair. "I have told you the honest truth!"

"Honesty is a word that comes far too glibly to lying lips," he responded harshly.

Her fists clenched. She longed to strike him, but that would solve nothing. Trying to speak as calmly as she could, she said, "I suggest that you speak to Lady Cassandra. She will corroborate every word of what I have told you." It occurred to her that Cassie would not only corroborate her story, she would be immensely gratified to learn that Verity had reached home safely. She must have been frantic when she and Reggie failed to find her in the box. However, they should not have left her alone so long, she thought resentfully. Everything that had happened to her last night had been their fault!

"I intend to speak to Lady Cassandra," Derek said coldly. "I am going there now. Meanwhile, I want you to go to your room and remain there until I return."

She glared at him. "I have no intention of leaving." She could not keep herself from adding sarcastically, "The Vauxhall Gardens are, I understand, closed on Thursdays."

The slam of the library door was her only response. Her fury increased. That he actually intended to abide by what had been an ironic suggestion seemed incredible to her, and even more incredible was his accusation. Yet, given his ridiculous jealousy, it was not. And oh, God, why had he arrived here on the very night she had gotten into this horrendous scrape? He had been gone such a short time, too. She could not think about that. Tiredness was descending upon her again. She had to lie down.

Coming out of the library and crossing toward the stairs, Verity was aware of an undercurrent of laughter and whispers on the ground floor, or, rather, tittering, and she knew it came from the parlor maids and the footmen, gossiping about the spectacle she had made of herself coming home at such an hour. She shuddered as she remembered Cassie's warning that the servants not be alerted—for the news would spread. As she mounted the stairs, she considered begging them to say nothing, but she knew that would be futile. They would egard her politely and chatter as they chose. She had the sudden feeling that she had fallen among enemies—not excluding her husband.

Reaching her chamber, she sank down on her chaise longue and put her head on the pillows. She was about to drop off to sleep when Kitty hurried into the room, her eyes wide with distress.

"Oh, milady," she blurted. "What 'appened? I don't beeve nothin' o' wot they're all sayin'!"

"What they're all saying?" Verity repeated. "What are they saying?"

"Oh, as 'ow you sneaked out to meet some gentleman. I old them 'twasn't true, but there was no talkin' to 'em. Oh, milady, what really 'appened?"

Her weariness fleeing again, Verity told her story a second time.

Kitty listened quietly, though several times she made little exclamations of anger or distress. As Verity finished speaking, she said hotly, "That Lady Cassie's a sad romp, milady. You shouldn't've 'eeded 'er. You should 'ear wot 'er Rosa 'as to say 'bout 'er goin's-on. And why didn't you take me, milady?"

"I wish I had." Verity ran her hands through her hair. "And now I suppose it'll be all over town."

"Oh," Kitty burst out. "It's wicked 'ow people talk. I told em there wasn't a particle o' truth in wot they were sayin'."

There was a heaviness in Verity's chest and a throbbing in her throat. The tale would spread, she knew, and everyone would believe she had crept out to some assignation! And Derek . . . would he believe it, also? No, he could not once he had spoken with Cassie.

"Milady," Kitty said mournfully. "You look all wore out. Let me 'elp you get out o' them clothes, 'n' sure you'll be wantin' a bath."

"A bath, yes. I must have a bath," Verity agreed.

"I'll bring the water up, milady," Kitty hurried out.

As the door closed on her abigail, Verity had a vivid image of the girl descending to the ground floor and all the staff crowding around to hear what she would report. She did not believe that Kitty would tell them anything. She was more than a servant, she was a friend. She had never felt that as strongly as she did at this moment. She smote her palm with

her fist. Why, why, why had she not brought Kitty with her
last night? She never should have listened to Cassie's protests.
If Kitty had been with her, nothing untoward would have
happened. Now, even with Cassie's corroboration, she would
be in trouble. Probably Derek would insist that they return to
Northumberland, and she would be treated like an outcast or
even a prisoner by his mother. Unwillingly, she remembered
her so-called savior's remarks about her husband's depen-
dence upon the dowager marchioness. That had been only too
evident while they were at the castle. Indeed, it had surprised
her that Derek had been willing to come to London without
his mother. Certainly, he never would again, and . . . but she
could not keep dwelling on what would happen. Perhaps she
was only borrowing trouble. Perhaps, once he calmed down,
Derek would listen to reason.

"Milady . . . milady . . ."

Verity awakened from a sound sleep to find Kitty standing
by the bed. She looked at the abigail vaguely, and then,
memory returning in a rush, she sat up. "I did not mean to
fall asleep. What is the hour?"

"It's close on two, milady."

"Two in the afternoon!" Verity exclaimed. "I slept that
long?"

"Yes, milady. And . . . his Lordship has just returned and
wishes that you will join him in the library."

"He has just returned? But—he went out so early." Verity
stared at her incredulously.

" 'E came back 'n' went out again."

"Why does he want me to meet him in the library? Could
he not come here?"

" 'E most particularly wanted you in the library, milady,"
Kitty said nervously. " 'E . . . 'e . . ."

"Well, come, what's the matter?" Verity demanded. She
was finding Kitty's manner very strange.

"Oh, milady," the girl burst out. " 'E was in a rare
takin'. I 'ave never seen 'im so angry. 'E were snarlin' like a
. . . lion wot I saw in the Royal Menagerie."

"I do not understand." Verity slipped out of bed, thought
of going to the library in her peignoir, and decided against it.

"No more do I, milady," Kitty quavered. " 'E says as

'ow 'e wishes you to come at once. I said you was sleepin' an' 'e said I was to wake you.''

"Well, you have. I will come as soon as I am dressed." Verity saw fear flare in Kitty's eyes and found that it was catching. She could not imagine why he would be more angry now than he had been earlier that day, and she found herself most reluctant to hear his reasons. Still, since there was no avoiding a confrontation, she was positive she would feel better able to deal with him if she was dressed.

As Kitty hurriedly helped her into a plain round gown, Verity's trepidation increased. She did not relish the sensation. If her fear was evident, he would assume that she felt guilty. Guilty of what? By now he must have heard the truth from Cassie—but what had kept him so long away? Where had he gone that second time, and why was he so angry? If she did not go down to the library, she would not find out. With what she hoped was a reassuring smile for Kitty, Verity came out of her bedchamber. She wished she did not feel like Mary, Queen of Scots, on her way to her execution.

Reaching the door to the library, she hesitated, and then opening it came in to find Derek pacing up and down the long length of floor that stretched between the window and the door. As she entered, Verity, looking at his face, caught her breath. Never in all of the time she had known him had she seen him so deathly pale. His expression was grim, and the look in his eyes chilled her to the bone. She had a feeling he had suddenly turned into marble.

"I sent word that you were to come immediately," he said in a voice as icy as his appearance.

"I needed to dress."

"I see—naturally you would need to dress for your husband."

She found that comment extremely mystifying. "I do not understand you, Derek."

"I am sure you do not," he returned, still in that icy tone. "But murder will out."

"I . . . do not understand you," she repeated. "Did you not speak to Cassie?"

"Yes, I spoke to Lady Cassandra. But it is not on Lady Cassandra that I wish to dwell. That was bad enough—but your conduct, madame, I can find no way to understand it. I suspected that there was something afoot—but to act as you have done! Oh, God, and this is the woman to whom I have given my name." He raised his two hands and actually tore his hair.

"Derek . . ." She moved toward him.

"Silence!" He stepped back. "Your behavior, and . . . and with a man I know to be a . . . a reprobate of the deepest dye where women are concerned. And that I should have to lie through my teeth and pretend that I did indeed have a mistress—for sure I could not own that the doxy with whom he consorted last night was, as she told him, my wife!"

She felt as if the floor had suddenly opened and dropped her into the bowels of the earth. "He . . . t-told you . . ." she stuttered.

"Yes, madame, he told me all that happened, after he found you parading through Vauxhall Gardens last night . . . quite alone, madame!"

"I was not alone," she cried. "I . . . I was running from this . . . this person, who came to the box . . . and I . . . I told you how it was . . ."

"Why did you hire a box? You did not tell me the reason for that, madame!"

"I did not hire it. Reggie hired it. Surely Cassie told you . . ."

"I pray you will not keep trying to blame an innocent young woman for your misdeeds—or did you imagine I would believe you without question?"

"Innocent . . . young . . . woman? What can you mean?"

"Your stratagems will not serve, madame. Did you actually imagine that a friend, no matter how friendly, would condone your scandalous behavior and moreover place herself in jeopardy for your misdeeds? You are a most peculiar mixture of deceit and naiveté."

She was hardly listening to him. Uppermost in her mind was the fact that Cassie had lied—Cassie and the man who had pretended to help her. They had both lied to her husband. She said furiously, "It was Cassie came to me and begged me to chaperon her because of Reggie . . . who was being s-sent to . . . to Jamaica."

"So you explained before, madame, and so I explained to Lady Cassandra and her brother, who laughed my face. Lady

Cassandra expressly told me that she had not seen Reginald Delaville in years. She said—and her brother corroborated her statement—that she had not left the house all night. But enough. How could you, madame, how could you accost a strange man and let him bring you to his house and have his way with you?"

"He did not have his way with me!"

"I believe you told me that you were in Chelsea Village last night—by the statue of King Charles II? The gentleman who picked you up at Vauxhall Gardens lives in Cheyne Walk, which is in Chelsea. Madame, he lives in the house you have sworn you did not visit, but after your night of love, he found this. He thought you might want it—just as he thought that I might want to know the character of the woman I am supposed to call mistress. He was doing me a service, you see." Reaching into his pocket, he brought out her reticule and threw it down on the floor. "He found it by the side of the bed."

"He did not. He must have found it by the washstand!" she retorted furiously.

"Ah!" Derek cried triumphantly. "You admit it—finally you admit that you were in his bedroom!"

"Yes, yes, yes, I went there to—to freshen up. My hair was much tangled and my face was smudged. He showed me the . . . the ewer and b-basin and left me alone. I didn't tell you about this before because I . . . I realized afterwards that I never should have g-gone to his house . . . only he said he would not stay long and he would t-take me home. Instead he . . . he tried to make love to me and . . ."

"And what did you do, madame?"

"I flung a pitcher of water in his face."

"Ah, and that, I expect, cooled his ardor?" Derek retorted with awful sarcasm.

"It shocked him, and I was able to get out of the chair where he was h-holding me and . . . k-kissing me." She shuddered. "I . . . I never should have trusted him. But he . . . he was kind to me in the Gardens, and that man was running after me and t-trying to . . ."

"Does that surprise you, madame? It should not. If you did not expect to be taken for a Cyprian, you should not have gone strolling in Vauxhall Gardens, alone."

"I did not stroll in them!" Verity stamped her foot. "Why will you not believe me? Why do you take Cassie's word against mine and the word of one whom you have said is a . . . a reprobate with women and who no doubt was trying to do me a disservice because I escaped him?"

"I find it very difficult to believe in the veracity of one who has already proved herself to be a liar—not once but many times!"

"Many times?" she cried.

"You must think me very dull indeed, madame. Or else your eagerness to join your . . . numerous lovers has rendered you incautious!"

"My lovers? I . . . I am supposed to have had *lovers*?" She was breathing quickly now, and mingled with her shock and fear was a rising anger. "And who are they, my lord?"

"Damn and double damn you for a brazen-faced trull!" he cried. "Did you imagine I did not see that sly little exchange of looks between you and your sister the other day? Being younger than yourself, she lacks your expertise in lying! I must tell you, madame, that you have been found out. I have been informed about all your recent escapades!"

"My . . . escapades?" she repeated. She was beginning to shake, and not with fear but anger. He had called her a brazen-faced trull, and he would pay for that. As for her sister, if she had to tell him the truth about that, she would.

"You may well tremble, madame . . . for it is no longer possible for you to deceive me as you have been doing with your clever communications with your lovers and your assignations in Leadenhall Street."

"My . . . my *assignations*!" Serious as the situation was, Verity could not keep from smiling.

"You dare to mock me!" he demanded furiously. "You'll be grinning on the other side of your face, madame, and soon. I have evidence of your follies! 'Twas supplied to me by the Bow Street Runners!"

All desire to smile left her. "The Bow Street Runners," she repeated incredulously. "You are telling me that you . . . that they . . ."

"They have been watching you ever since that day I caught you lying to me!"

"You . . . set the Bow Street Runners to . . . to follow me? How dared you do such a thing? How dared you?"

"You have the effrontery to ask that, madame? Let me ask you who Anthony Hunter is. And tell me what this means." He strode to his desk and scooped up a volume that lay on top of it. Opening it, he read, " 'From one to another.' Pray tell me what that means!"

"It means that he is my lover, of course," she retorted caustically. "One of the many millions I have entertained in your frequent absences, my lord."

"You admit that he is your lover. Good. I shall have my seconds wait on him!"

Verity paled. Her anger had wrought on her common sense. She never should have made such an admission, not with Derek in his present mood. "He is not my lover," she cried. "He is an author. He wrote a book on travel. But you know what it is, since you have obviously scanned it. You had no right. It was in my escritoire. You went through it!"

"*Your* escritoire, madame? There is nothing in this house that is yours . . . all that lies beneath this roof is mine—until I choose to discard it, as I will this book when it comes time to discard it. Where did you meet this man you call your lover?"

"He's not my lover. I only jested."

His blue eyes were frigid. "Many a true word is spoken in—"

"Spare me your platitudes, my lord. Anthony Hunter's nothing to me—and the translation of the line he wrote in that book is as follows—'From one author to another'!"

"Author? You? I do not understand you, madame. Or rather I do . . . it is only another of your lies."

"It is the truth. Mr. Hunter is an author. He and I met by accident at the Minerva Press, which is in Leadenhall Street, as your spies have informed you."

"They informed me that you were laughing and jesting with a young man whom I suppose to be this Anthony Hunter or possibly another . . ."

"Of my millions of lovers, my lord? I now remember the man who came bumbling in and out of the office while I was conversing with Mr. Hunter and my publisher, Mr. Newman—Anthony K. Newman, proprietor of the Minerva Press, for which I have written two books and am currently writing a third!'' she said defiantly, thinking that it was well he had not found the chapters she had hidden in the bottom of her portmanteau.

"You . . . you write that pap!'' he thundered.

"I do.'' She lifted her chin and looked him straight in the eyes. "I am proud of every word I have set down.''

"It seems there is much I do not know about you, madame.''

"Really? I was under the impression that you believe you know all there is to know about me. It's a marvel your vigilant Runners did not tell you that I joined Cassie last night, meeting her in a post chaise that stood at the end of the street. The one with a yellow ribbon dangling from the window.''

"They saw you being helped into a closed carriage. Unfortunately, they lost sight of it in the crush of vehicles near the Gardens. I might mention to you, madame, that they did not see Lady Cassandra.''

"How might they have seen her in a closed carriage?'' Verity demanded. "Oh, it is outside of enough . . . that you dared to have me followed.''

"My wife, madame, must like Caesar's wife be above suspicion!'' He sighed and shook his head. "I wish that you might have been all that I once believed you to be. When I went to my club two nights ago, I hoped against hope that my suspicions would remain unfounded.''

"You . . . went . . . to . . . your club?'' Verity looked at him through narrowed eyes. "You have been in town all this while?''

"I have been in in town, madame.''

"And all because you thought you caught me in a lie with my sister?''

"I had more reason than that.''

"What reason? I never gave you cause . . .''

"Your mother . . .'' He paused.

"My mother!'' she exclaimed. "What has she to do with . . .''

"I have been told, madame, that she . . .''

"Ah! You need say no more, my lord. My mother was known to be promiscuous . . . and where had you that information? From that wasp-nosed old fidget you call Mother, no doubt, since it was all a long time ago with mine in her grave and all the gossips silent—because there's precious little sport in maligning the dead!''

"How dare you speak of my mother in those scurrilous terms! You are impudent, madame. And furthermore, she meant only to warn me!''

"You should have heeded those warnings, my lord," she said contemptuously.

"I wish I had!" he retorted bitterly. "I'd be spared this sorrow and disgrace. Can you imagine what they are already saying in town—and what they will say? And what they'll be printing in lampoons? No doubt, the whole ugly tale will be in the *Morning Post*! Your reputation, madame, will be completely destroyed and mine with it. I never thought to be known as a cuckold!''

"You can remove those horns quite easily, my lord. All you need do is divorce me, and speedily."

"That, madame, is my intent. This afternoon I have consulted with my solicitor. He is ready to make all the necessary arrangements."

"Good," she snapped. "The sooner the better. Isn't it fortunate that our home has not been blessed with progeny."

"I consider that most fortunate, madame, since I would be very doubtful as to who had fathered them."

She glared at him. "And I, my lord, would be very doubtful as to their mental prowess!" Whirling, she sped from the room, slamming the door violently behind her.

Still in the high heat of fury, Verity, coming into her chamber, was glad to find her abigail there. "Kitty, you will pack my portmanteau—take such gowns as you can fit into it, but leave all jewels behind save those that were mine before I entered into this ill-omened alliance!"

Kitty regarded her in horror. "Milady, you'll never be telling me . . . that . . .''

"I am leaving as soon as possible. I will go to my grandmother's house. As for you . . .''

"I'll go with you," Kitty cried.

"Kitty, my dear." Verity made an effort to speak calmly. "Before you make so hasty a commitment, you must know that his lordship will be suing me for divorce—and the charge will be, of course, adultery."

"Milady!" Kitty regarded her in horror. "Did you not tell him . . ."

"I told him all that I told you, Kitty, but unlike you, he did not believe me." Verity began to tremble with rage. "You see," she continued between her teeth, "he has had the Bow Street Runners following me, and so feels himself fully justified in this action. My unfortunate adventure of last night has had ramifications which have served to confirm his worst suspicions. Now, I know it cannot add to your consequence to remain in the employ of one who must soon be both debased and disgraced in the eyes of all society. So I beg you will think well before you come to any decision."

"Milady, I'm goin' with you," the girl said staunchly. Her eyes, a bright blue, blazed with anger. "I'll not stop another night under this roof."

"Kitty." Some of Verity's white-hot fury left her. She spoke over a lump in her throat. "Think well what you do."

"I 'ave thought well, milady. I'd go with you as . . . as far as China!"

"Oh, Kitty." Tears stood in Verity's eyes. "You believe me, do you not?"

"As I believe wot's wrote in the Bible, milady."

"Oh, my dearest Kitty . . ." Verity determinedly swallowed a sob. "I do thank you. Now let us be quick. I wish to leave his house as soon as possible."

Standing in the drawing room of Harcliffe House, Verity, pale and shaken, stared incredulously at her grandmother's implacable countenance. "You cannot let me stay here?" she repeated.

Lady Harcliffe's faded blue eyes were as stern as those of Derek. Her thin body was taut, and her face had never appeared more austere. She said coldly, "I am sending Caroline to the country, and as for Miss Marshall, I gave her notice directly your husband informed me of her complicity in your schemes."

"You . . . gave her notice!" Verity repeated in horror. "But she has done nothing. She only accompanied me to . . . to Leadenhall Street."

"Clandestinely," Lady Harcliffe said frigidly. "Aiding you and abetting you in . . ."

"In what? The fact that I have written two novels and have told no one about them? Is that so shocking? Have I ruined my reputation and that of my family because I used an assumed name?"

"Miss Marshall was in my employ. It was her duty to . . ."

". . . to betray one whom she has known since she was in pinafores? I presume you dismissed her without references?"

"She was not entitled to references!" Lady Harcliffe responded.

"Oh, God, and she is the sole support of her crippled brother and her old aunt. How could you be so cruel?"

"I expect loyalty from those who serve me," Lady Harcliffe said icily.

"Oh, where is she? I must go to her."

"She has gone. As far as I know, she took the stage back to Clavering."

"So soon?"

"I told her that she was to leave immediately she was packed," Lady Harcliffe said. Moving to a table, she opened a drawer and took out a letter. "She left this for you. From the weight and feel of it, I would say there is currency inside. I have no idea why she would be giving you money."

"She is undoubtedly returning the—fruits of my pen, from my novel *Elvira*, which monies she said she would hold for me. I wish she had taken them with her. Give me her direction and I will send them to her."

"I do not have her direction," Lady Harcliffe replied.

"He will have it, Mr. Newman!" Verity exclaimed. "Oh, I must see him, and Mr. Parry . . . he must know he is in danger. Still, I did not give his real name, and . . ."

"What are you babbling about?" Lady Harcliffe demanded crisply.

Verity's eyes hardened. "Nothing that would interest you, Grandmother, who'd turn away a poor woman without cause."

"There was cause. There was prevarication and dishonesty. Hold," she added sharply as Verity started for the door. "Where are you going?"

"Why should you care, Grandmother? You've just told me I am no concern of yours, since you choose to believe my husband rather than myself. What I have told you is no more than the truth, but . . ."

"Whether I believe you or not makes little difference. It is what will be believed by the *ton*, once you are divorced." Lady Harcliffe grimaced. "That your folly should bring you to this!"

"My folly! I have done no wrong!" Verity flared.

"If you have done no wrong, you have been uncommonly foolish and deserve all that happens. I am truly sorry for you."

"You are not sorry for me. No doubt you agree with my husband that because I resemble my mother, my morals are the same!"

"If they are not, you have been hard put to convey that impression. But enough, I'll have my coachman convey you to Gordon's Hotel. 'Tis in Arlington Street. I'll give you a letter to the manager, who is known to me."

"I do not want . . ."

"Silence!" exclaimed Lady Harcliffe, her eyes flashing. "Would you sleep in the street, girl? You'll need some manner of habitation until this miserable business is at an end—and afterwards, well, we'll see. You'll need money, too. I'll provide you with fifty pounds, which will see you through for the nonce."

"I do not want your money!"

"Good Lord." Lady Harcliffe raised her eyes toward heaven. "I do believe the chit was weaned yesterday. What will you do without it, pray? You cannot live on air. You are a child, Verity, and I can well believe you write romances. You have the head for 'em and little else. You'll need money—and more later. But we'll talk about that when the time comes. I am too weary to think about the future at this time." Much to Verity's surprise, Lady Harcliffe's voice quavered, and coming to her side, she put an arm around her. "Take heart, child. I wish I could keep you with me. But there are your sisters to consider. But believe me, you are nothing like your mother. She had the wisdom of a serpent, and I doubt you have the wit of a sparrow."

"Oh, Grandmother." Tears shone in Verity's eyes. "Is it possible that you do believe me?"

"I suppose I must," Lady Harcliffe said grudgingly. "But that will help neither of us now. I'll call my coach, and in the meantime write a note for you to give to Mr. Soames, the manager. I will have him send his bill to me, and do not give me an argument about that, I pray you.''

Once she was situated at the hotel, it had been Verity's intent to hire a hackney and drive at once to Leadenhall Street—but it was already thirty minutes past the hour of six when she and Kitty were finally settled in the chamber and dressing room allotted to her. Furthermore, once her fury had abated, depression coupled with a stultifying weariness overcame her, and Kitty, fixing her with an appraising eye, insisted she must go to bed. She did not argue—and she fell asleep within a minute of retiring.

Verity awakened to sunlight streaming through a gap in the curtains that hung at the two windows facing the street. For a moment, she was confused to find the walls so much closer and the dim shapes of the furniture so different from what she was used to seeing. Memory returned, bringing with it some of the numbing shock she had experienced the previous day, together with the sense of betrayal from Cassie and from Derek. She was glad she need no longer include her grandmother and make that duo a trio. But, she recollected, there was her would-be seducer to put in Lady Harcliffe's place. Anger welled up in her breast as she thought of the man, whom she had momentarily bested and who had exacted so craven a revenge!

How furious he must have been—but that was nothing to Derek's rage at having his suspicions so readily confirmed, at least in his own mind. And how dared he have her followed as if she were a proven adultress and, without giving her a chance to explain, willfully misconstrue the reasons behind her meeting with Mr. Newman and Alan Parry? Thank God, Mr. Parry had signed his *nom de plume* instead of his real name! But despite that disguise, could not her husband ferret him out? She remembered her resolve of the previous evening; she must abide by it, and soon! She prayed that Derek had not already gone there—but a glance at the clock on the small mantelpiece to her right showed her that it was only a little past the hour of eight.

She put her hand out for the bell with which she usually summoned Kitty but did not find it, seeing only a nightstand that was unlike the one in her bedchamber—not *her* bedchamber! Shock ran through her again. In her mind, her husband declared, "Mine . . . there is nothing here of mine!" But there had been her dowry, thousands of pounds. She had not come to him a pauper. Why could she not have reminded him of that? There were so many things she could have told him but had not and could not. And now he would shine like St. Michael at the gates of Paradise and she would be driven forth—a sinner, an erring Eve, who had not even tasted of the apple, had done nothing save to help a sorrowing friend—not a friend, not a *friend*! She turned over, pressing her face into the pillow, and turned around again just as quickly, remembering that she had no time for tears. She must get to Leadenhall Street. Rising, she moved to the dressing-room door, where a bed had been set up for her abigail, but before she could knock, Kitty emerged, looking at her anxiously.

"I 'eard you stirrin'. I 'ope you slept well, milady."

"Very well, Kitty," Verity said calmly and explained her mission.

Kitty regarded her in alarm, "Oh, milady, do you suppose 'is lordship'll call that poor young man out just for 'im signin' 'is name in a book?"

"Othello strangled Desdemona for a dropped handkerchief," Verity said dryly.

"I don't believe I know 'im." Kitty wrinkled her brow.

"I'll explain while I'm dressing," Verity told her.

A short time later, Kitty stepped back, saying, "Seems to me that Othello were a rum sort, but I've 'eard tell that foreigners can be tetchy." She regarded Verity's gown fixedly. "That green's becomin' to you, milady."

"Thank you, Kitty." Verity regarded herself in the full-length mirror that stood to the left of the armoire. She was arrayed in her newest walking dress, a French washing silk in a Nile green that added a touch of that same color to her eyes. Her gloves, the plume on her close-fitting bonnet, and her little kid shoes were also green, a hue that in *Othello* had been associated with jealousy. She had not thought of that when she had decided to wear it, but, she decided with a wry smile, she was well garbed for an occasion in which she must needs warn a man as innocent as Cassio of her husband's possible intentions.

"Are you sure you wouldn't like me to order up some

eggs 'n' bit o' steak? Doesn't seem to me that chocolate 'n' a roll's much of a breakfast, milady," Kitty said worriedly.

Verity shook her head. " 'Twas more than enough," she insisted. Shock, she guessed, had robbed her of her appetite. In fact, the more she dwelt on the cataclysmic events of the past twenty-four hours, the stranger she felt—as if, indeed, nothing were quite real, not the chamber, not the hotel, not the fact that soon Derek would no longer be her husband, and all because . . . but she could not think of those either, the reasons, the terrible reasons for a fall that was akin to that of Humpty-Dumpty, whom all the king's horses and all the king's men could not put back together again. And what would happen *now*? She would not think of that, not yet. Determinedly, she said to Kitty, "Please instruct the clerk at the desk to hire me a hackney. We must go to Leadenhall Street."

"Yes, milady." Kitty hurried out of the room.

As Verity started to follow her, she realized she had not changed reticules, and upon opening the one she had carried the previous day, she found Miss Marshall's letter. She winced. For all her outspoken concern over the fate of the governess, she had not even read it!

Opening it, she found coins amounting to forty shillings, the sum she had been paid for *Elvira*, which she would forward to Miss Marshall as soon as she obtained her direction. She hoped she might have put it in the letter, she had just unfolded.

My dearest Verity [she read]. First and foremost, I wish to assure you, though it hardly needs saying, that I cannot believe your husband's cruel accusations. He mentioned Lady Cassandra, whom I know to be an out-and-out liar as well as a mischief-maker. I endeavored to speak for you but was roundly castigated by him for aiding and abetting you in what he termed your "assignations." Since I knew that I would be no longer in your grandmother's employ once he had quitted the house, I dared to defend you, but to no avail. He was in no mood to listen and dismissed me in terms that made me long to strike him. I wished that I had been a man and might call him out, both for what he said of you and to me. No doubt, I should not be telling you all this, but I am writing in anger and disgust for a man who, having lived with you for the better part of two years, should surely know that you are the soul of integrity. Yes, I am aware that you have not always told him the truth, but prevarication was forced upon you through his own conduct. And I must say that terrible as the circumstances attendant upon this severing of your relationship are, I cannot help but feel, my dearest child, that you are well out of an alliance with one who cannot possess a fair share of that faculty we call reason.

I would I might remain beside you in this hour of trial, but rather recently my brother's condition has worsened and I will be needed to nurse him. Consequently, my dismissal was fortuitous, as I must have resigned my position at the end of the month at the latest. I might add that Lady Harcliffe, though she was most angry at what she termed "our gross deception and reprehensible abuse of her trust," was more generous than I had any right to expect. She said that in view of my long service with the family, she would write me a reference, and furthermore, she presented me with ten pounds in addition to my salary and added to her generosity by paying for my fare back to Clavering.

Dearest Verity,

I fear you are in for some difficult times, though judging from her actions regarding myself, I feel that your grandmother will help you—and knowing your strength of spirit, I beg you to be of good cheer. Rather than bemoan the change in your circumstances, I charge you, continue to write. You have real talent, and I have much decried the fact that you have been forced to hide your light under a bushel as it were. I know my good friend Mr. Newman will be pleased that you will now have the leisure to pursue the occupation for which nature seems to have designed you. I would I might have seen you before I departed, but I am sure we will meet again one day.

All my love,
Aurelia Marshall,
19 Grey Street,
Clavering

"Oh, Miss Marshall." Verity pressed the paper to her lips. At least the governess would not suffer because of her folly, and while Verity would miss her, she could think of her being relatively comfortable at home. And she would send her some of the money her grandmother gave her. A few pounds could not last her forever!

"Milady?" Kitty stood in the doorway. "The 'ackney's below."

"Thank you, Kitty. Come, then."

As she walked through the lobby of the hotel, Verity had an uncomfortable suspicion that she was being covertly observed, even though the manager and the various clerks were almost obsequiously polite. Coming out on Arlington Street, she was about to enter the hackney when she saw the Earl and Countess of Prestbury, with whom she and Derek had dined two weeks ago. Without thinking she smiled at them, and was shocked to see Lady Prestbury continuing to stare straight ahead as if she had not seen her. His lordship, on the other hand, continued to smile, but in a knowing and roguish way that made Verity long to slap a face that had always reminded her of an overripe peach, covered as it was with a light fuzz.

Fortunately, the footman was waiting to hand her into the hackney. Followed by Kitty, she settled down in a corner of the carriage and composedly gave her direction.

Kitty, huddled in the other corner, was frowning. "That whey-faced old 'arridan . . . and 'im . . ."

"Hush," Verity murmured. "If you will become upset over that, my dear Kitty, your days will be spent in moping, for we can expect the same from every member of the so-called polite world. I shouldn't be surprised if the story were not already in print."

"It is," Kitty corroborated mournfully. "They was all talkin' about it when I come down to instruct the porter 'bout the 'ackney. It's them wot works in that 'ouse spread it about. Couldn't 'ardly wait to start blabbin' . . . Milly 'n' Maggie 'n' Bob . . ."

"Oh, I pray you'll not blame it on the parlor maids and one footman. You might as well include the housekeeper, the butler, the cook, and the coachman. I am sure they have all made the most of it," Verity said caustically.

"I am sure they 'ave, milady. An' . . ."

"Kitty, dear, please don't let's dwell on their perfidy. It will not alter the circumstances. The cat and several kittens are out of the bag and in print." Verity managed a smile, but there was a heaviness in her chest. Though she had been girding herself for such confrontations, this one had been harder to bear than she had imagined they would be. The icy look in her ladyship's eye, the grim set of her mouth. That was what she could expect from all those women she had had so little opportunity to know—mainly because Derek was unwilling to go about in society. If they *had* known her better, would they have been less eager to pass judgment? She doubted it. The shredding of reputations was a popular sport among the idle members of the *ton*, and among most of London, as witness the eager purchasing of lampoons and cartoons. No one was safe from the satirists—not the royal dukes and especially not the Regent, whose increasing girth and penchant for elderly mistresses was a subject of which they never tired. The lot of them needed only a whiff of smoke to kindle a major conflagration. Her so-called adventures would keep the town titillated for, perhaps, two days— maybe even a week. Then something equally shocking would take its place, but meanwhile, she would be disgraced and shunned for life!

"Caesar's wife," Verity muttered, trying to quell her rising anger at the injustice of her position. If she had Cassie Dilhorne here she would have strangled her, she thought fiercely—Cassie Dilhorne, who, she remembered bitterly, would be in her debt forever and ever, ask of her what she would, etc. She could not even ask her to clear her name— because Lady Cassandra had proved to be a coward, a mealy-mouthed coward, who had lied to Derek to save herself.

She leaned forward impulsively, wanting to tell the driver to turn around and bring her to Lady Cassandra's door. No. She settled back in her seat. In her mind's eye, she could see herself being politely turned away by the butler, who would announce that her ladyship was unable to see her.

Cassie, of course, was not entirely to blame for what had happened. She never should have agreed to go. It had been against her better judgment. She should have taken Derek's terrible jealousy into account. She might have guessed that he might find out, he, who only needed a glance, a smile, a wink on which to build a mountain of suspicion! Well, he had had his worst fears confirmed. He had found that his wife was all he suspected, the erring daughter of a whoring dam! She released a long hissing breath. That he should throw her mother's sins in her face! It did not bear thinking about, not now when she needed to be in control of herself. No doubt the publisher would have read the *Morning Post*—and Alan Parry, too. And the clerk, whose obsequious attitude would turn to disdain. She could not think of anything so trivial as his attitude! She must concentrate solely on her mission, which might be to save a man's life!

Finally, they were at the publisher's office. On coming into the anteroom, Verity was startled to see the clerk descend hastily from his high stool and knock on Mr. Newman's door. In another moment, the publisher came hurriedly into the room, followed by Alan Parry. One look at their grave faces and Verity knew that Derek had preceded her. Had he gone? Mr. Newman's office door remained open, and there was no one inside. Her first sensation was one of relief, but that was soon surmounted by apprehension.

Impulsively she turned toward Mr. Parry. "Oh, you are here. It cannot be another coincidence."

A brief smile glowed in his somber eyes. "It is never a coincidence. I work closely with Tony editing manuscripts, but today is different."

"Different? My husband's not called you out, has he? Oh, I pray he has not. I did so want to come here last night, but 'twas growing late, and I . . ." To her annoyance, tears came into her eyes. She tried to blink them away, not wanting to weep in front of them.

"My dear Lady Unger." Mr. Newman strode forward and took her hands. "Please come in here," he said gently.

"Yes, yes, of course. Kitty, dear, please wait out here."

"Yes, milady," the girl replied.

"Sit here, child." Alan Parry indicated a chair and received a grateful look from the abigail as she obeyed.

"I do thank you, sir," Verity murmured, appreciating his courtesy. "I . . . I . . ." Again she found it difficult to speak, and hurrying into the office, she sank down on the chair that the publisher offered her. Mr. Newman took his seat at the desk, but Mr. Parry remained standing. Verity glanced at him and looked down quickly. She scarcely liked to address the two men, primed as they must be on her husband's story. Unfortunately, there was no help for it, but first she had to know if Derek had succeeded in challenging Mr. Parry to a duel. "*Has* my husband called you out, sir?" she demanded nervously.

"No. Tony, here, told him that I was traveling in Egypt and will not be home before the year is out."

"Oh, I am glad." She met his questioning glance and flushed. " 'Twas all my fault that such an idea ever entered his mind. But you must hear what happened."

"We do want to hear," the publisher said. He favored her with a rueful smile. "Had I been expert with either sword or pistol, I'd have been minded to call Lord Unger out for the calumny he heaped upon my firm this morning, dubbing us a twopenny operation aimed at babes and fools. He suggested that London would be the richer and the warmer were my wares heaped on a bonfire and burned in the public square. I had the distinct feeling he felt I should be incinerated with them."

"Oh, dear, I wish I might have prepared you for his visit, but I had hoped against hope he'd have grown calmer and perhaps more reasonable than yesterday. I never should have said what I did, knowing how eager he was, not only to have his suspicions confirmed, but to find someone on whom he could vent his fury."

"And furious he was." Mr. Newman rolled his eyes. "He frightened my poor clerk half to death. Lord, the man seems scarcely sane."

"Let us hear what you have to tell us, Lady Unger," Mr. Parry prompted.

Very was finding herself increasingly reluctant to give them an explanation they, too, might find unbelievable. After all, neither of them knew her. Still, there was no help for it, and perhaps the bad impression Derek had made when he stormed into the office would stand her in good stead.

Fixing her eyes on a silver ornament that stood on the publisher's desk, she began hesitantly, feeling extremely foolish as she described Cassie's visit and request. Thinking about it, she feared her wits must have been wandering that day. Why else would she have consented to visit so notorious a spot, and in company with another female? However, as she explained defiantly, Reggie was to have met them, and he'd have seen them home. It was a little easier to describe her encounter with the lout—but telling them how she had been persuaded to go to her "rescuer's" house was very difficult. Probably they would be just as incredulous as Derek—more so, for they did not know her and Derek did. No, she reasoned bitterly, he could not have known her either, else he never would have doubted her.

It was equally difficult to describe her quarrel with her husband, for she was forced to cite her ironic references to "Mr. Hunter" as one of her "millions of lovers." Soon after, she faltered to a close. "He'd believe all that was said against me and nothing I told him, save my mention of Mr. Parry. It . . . was very foolish of me to make so provocative a statement—especially in view of what he'd said about the Bow Street Runners. But I . . . I was past caring what I said. I was so very angry." A long sigh escaped her. "That's the whole of it."

"That damned fool!" Alan Parry exclaimed explosively. "I wish I'd been present when he arrived. I'd have answered his challenge readily enough on the mere suggestion of her infidelity. And that without any prior knowledge of the situation!"

"Come, my boy," Mr. Newman said soothingly. "One does not fight with fools or madmen, and if he's not the one, sure he must be the other."

"Yes." Mr. Parry strode back and forth across the room. "But she should not need to suffer the brunt of his madness. If I'd heard how this scoundrel, this wolf in sheep's clothing, under pretense of rescue, had dragged her to his house and tried both to insult and assault her—that's where my challenge would have been sent. As it is, I've half a mind to call this idiot out—if only for his arrant stupidity!"

"I beg you will not!" Verity leaped to her feet. "He's an expert with rapier and pistol."

"Yes, Alan, remember that if you were to meet him, Lady Unger's reputation would be in the basket."

"And is it not already, with him bruiting his supicions all over town? Were I wed to this innocent, no one could make

me believe that she was anything save virtuous." He looked
at Verity, and his voice softened. "Come, my dear, you must
not weep." Moving to her side, he put a comforting arm
around her shoulders.

Tears she could not check ran down her cheeks. She
realized that she had not expected them to believe her story
any more than Derek had. "I do thank you," she whispered.
"I f-feared neither of you would credit my tale."

"Only a man whose jealousy is greater than his acumen
could doubt you," Mr. Parry said hotly. Moving away from
her, he addressed the publisher. "Good God, to threaten
divorce upon such flimsy evidence! Even used as a plot
device in one of your romances, Tony, I would find it hard to
swallow."

" 'Tis more than a mere threat," Verity said in a small
voice. "His solicitors will probably be calling upon me at the
hotel. He's already consulted them. And my grandmother
seems to believe that he will divorce me."

"Ah, your grandmother! Could she not have given him the
lie in his teeth?" Mr. Parry demanded.

"My grandmother has said she thinks I am telling the
truth, but Mr. Newman, she's dismissed Miss Marshall on
the grounds that . . . that she conspired with me in my deceit
of her—not my husband alone. She has sent her back to
Clavering."

"Thus dropping yet another faggot on the fire!" the publisher said grimly. " 'Tis not such hard lines for Miss Marshall,
as you might believe. Her brother's ailing, and she's needed
at home."

"I know—she told me as much in her letter. My grandmother was generous, at least by her standards, and she gave
her a reference as well as ten pounds—but I must send her
more. My grandmother has given me fifty pounds. I can
spare some of that."

"No, wait." Mr. Parry frowned. "Why will your grandmother not let you stay with her?"

"Because of my sisters. She fears they will be hurt by the
scandal, as indeed they would be, were I to remain with her.
I see it now. Their reputations might be colored by that same
brush that has already blackened mine. But I think that

afterwards, she will let me stay in the country. She hinted as much, or at least that is how I interpret her remarks."

"Oh, generous!" Mr. Parry said sarcastically. "And you'll live like a penitent for the rest of your days, punished for a crime you did not commit, watched and excoriated at every turn. There's no reason why you should suffer that, my poor girl. You are an artist."

"Indeed she is. One of my most gifted writers," the publisher put in.

"And you should be among her own kind. Your husband, though—is there no chance that he'll not relent and take you back, once he comes to what must be charitably termed his 'senses'?" Mr. Parry demanded harshly.

Verity drew herself up. "Even if he were to relent, I would not. I have not told you all he said—nor will I. Suffice it to say that I could not live with him again. I prefer disgrace."

"And you will have more than your share of it—if you remain in London." Mr. Parry's eyes were filled with an almost savage anger. "God, I wish I were in more of a position to help you."

"That you should want to help me is enough," she said gratefully.

"No, it is not enough," he returned slowly. "But there is an alternative, you know, if you care to avail yourself of it."

"An alternative?" she repeated unbelievingly.

"You need not suffer the importunings of his solicitors. What he has set in motion will continue with or without your presence, and though it would seem an admission of guilt, it would be no more damning than the position you occupy already."

"I begin to see what you mean, Alan," Mr. Newman murmured. "And yes, I think it would serve."

"I do not understand," she said.

"You can do as a friend of mine once did, when in a similar situation—though that was of his own devising and none other involved. You could simply disappear. You've quite a bit of money and stand to earn considerably more through your writing. Tony will see to that."

"Yes, indeed, I will. I am still receiving requests for your *Elvira*," the publisher told her. "And that, I might mention, does not happen with many of our books. There's such a great flow of 'em.''

"It . . . it is kind of you to tell me so," she murmured.

"I am not kind," the publisher said earnestly. "No one in my position's ever kind, and often I am cruel when I am presented with manuscripts I find inferior."

"Enough. Do not alarm Lady Unger with the ogrish aspects of your reprehensible character, Tony." Alan turned back to Verity. "Have you ever been up near Hampstead Heath?"

"I've seen it—but never walked upon it. 'Tis a pretty spot . . ."

" 'Tis a spot that might suit you well, were you to settle in the adjoining village. Many writers have their homes there. You may have heard of Leigh Hunt."

"I have, of course." She knotted her forehead. "Yes, the editor of the *Examiner*. He was sent to prison for calling the poor Regent an 'Adonis of fifty,' Miss Marshall told me."

"For a trifle more than that. The article was long, scurrilous, and well deserved, though I can see by your frown you're not quite in agreement with me."

"The Regent was uncommon kind to me," she murmured.

" 'Twas undoubtedly no more than you deserved. But I am straying from my text. Leigh Hunt has lived in Hampstead and undoubtedly will be returning there. Many other writers have homes in and around the village, including myself. It possesses a most felicitous atmosphere. Its quiet lanes and that broad heath furnish inspiration. It is as charming an oasis as you are like to find within so short a distance from the city . . . 'tis no more than four miles. Yet, for all its proximity to London, it is peaceful and sequestered enough to shelter you and none the wiser as to your whereabouts."

"It does sound inviting," she said. "But sure they must read the *Morning Post* even there."

"Of course, but you'll not be calling yourself Lady Unger . . . or even Verity Stratton. I'd not like to see you drop the name of Verity, though."

"Why not?"

"Because it suits you. It means 'truth.' "

"Oh," she murmured gratefully. "You are kind."

"I am not kind, either. I am honest," he corrected. "What should she be called, Tony?"

"Maiden's her *nom de plume*," the publisher mused. "But perhaps it were better if she did not use it."

"Verity Lost." She managed a laugh.

"Verity Farwell, rather," Mr. Parry suggested. "For you'll not be lost but only saying farewell."

"Verity . . . Farwell?" she murmured. "It has a pretty sound. And," she added wistfully, "I should like to say farewell to all I wish I might leave behind me."

"Let the wish be father—or mother—to the thought," Mr. Parry urged.

"Could it be done?" she asked dubiously.

"As I have told you, it has been done by my friend, who had lived in London longer than you and had a wider acquaintance as well as a fine old name. One does not need to flee as far as America to find anonymity."

"Anonymity. Oh, I should like that above all things," Verity said wistfully.

"You could have it, and within four miles of this seething city. There are lodgings to be had in Well Walk, which is just below the Heath."

"Well Walk?" she repeated. "I remember something about Hampstead. It was famous for its healing springs, was it not?"

"In the early part of the last century, mainly. But the great Dr. Johnson went there for his health, and currently it is a place of poets."

"Poets! Oh, I do love poetry!" Verity exclaimed. She fastened her eyes on Mr. Parry's face. "Do you suppose it could be done? Could I drop out of sight so easily? The idea frightens me, rather."

"I expect it must." There was sympathy in Mr. Parry's dark gaze. "It will mean an entire change in your way of life. You've been used to luxury, servants, horses . . . all that goes with your high position. I'll wager you've never even set foot inside a lodging house."

"You've won your wager, sir," she said. "But as for the changes in my existence, you're right. They'll be there whether I go or stay. As of yesterday, I ceased to be a marchioness. It wants only for my husband's solicitors to do his bidding."

"Such a tempest in a teapot!" Mr. Newman sighed.

Mr. Parry's look was commiserating. "His attitude is certainly excessive. However, though you may not believe me at this moment, Lady Unger, you are well out of a situation which would only worsen with time. The most unfortunate aspect of the matter's that the blame could not be fixed where it is most deserved. In my novels, I have yet to let the guilty go unpunished."

"Oh, so do I," she said earnestly. "But that is why we're read, is it not? Because life is so full of the sort of contradictions we would as soon not contemplate—and reading offers the solace of a happy conclusion."

"Granted." He smiled ruefully. He added, "Are you willing to take the step that will bring you out of this morass, Lady Unger—or will you need more time to think about it?"

She was silent for a moment. Then, she said, "I must ask you to stop addressing me as Lady Unger. In view of the change of my circumstances and remembering my married state—I think you must call me Mrs. Farwell."

Part Three
ℜ ℜ

One

The deed had been done, or, rather, the move had been made. In a matter of a few hours, Verity Vane, Marchioness of Unger, resident of Unger Castle and Great Jermyn Street, London, had been transformed into the widowed Verity Farwell of Hampstead Village. She occupied two rooms on the second floor front, of a tall old house in Well Walk, and Kitty had been given a cubbyhole at the top of the house. It was owned by a Mr. and Mrs. Staples, who were, Mr. Parry had told her, a retired butler and housekeeper. The rent was minimal, no more than two pounds a month, including Kitty's accommodation.

Though they faced the lime-bordered street, her rooms were extremely quiet. She could not hear the cries of peddlers, the curses of coachmen or drivers of drays stranded in traffic, and all the other multitudinous noises indigenous to the city proper. Through her open window she could hear the birds in the trees and the occasional shouts of children at play. There was a family of four boys in the house next door, who were very rambunctious, Mrs. Staples had said regretfully. Their mother, a Mrs. Bently, also kept rooms, and currently her lodgers were a young poetic gentleman and his brother, who was suffering from consumption.

Verity was sorry for the brother and wondered about the "young poetic gentleman." Was he one of the poets she would be meeting in Hampstead? Staring out of the window at the road patterned by the leafy shadows of the lime trees, she forgot about him in wondering how long it would take for her to become accustomed to this startling change of circumstances. She was conscious of an emptiness in her chest, or perhaps it was farther down in the region called her solar plexus. The location was not important. It was not really there, that feeling. It was symptomatic of the sense of loss she was experiencing, and she could not help but be aware that she had made a move just as impulsive as the one which had caused so abrupt and alarming a change in her life.

She had not expected to feel quite so much at sea, nor had she anticipated the hurt and anger that had invaded her earlier in the day when, on telling the manager of Gordon's Hotel that she was going into the country, she had read relief in his eyes. He had been as obsequious as ever, but, of course, it was false. Two days earlier, he would have been ecstatic and boastful because the Marchioness of Unger had deigned to patronize his hotel. Now, with tongues wagging and covert glances following her as she walked through the lobby, he could hardly wait to be rid of so unwelcome a guest. At that moment, she had been conscious of a futile wish to be several inches taller. If she were only stately, she could have swept through the lobby as Derek often did, looking chill and unapproachable. It was very difficult to sweep or even to look unapproachable when you were but an inch over five feet!

Derek.

What would he think when his solicitors returned to him with the news that his prey had fled? Prey? She considered her almost unconscious employment of the term. Yet, it was apt. Knowing him as well as she did, she was quite sure he would have done all in his power to wound her. In other times and climes, he might have had her stoned in the public square! In a sense, that was what he had done by airing his suspicions in the hearing of his servants—and no one more aware than he of how swiftly the news must spread. Subsequently, he added injury to insult by consulting his solicitors as soon as he imagined his unworthy suspicions corroborated. He had not even given her a chance to speak in her own defense!

To refer to her mother, casting that lady's sins in her face, completely ignoring the equally well-known fact that her father, rather than being a wronged cuckold, had had more than his share of mistresses—not excluding the infamous Hariette Wilson with whom he had dallied in her box at

Covent Garden, with all the polite world looking on! Yet it was her mother who had been held up to scorn while her father's actions brought only tolerant and, possibly, envious chuckles from his friends. It would have served Derek right had there been fire beneath the smoke!

She blinked at a vista suddenly grown blurry and found to her surprise that there were tears of anguish in her eyes.

How could Derek have mistrusted her so completely? How could this man to whom she had been wed for the best part of two years have been so willing to believe in her guilt? If it had been the other way around, she would have demanded more proof, and then she would have been dubious, knowing how much he cared for her, *had* cared before the frost withered the rose. Even Mr. Parry, whom she had met no more than four times in her whole life, had believed her implicitly, and so had Mr. Newman. Their trust had comforted her, and more than that it had given her the courage to sever her connections with her former life.

"A clean thrust"—those were the words Mr. Parry had employed when he found her a hackney. "Cut yourself off from your former existence. It may hurt at first, but you'll be surprised to find how quickly all wounds will heal. You have the benefit of a clear conscience—which is more than my friend had when he severed the strings that bound him to his old life."

She wondered about Mr. Parry's anonymous friend. Might he not be speaking about himself? No, she could not believe that. He had strength of character and purpose. She could not imagine him making disastrous missteps such as the one that had plunged her into this morass. She doubted she could have carried off her departure from the hotel with such aplomb had it not been that she knew him to be waiting for her near St. Martin-in-the-Fields. She had felt very strange, and she knew that Kitty, though well primed as to her intentions, had been shocked when, upon calling her driver to halt, she had had him unload her bandbox and portmanteau. Hardly had they descended when Mr. Parry had arrived in another hackney and, instructing the postboy to pick up her luggage, had directed the coachman to drive them to Hampstead. If the Bow Street Runners had still been on her trail, they would have reported an elopement to Derek.

A smile played briefly about her lips as she thought of her rescuer, whom she must remember to address as Alan, because he had suddenly become her "cousin" and also "the boyhood chum of her late husband."

"For it would be better if we had some family tie," he had explained. "Otherwise it will be difficult for me to procure you lodgings in Hampstead and introduce you to my friends."

It was really ironic that Alan should be her champion—she had searched her mind and remembered now that less than two years ago, she had thought herself madly in love with him! She, had, in fact, wept bitter tears over him, and all the way up to the time when Kitty was helping her dress for her wedding, she had wondered about the moody glance she had seen on his face during her last visit to Mr. Newman's office. She had actually succeeded in convincing herself that he was as heartbroken as she herself—over their brief meetings and final parting. She had been positive that Alan Parry's image would be enshrined in her heart forever and ever. She had stepped from the carriage that brought her to the church, stubbornly bemoaning the cruel fate that was catapulting her into the arms of a man she was positive she loathed.

She did loathe him! He deserved to be loathed for his cruelty, his disbelief, his untoward actions . . . but for nineteen months, he had been the most important person in her life, practically the only person, but she had not minded that. When they were alone together, he had shed the austere face he turned to the world. He had been so tender, so loving—how could he have turned on her like a . . . a mad dog?

Easily, provided with the seeds sown by the dowager marchioness. And now . . . now what was going to become of her?

That had not occurred to her before. Yes, it had. She was going to settle down and write in earnest. And for the first time, she need not keep her work hidden, and also, she would be meeting other authors and poets. She would be a member of an artistic community! Unfortunately, at this moment she felt singularly uninspired—but that, of course, would pass once she was more accustomed to her new life. She shivered, finding to her regret that some of her courage seemed to be deserting her. She feared change. Her existence had been so *ordered*. Until two days ago, she had expected that Derek would calm down eventually. She had expected, too, that they would have children. Not everyone conceived during the first few years of marriage. Derek's mother had been thirty-six when he was born. She had not even suffered a miscarriage until then. A sob shook Verity. She had wanted to give Derek children, she recalled.

Children.

Why was she weeping when he had pronounced himself *pleased* because there had been no issue? He had said he would have doubted their legitimacy! Damn him! It had been a great shame she had not been unfaithful and presented him with a collection of bastards! Furiously, she blinked her tears away. How ridiculous to be mooning over her heartless husband when he did not merit so much as a single tear! Better to dwell upon his amazement when he learned she had left the hotel and seemingly vanished into thin air. Of course, in cutting herself off from Derek, she had also estranged herself from her grandmother, whose anger upon learning of her departure would be great. Verity had considered leaving a note for her, explaining where she was going and why she was leaving—but second thoughts had intervened to assure her this was madness. Lady Harcliffe would have wasted no time in turning the information over to Derek.

There was a tap on the door of the small passage lying between bedroom and sitting room. Recognizing Kitty's knock, Verity said, "Come in."

Looking at the abigail, Verity saw that her eyes were bloodshot, and with some compunction she realized that Kitty was probably just as upset at the change in their circumstances as she. "Oh, Kitty," she cried. "I pray you'll not be too unhappy here."

"Oh, no, milady," the girl assured her. " 'Tis a pretty spot, and no doubt I'll soon get used to it."

Verity's concern increased. Kitty was being brave. She wondered if the girl might not have left a sweetheart behind in London. She was on easy terms with the other servants, and it seemed to her that she had noticed Kitty being particularly friendly with Mark, a young groom whom they had brought in from the country. It was on the tip of her tongue to ask her about him—but perhaps such a question would only serve to make her more miserable. She said, "Are your quarters comfortable?"

"They are that, milady, and much larger than I 'ad in London. I pray you'll not waste any time frettin' about me, milady. May I unpack for you now?"

"Unpack, oh, yes." Verity looked at the portmanteau and the bandboxes curiously, wondering what garments Kitty had included. She herself had been in such a confused state of mind she had never thought to supervise the packing. Consequently, she watched rather apprehensively as Kitty opened the armoire. She winced as she saw the lacy ballgown she had had made in Edinburgh last year on the occasion of their visit to Lady Campbell-Stuart, an aged and distant cousin on the dowager marchioness's side of the family. She had, Verity recalled wryly, never ceased discussing her ancestors, with emphasis upon Bonnie Prince Charlie and with many reminiscent tears for the dead of Culloden, the which she professed to recall as though it were only the day before yesterday and she an interested observer, a circumstance that she and Derek doubted, since the battle had taken place in 1745 when his cousin was but eight months old. When they were alone, he had talked pridefully of those Scots who preferred not to cast their lot with a failed cause, and scathingly of the later years of the Bonnie Prince, who, in 1789, had died drunken and debauched in Rome.

She approved the patterned muslin. It was simple and would suffice for walks through the village. The turquoise satin was a trifle too flamboyant for village life. Derek had never approved the fact that it was so low-cut, and she had worn it only twice. He had liked the blue lutestring which she had had before her marriage, and she was glad that Kitty had also packed her new morning gown in lavender poplin. She bit down a sigh as she saw the long hooded cloak she had worn to the Gardens—the night before last! Had it been such a short time ago? She was minded to present the garment to Kitty, but caution intervened. It was comfortable, and she would no longer have access to funds which would purchase anything half so fine.

What would she do for clothes when her own were worn out?

The gowns Kitty was still removing from the portmanteau

were worth many times more than the money she would receive from the sale of her book. A curlicue of fear stirred at the bottom of her throat. Fifty pounds had seemed a large sum when her grandmother had presented it to her—but how long would it last? Still, she did have the money from *Elvira*, and she would be selling more than one book. The publisher had pronounced himself eager to receive as many manuscripts as she could produce, but one could not write them overnight. In severing the strings that bound her to the past, she had not given much thought to the fact that she could no longer depend upon her husband or her grandmother. She would have to watch what she spent. . . .

A knock at the door interrupted these speculations. Kitty quickly opened it, and Verity glimpsed the mop of brown curls and the big blue eyes of Betty, the all-around maidservant, who did for Mrs. Staples. She spoke breathlessly, as if she must needs be on the run to perform all that was expected of her. "Beggin' yer pardon," she panted. "But Mrs. Farwell's cousin's come an' wants to know if 'e may see 'er."

Verity started up. "Oh, yes, of course. I'll be there in a minute."

"I'll tell 'um." Betty sped off.

"I'll go with you, milady," Kitty said.

"No, you need not." Verity looked in the mirror over her small dressing table. The glass was not of the best quality and she appeared rather wavy, but it did tell her that her locks were sadly tumbled. "You can smooth my hair a bit, Kitty. And my gown . . . I ought to change it, for this is wrinkled. That sprigged muslin you just unpacked . . . and my shawl, 'twill suffice. But we must hurry, for I said I would not be long."

Kitty, helping her from one gown to another, said stubbornly, "I think I ought to go with you, milady."

"No, you need not, for he is known as my cousin, and it's quite proper for me to be seen with him." Looking into her abigail's dubious contenance, she added, "He is a gentleman."

" 'Tis late for a walk," Kitty said insistently. "The sun's nearly down."

"But not entirely—and he did promise to show me something of the village. I had quite forgotten. And Kitty, dear,

remember that you must not continue to address me as milady.
I am plain Mrs. Farwell."

"Oh, milady." Tears sparkled in Kitty's eyes. "It be all so
different, an' you innocent as any lamb."

"Come, my dear," Verity said bracingly. "Crying will not
alter the circumstances. Be of good cheer, and meanwhie
please try to do something with my miserable hair. I have
half a mind to cut it."

"Oh, I pray you will not, mi . . . Mrs. Farwell." Kitty put
protective hands on Verity's golden curls. " 'Twould be a
shame!"

"Well, for now, just brush it," Verity directed. She added
a trifle anxiously, "Oh, I almost forgot . . . you did take the
portmanteau that contained the leather box which has my
stationery in it?"

"Oh, yes, milady, 'tis at the bottom."

A few minutes later, descending the stairs that would bring
her to the ground floor and the front parlor, Verity wondered
at the lift in her spirits. Probably she was all cried out, she
decided. However, upon reaching the parlor and seeing Mr.
Parry smiling at her, she experienced an even higher surge of
good spirits and had no trouble tracing both the former and
the latter to the proper source.

"My dear Cousin Verity." He came forward and took her
hand, starting to bear it to his lips, only to flush slightly and
press it warmly instead. "You are looking very well. I hope
you were able to rest."

Verity, her hand still imprisoned in his grasp, was, much
to her astonishment, reminded of the first time she had ever
seen him. Though she was not prey to the same childish
emotions that had gripped her then, she could not deny that
his presence seemed to brighten this meanly furnished and
dingy parlor. Coupled with that realization was another even
more pleasant. She could walk with him through the vilage
without fear of Derek's reproaches to herself and threats to
her companion. She said, "I am well rested and I am looking
forward to seeing some of those points of interest you mentioned to me."

At last he released her hand. "I am looking forward to
showing them to you."

Coming out of the house, Verity did feel a little disoriented.

Aside from her regrettable experiences in the Vauxhall Gardens, she had never been abroad without the protective presence of her husband, an older relative, her governess, or her abigail. To walk with a man she had met only a few times was certainly unconventional! But he wasn't quite a stranger. She could not attach that description to one who had rescued her from what amounted to a trial by fire.

She could easily liken him to Sir Launcelot rescuing Queen Guinevere from the stake where popular suspicion had put her—with the one difference that the Queen's dalliance with that same knight had placed her in that precarious position. She winced, recalling that her supposed dalliance with "Anthony Hunter" was a factor in her own downfall. It was extremely fortunate that his assumed identity had saved him from a duel!

She glanced at him and again was pleased because it was not necessary to crane her neck to see his face. Rather than being at least three inches below it, her head topped his shoulder. Consequently, it was easy for her to admire the crisp curl of his blue-black hair, his heavy but well-shaped eyebrows, and his eyelashes which, she now noticed, were long and curling. She had remarked his olive complexion when she had first seen him, and once again she wondered if he might be of foreign extraction. He dressed well but not ostentatiously. She liked that about him, too, and realized in that same moment she was staring at him.

She glanced down quickly, saying self-consciously, " 'Tis very quiet here."

"Monstrously quiet," he agreed.

"Monstrously, sir?"

"After London," he clarified. "You'll probably go through a period when you'll feel much at sea. The quietness might seem almost as oppressive as the turbulence of the city. My friend found it so."

"Ah, your friend! Will I meet him?" She fixed her eyes on him, wondering if he would betray himself or, rather, reveal himself as his so-called friend.

He said merely, "I doubt it, for he has gone abroad. His name is Henry ffolkes." He glanced at her almost as if he expected her to know the name—but she did not. Her curiosity was and was not satisfied. She scented a mystery about

Alan Parry and wondered if it would ever be unveiled. Now was not the time to think about it, she decided, and looking around her she saw a long low brick building.

"Gracious, what's that? 'Tis too large to be a private house and too small to be a palace."

"It is known as the Long Room. You should revere it."

"I? Why?"

"It was mentioned by one of those intrepid ladies who paved the way for you and other female writers. I am talking about little Miss Fanny Burney, or Madame d'Arblay, as she is presently called."

"Oh, dear, yes!" Verity exclaimed. "Hampstead *was* mentioned in *Evelina* . . . her heroine attended a dance in the Long Room. 'Twas an assembly hall. And now no longer?"

"No, for the waters have receded, or, at least, they are not being touted as being the equal of those at Tunbridge Wells and Bath. There is the place that was once used as the Pump Room, and . . ." He paused at the crunch of a foot on the gravel behind them.

Verity turned swiftly, her heart beating faster and the idea of surveillance rising in her mind along with a vision of that small angry man who had bounced into the publisher's offices that day, but it was only a slight, pale youth, rather unfashionably dressed, who smiled shyly at her companion.

"Tom," Mr. Parry said, "good afternoon. I am glad to see you abroad again. You are feeling better, I hope?"

"I am that, Alan." He spoke hoarsely, as if troubled with a sore throat. His eyes rested on Verity's face.

"Verity," Mr. Parry said, startling her with her use of her given name, "I should like you to meet Mr. Thomas Keats, who is your neighbor. Tom, this is my cousin, Mrs. Farwell, newly arrived from London. She is lodging with Mrs. Staples."

"Delighted, ma'am." The young man took Verity's proffered hand and smiled at her shyly.

"I, too, Mr. Keats." She managed to conceal a start at the touch of his hand, which was hot and dry. He was very thin, too, and his eyes were preternaturally bright. She was unhappily reminded of Clara, a maid at the castle who had had the same hoarse voice and bright eye. She had died early from consumption, and now she remembered Mrs. Staples's references to Mrs. Bently's lodgers.

"Have you heard from your wandering brother?" Alan asked.

The boy's eyes brightened. "Yes, I received a letter just the other day. He seems to be enjoying Scotland."

"Oh, what part of Scotland is your brother visiting?" Verity asked.

"He's on a walking tour and hopes to cover two thousand miles, mostly on foot, though he says that sometimes it's hard going, for he's traveling with a friend, and with their knapsacks on their backs they are often mistaken for peddlers. The Scots don't seem to fancy peddlers." Tom laughed, and coughed, quickly pressing a handkerchief to his mouth. "He says," he continued after a moment, "that he was much impressed by the view from the top of Skiddaw but disappointed by the Falls of Lodore."

"As Mr. Southey was not," Mr. Parry commented. "But no doubt John will find inspiration beyond the famous Cataracts."

"He says that he has," affirmed Mr. Keats. "Though I wish he might have found more here in Hampstead. I do miss him."

"I am sure you must," Mr. Parry said sympathetically.

Listening to them, Verity made a connection in her mind. "John . . . Keats," she said tentatively. "*He* is your brother? The poet?"

"Yes," the young man acknowledged proudly. "Are you acquainted with his work?"

"Oh, yes, my husband . . . was very fond of poetry. I've learned some of your brother's poems by heart." She repeated softly:

> "Then I felt like some watcher of the skies
> When a new planet swims into his ken
> Or like stout Cortez when with eagle eyes
> He star'd at the Pacific—and all his men
> Look'd at each other with a wild surmise—
> Silent, upon a peak in Darien."

"Oh, how well you spoke John's verse!" Tom Keats exclaimed, his sunken eyes glowing. "I do wish he'd been here to listen."

"I am glad I was here to listen." Mr. Parry looked at her

with considerable interest. "You did not tell me you were so well acquainted with young Keats's works, Cousin Verity."

"Did I not? We had so much else to discuss, meeting after so long a time."

Tom coughed. "I think . . . I must be going inside," he said disappointedly, his voice half muffled by the crumpled handkerchief he pressed against his mouth.

"You must," Mr. Parry agreed, concernedly. "The breeze is rising. Have you taken your physick?"

"Oh, I have." The boy spoke wearily. "I live upon it and not much else. There are times when I might wax poetic myself over a piece of underdone beef or pasty. But I am feeling a bit better, so I must continue with the treatment." He visited a singularly sweet smile on Verity. " 'Twas a pleasure to have met you, Mrs. Farwell . . . and Alan, I hope you'll come and see me soon."

"Of course, I will," Mr. Parry returned.

Verity watched as Mr. Keats walked toward the tall gray house where he lodged. "He's very ill, is he not?"

"Very. And John's delicate, too."

Her hand flew to her throat. "I pray you'll not tell me that he . . ."

"I do not think so. But I cannot believe that so strenuous a walking trip is good for him."

"Nor I," she said on a breath. "Nothing must happen to him! He is so brilliant . . . and he must be very young, too."

"He's twenty-three."

"Oh, dear." She looked at him ruefully. " 'Tis enough to make you want to throw your pen away and send him all your writing materials for his use."

"I've often had the same feeling, but each of us has something to say, even if we cannot be a Keats or a Shakespeare."

"Or an Austen," Verity sighed.

"Or a Scott," he agreed. "Yet, one need not write for the ages, you know. It's enough to have the assurance that what pleases us to scribble pleases other when they read it and lets them soar for some short distance on the wings for our inspiration."

"Oh." She smiled. "That was most felicitously put, sir."

"Truthfully, too, I hope you agree."

"I must . . . if I am to continue scribbling," she returned and felt a little throb of fear. When she had been working on *The Canadian Cousin* three days ago, she had felt full of enthusiasm, but oddly enough, the idea of settling down to continue working was not giving rise to a similar sensation. She hoped that the feeling would vanish and expected it must. She only needed to rest and to acclimate herself to her new surroundings, her new position, or, rather, the lack of any position, something she had occasionally desired, she recalled. She felt immensely older than the girl who had chafed at the restrictions of her existence and who had not known how very easily they could be lifted, how easily, how disastrously, and herself become an object of opprobrium just because . . . but she must not, must not, must not allow herself to fall into the slough of self-pity. She said brightly, "We passed the Heath coming here . . . might we walk up there now?"

"We will, but shouldn't you like to know something about this bit of earth where you are standing now?"

"Indeed, I should," she replied eagerly.

He spoke as he wrote, she discovered, giving her fascinating little anecdotes concerning the days when the Pump Room, which lay across the street from an old inn called the Green Man, had been full of people taking the waters for every ill from gout to goiter. She could pity the scrofulous Dr. Samuel Johnson with his swollen neck and laugh at a certain lithe, lovely countess who insisted on wearing no more than her shift when immersing herself in the waters. She had shocked her feminine contemporaries while titillating her masculine admirers. "She was known as the Swimming Siren," Mr. Parry said.

"You make me wish I'd been here then."

"I am glad you were not," he said quickly. " 'Tis not often I have so interested an audience."

She was a trifle sorry he had qualified what might have been a provocative remark—but it was better that he had, she reminded herself. She was no longer attracted to him in the same way that she had been on their first meeting. He was a very pleasant companion, though, especially when contrasted with Derek.

She wished she knew more about him, and surely as his "cousin" she ought to have enough information to counter questions which might be put to her. It was on the tip of her tongue to demand a few particulars, but perhaps it would be too soon. Possibly when they knew each other better, he would volunteer that information.

"You wanted to see the Heath. 'Tis not possible to traverse the whole of it, but we may see a portion of it, and I'll point out the Vale of Health, where Mr. Hunt used to live—that is, if you're interested in one who slandered your beloved Regent. He, by the way, discovered John Keats and printed his early poems in the *Examiner*."

"Oh, for that I can forgive him anything!" she said fervently.

"I must suspect you of harboring a secret passion for our John," he teased.

"There's nothing secret about it, sir. I am far more in love with his versifying than with that of Lord Byron."

"We mustn't let wee Geordie hear that—'twould put him quite out of countenance, not to possess the heart of every beautiful woman."

"Now you're teasing me!" she accused.

"On the contrary. Byron values his reputation as a heartbreaker."

"How tedious."

Admiration flared in his eyes. "You are an original, cousin."

"I hope you are paying me a compliment, cousin."

"Your hopes are realized, cousin. Now come, if we walk up this street we will soon be on the Heath."

The glimpse she had had of Hampstead Heath as she rattled past it in the hackney, bracing herself against the jolting and with the scenery seemingly going up and down, had not prepared her for the wild and apparently untrammeled beauty of the place. She had seen the tangled grasses from the window but had barely noticed the spiky leaves of yellow gorse among them or the upstanding purple heather or the dog violets or the white-and-scarlet pimpernel, closing now that the sun was on the wane. Miss Marshall had taught her to identify these wild flowers a hundred years ago or so, it seemed, though only four had passed since she left the country. She repressed a desire to run through the grasses and fling herself down among them as she had been wont in those days, when she had enjoyed a freedom she had not really appreciated.

She smiled at Mr. Parry. "Oh, it is lovely. I like it much
better than Hyde Park . . . and to live so near. I will come up
here often!"

"But not alone," he cautioned.

"Why?"

"You must know that half a century ago, this place was
much frequented by highwaymen. A hundred years ago or
perhaps a little more there was a French villain who, when he
held up a coach, would bid the men and invite the ladies to
dance a minuet with him. Eventually he did his dancing alone
at rope's end."

"Oh." She shivered. "But there are no highwaymen about
here now that the spa's shut down, are there?"

"There are always vagrants in lonely places. And gold's
not always their objective. But I do not mean to frighten you.
It's just that you are so small and slight, so delicately
fashioned."

"Oh, dear, I pray you will not say so," she protested.

"I beg your pardon if I have presumed," he began quickly.

"Oh, no, it's not that. I do hate being so *little*. All my life
I have prayed that I might grow taller."

He laughed. "I am glad those prayers went unanswered. I
should not like to see you one whit different than you are
now, fair cousin."

She blushed. "You are kind, sir."

"My reputation's less for kindness than for honesty."

"I'll argue with that. Look what you've done for me in
aiding me to get away from . . . from everything."

"I could do no less for a fellow author."

It was a perfectly satisfactory answer, an honest answer,
and to be disappointed by it was ridiculous, especially since it
helped her to understand his motives and put her own feelings
in the proper perspective. With that in mind, she was able to
reply in kind. "I hope that I can justify your faith in me,"
she said.

"You've already done that. I look forward to the comple-
tion of your new book. I am sure I'll not need to wait very
long—now that your time is less constricted."

"I am sure you are right," she said staunchly. "Once I am
acclimated, I do not see how I can want for inspiration here. I
know I'll not need to seek it in Scotland—but I have less than

a passion for the place. It lies very near my husband's holdings in the North, where I have been for nearly the whole of my marriage."

"Oh, Lord, that can be gloomy, particularly in winter with the north winds howling and the snow drifts piling high."

"You know the North, I see."

"As a boy. I have cousins who live near Norham Castle."

"Oh, I have seen that," she said, and with a mischievous smile added:

"Day set on Norham's castled steep,
And Tweed's fair river broad and deep . . ."

"Ah." He also smiled, and continued:

"And Cheviot's mountains lone;
The battled towers, the Donjon Keep . . .
The loopholes grates, where captives weep,
The flanking walls that round it sweep,
    In yellow lustre shone.
The warriors on the turrets high,
Moving athwart the evening sky,
    Seem'd forms of giant height:
Their armour, as it caught the rays,
Flash'd back again the western blaze,
    In lines of dazzling light."

Verity applauded. "You said that thrillingly. You could be Edmund Kean, and you have a head for poetry, too."

"I thank you for your most flattering comparison. I might have a head for verse, but not the pen." He sighed.

"Your pen's used just as felicitously."

He flushed. " 'Tis more a matter of struggle than of inspiration, I assure you. My versifying always turns into doggerel."

"But poets," she said warmly, "must, I am sure, struggle with prose."

He favored her with a grateful smile. "You are determined to argue me into a good opinion of myself—and for that I thank you, cousin."

His reference to their assumed relationship reminded her that she wanted to know more about him. "If anyone thinks to ask how we are connected, or, rather, to which branch of the family I belong, what may I tell them?"

He hesitated, a slight frown in his eyes. "You may say that

you are the daughter of my Uncle Stephen, who used to live in Bath. He's dead now. However, I do not think they'll question you further.'' He glanced up. "The sun's near setting now, and I must take you back, I think.''

"It is,'' Verity discovered, wishing that she dared probe for more information about this newly acquired relation, but at the same time she had a feeling he begrudged her even that peep into his life, if peep it had been. She was ashamed of herself for prying, yet deeply curious about the man who strode at her side. It occurred to her that he could easily pass for that "mysterious stranger'' who figured in so many of the romances she had read. Usually these gentlemen were possessed of a "dark secret.'' Was he? She giggled, thinking herself a sad scatterbrain for comparing her so-called art to life. The chasm between the two was enormous, for the former always came equipped with a comfortable solution to all the heroine's problems.

"What has amused you?'' he demanded.

"I was thinking of my newly acquired 'father.' What is his last name?''

"Parry. However, if I were you, I'd limit my discourse to my dear departed husband, the late Mr. Farwell.''

"Oh, dear, I'd forgotten about him!'' she said. "Of course, you're right. Gracious, should I not be wearing widow's weeds?''

"No, I'd not like to see you drowned in sable. Let him be dead at least three years . . . which would take us back to Waterloo. He could be a . . . captain in the Eighteenth Hussars. That will bring you out of blacks and violets, grays and whites as well—and into blue. You look exceptionally well in blue, cousin.''

"I thank you, cousin. 'Tis one of my favorite colors.''

"It should be—for it matches your eyes.''

"And those of nearly everyone upon this island,'' she pouted. " 'Tis terribly usual to have blue eyes. I'd much rather have green or dark brown eyes like yours. Gracious, we do not resemble each other in the slightest. You look as if you might have had some Spanish ancestor.''

He gave her a rather startled look. "No, rather call it Roman, a throwback to the brave centurion who deserted Caesar's legions to woo a Saxon maiden.''

"Fie, sir, that is the very fabric of romance!" she exclaimed, nettled by his smooth evading of what she had believed to be a reasonably subtle probe.

"It's a fabric that has clothed and fed me for some years and consequently comes naturally to my lips as well," he said lightly.

"I hope it will come naturally to mine." She frowned, not having meant to voice her fears aloud.

"It already has," he pointed out. "Or would have if you'd needed it."

"If I didn't need it to keep me in clothing and food, it sustained me in other ways," she said gently.

"I believe that as I believe you are an artist," he assured her. "Now . . . before we begin our descent, let me show you the Vale of Health. I wish Hunt were still in residence. 'Twas a pleasure to be in his house, even though it was much cluttered with books and his wife Marianne's sculptures, always in a half-finished condition, and his children underfoot and hordes of friends thronging every room and arguing on such diverse subjects as the state of the king's health and farming in the West Indies. Still, you'll enjoy meeting Charles Dilke. Our next meeting will be at Wentworth Place, where he lives. He's an author and an editor. Also a friend of Keats. But come . . ."

Even if her curiosity had not been satisfied, Verity, parting from Mr. Parry, or Alan, as he insisted she, as his cousin, must address him, was feeling considerably happier than before. In addition to showing her the Vale of Health nestled in its hilly stronghold, he had promised that she would be present at the next poetry reading, whenever that would take place.

It was wonderful to anticipate discourses on poetry and the arts. She would be meeting Mr. Hunt and possibly Charles and Mary Lamb, people who until today had been only illustrious names to her. However, she was determined that her own work remain a secret. She would have Alan introduce her as a mere listener. A writer from the Minerva Press could not hope to find a place on a literary Olympus—but her imagination was fired and her fears about continuing her book so far in abeyance that she was ready to take out her chapters this minute and begin work again.

Coming inside, she ran lightly up the stairs and knocked upon the door. It swung open so quickly that she guessed Kitty must have heard her step upon the stairs. Entering, she was startled to find her abigail actually wringing her hands. "Oh, milady," she moaned, her eyes wide and tearful.

"What is it, Kitty?" Verity demanded.

"Oh, milady . . . 'is lordship . . ."

"My husband?" Verity tensed. "Did he have me followed, then? And . . . and has he been here?"

"No, 'e's not been here but . . . but, oh, milady . . . come an' look." Without giving Verity a chance to ask any more questions, she turned and ran into the bedroom.

Following her, Verity saw that her leather portfolio lay on the bed. Something in her chest flew to her throat and began to pound heavily. She had no reason to be so sure that that was where the trouble lay, but, in another second, she opened the portfolio and found that her fears had been realized. The papers, forty of them, which had been covered with her neat writing, lay in shreds, or at least some were shredded. Others were merely crumpled. Her pens were broken and the whole stained black with the ink that had been wantonly spilled over everything. She trembled. She was angry, furious, but more than that, she was frightened—for surely the man she had called husband must be more than a little mad!

Two

Verity's anger passed quickly, and anguish settled like a dark cloud over her spirits. Glancing at the pitiful fragments that had once been her carefully written pages, she felt as if something inside of her had been as wantonly obliterated.

Yet, with returning reason, she saw a possible method to her husband's madness. The fact that she had hidden her portfolio inside her portmanteau would naturally have sent his already inflamed suspicions spiraling upwards. Then, glancing at them, he would have noted that they were written in an epistolary style, addressed to "My dearest and most beloved friend"—and what had been the first sentence? Something about "I have long wanted to set down the events which have complicated my life of late. But I must insist that you keep them secret. . . ." Had she mentioned secrecy? She was not quite positive. Yes, she was positive. She had mentioned it. More than that, she had emphasized the heroine's need for it. She doubted that Derek had read any further. Having concluded that they were love letters, he had destroyed them in a fit of jealous rage.

Yes, of course, that was what he had meant when he referred to her "communications with her lover"! These and "Anthony Hunter's" teasing and provocative inscription in his book had furnished the evidence that had rendered her culpable in her husband's eyes. She smiled ironically. The pursuit of literature was not without its perils.

Her smile quickly vanished as she realized she would have to compose these lost chapters again. For that she needed the outline she had left with the publisher, her own having also been destroyed. She must go and see him first thing in the morning. She knew he would be understanding, but the fear she had believed vanquished was back, nullifying her new confidence. She feared she would be unable to recreate the lost pages.

It was really ironic, she thought bitterly. Now that she was in a situation where no one could oversee, interrupt, or destroy her work, she was too upset and confused to concentrate. She moved restlessly around the room. Some of her pain might have been alleviated, she knew—if only she could have found a sympathetic ear and poured out all her distress. Alan? Certainly he would be sympathetic, but she could not burden him with this latest tale of woe. She was not his responsibility. The sooner she learned to depend upon herself, the better it would be. Resolutely, she summoned Kitty, and with a calm that amazed and pleased her, she bade the abigail dispose of her papers and portfolio.

On a morning a fortnight after her arrival in Hampstead, Verity, with Kitty beside her, stood with a group of people awaiting the stage to London. She was aware of curious glances and was glad of her bonnet with its innovative drawstring veil now pulled over her face. She had thought it very silly when Derek had made her purchase it as a defense against the eyes of interested and admiring strangers when sightseeing in Edinburgh. Oddly enough, it was only one more instance of the jealousy that was responsible for the journey she was about to take, the jealousy that was, in fact, responsible for practically everything that had recently happened to her and threatened to keep on happening.

She sighed. She had been doing quite a bit of sighing of late. She had never fooled herself into imagining that it would be easy to adjust to her change in circumstances. Still, she had not anticipated the difficulties attendant upon being a young woman alone—save for her abigail and in quarters which seemed to grow smaller by the day!

Waking each morning in such constricted surroundings, it was only natural, she thought defensively, that she should long for the spacious apartments she had occupied at Harcliffe Manor, at her grandmother's house, in Castle Unger, and in Derek's townhouse. There if she was troubled in mind, she could wander at will through marble halls, settle down in the libraries or the portrait galleries, and if it were a fair day, she could walk in the gardens or go riding. If only she might have ridden here over the trails running across the heath—but Kitty had not packed her habit, and besides, she would not like to mount a strange steed.

A tiny suspicion that she might have been better off at Harcliffe Manor was quickly banished. When she went for a stroll in the village people might regard her with the curiosity accorded any stranger, but they did not look *through* her. Besides, if she had gone to stay in the country, she would have been deprived of Alan Parry's companionship.

Though she knew no more about him than she had known two weeks earlier and though she was positive there was some mysterious reason why a man of his breeding and charm chose to live in relative obscurity, she was no longer quite so troubled by the mystery. Mainly she was glad he was there and willing to take some time away from his writing to visit with her and show her more of the village. He had also indicated some shops she might fancy, and he had given her the name of a Miss Catley, a talented mantua maker. Furthermore, though she had spent more time with him in the last fortnight than with any man save her husband, never by word or look had he indicated that he wanted to be more than her good friend. In fact, she was hard put to remember that he was not a cousin. It was a very comfortable situation, especially when contrasted with the jealousy and suspicion never absent from her life with Derek.

Of course, she had to remember that Alan Parry was not in love with her. He did admire her. He made no secret of that. However, she was positive that his admiration was based on her work rather than herself. He was always praising her writing. And yesterday, unbeknownst to himself, he had given her quite a jolt when he asked her how her book was progressing. She prided herself on answering calmly that it was going a little slower than usual, something he completely understood, given the travail she had undergone two weeks ago. He had really startled her by his use of the term "two weeks." It was accurate enough. No, actually, it had been two weeks and three days since she had parted from her husband. And in that time, she had not been able to write two sentences! She could blame that on her lost outline—which she should have reclaimed immediately, but she had not been in the mood to write. She had to write!

"Milady?" Kitty plucked at her sleeve, adding belatedly, "Mrs., uh, Farwell, the coach be comin' an' us'll 'ave to get us some inside seats."

Though it was only a matter of four miles, the coach ride to London was both tedious and uncomfortable. Thanks to Kitty's much-criticized but defiant and expert maneuvering, they had obtained the desired inside seats. Unfortunately, both of them being small and slight, they were squeezed together by a huge woman carrying a bird cage on the one side and a heavyset man on the other. The inside of the coach reeked with the odor of unwashed bodies, and upon alighting from it some two hours later, Verity, endeavoring to shake the wrinkles out of her stylish blue poplin gown, feared she had carried away some of that horrid odor on her own person. Kitty, who had been next to the woman with the bird cage, loudly complained that it had been resting mainly on her lap. However, their dismay was quickly forgotten when faced with a larger problem—the need to find Leadenhall Street. Inquiries of various pedestrians netted the information that there was no such street in London, or, if there was, as some admitted, it was nowhere around the Swan with Two Necks, the inn where the coach had stopped to discharge its passengers. Then finally someone was able to tell Verity that hackney drivers usually knew every street in London. And so it proved when they hailed one.

"Leaden'all Street, 'ave you there quick as that," said the accommodating driver.

She could not see Mr. Newman immediately. He had been in conference with another author when she arrived, and it was some forty-five minutes later when the clerk announced her.

The publisher greeted Verity smilingly, but when she explained her errand, his good humor deserted him. Though he decried Derek's action, it was with something less than his habitual politeness that he said, "I'd have thought that you'd have come here earlier, Mrs. Farwell. You must know that we operate on tight schedules, and your book is already intended for a January release, which means we must have the manuscript by the first of October at the latest. I hope you'll be able to recreate those chapters and finish the work on time. If it is impossible, I would appreciate hearing from you at the earliest opportunity."

He had never spoken to her like that. She could not help wondering if her change in status had lowered her in his regard, and she was immediately annoyed at herself for this base suspicion. Those authors whose manuscripts furnished them with a livelihood would never have let their private woes interfere with their work as she had been doing for two weeks. And as for Mr. Newman, his attitude was based upon the exigencies of his profession. Striving for a calm and businesslike tone of voice, she said, "I am am sure that I will be able to complete the novel in the time allotted. I need only to have my outline."

"Very well." Some of the tension left his manner. "Fortunately, I have an extra copy. I always have my clerk make one in the event of an emergency."

"Have other authors lost their outlines?"

"Oh, my dear Mrs. Farwell, yes, indeed, they have, though not usually in such unhappy circumstances. I am truly shocked and sorry that you should be forced to do so much work over again."

"It is of little matter, sir." She managed a smile. "I will not fail to met my deadline, you may be sure of that."

"I am not at all worried on that count," he replied.

She would begin work that night, she vowed, as she and Kitty came out into the street.

Once more it was a matter of hiring a hackney to convey them to the Swan with Two Necks, where they would need to wait until midafternoon when another stagecoach would be taking them back to Hampstead. The common room at the inn was large, and fortunately Verity was able to bespeak a table for herself and Kitty. A repast of cold chicken, bread, and tea whiled away some of the time, but after lingering over it as long as they could they finally had to return to the innyard.

Now that she was free from worry over the pending meeting with the publisher, Verity, standing far away from the masses of people walking back and forth, impatiently waiting for the various coaches that rumbled inside to disgorge or to take on passengers, was more alive to the sights and sounds about her. She was glad she had purchased a round-trip

fare. There seemed to be hundreds of disgruntled individuals
near the ticket offices all talking or, probably, cursing at
once, as a plump officious man in a livery she did not
recognize yelled back at them in a cross discouraging manner.
She was also pleased she was not going far, and she hoped
devoutly that such a necessity would never arise. Wistfully,
she recalled her recent journey from the North in her husband's
well-sprung coach. Its cushions had been covered with velvet.
There had been a strap to hold . . . it had not been a matter of
being squeezed and jounced in a huge lumbering contraption
that, from its appearance, might have been built somewhere
in the middle of the last century.

"Old clothes . . . old clothes . . ." someone bawled uncomfortably close to her ears. Verity turned to see a thin
elderly man carrying a pole on which hung bulging sacks of
what she deduced to be his wares, and, indeed, through a
hole in one of them she saw a tangle of materials, a sleazy
pink satin, a yellow muslin, and a bit of paisley shawl, all
extremely grimy. There were several coats over his back, a
selection of waistcoats over his arm, and a few pairs of shoes
tied together by their laces and hanging from his other arm.
She held her breath as he passed but still was repelled by the
smell that assaulted her nostrils, as well as by his thin lined
face, shaggy white hair, and wiry bristles that sprouted
from his ears. She remembered Miss Marshall's telling her
that in the noisome purlieus of Covent Garden there were
places where garments could be pawned and bought back
again when their owners were in funds. She had a moment of
missing the governess. How was she faring, she wondered.

" 'Ere, where are you puttin' yer 'ands?" Kitty suddenly
shrilled.

Verity started, feeling a yank at the handle of the reticule
hanging from her arm; she clutched it and, at the same time,
saw a small, ragged urchin darting through the crowds.

"You gotta keep your eyes open, milady," Kitty chided.
" 'E'd 'ave 'ad your reticule if I 'adn't caught 'im."

"He was such a little boy!" Verity exclaimed.

"They're the kind you gotta watch." Kitty rolled her eyes.

A shrill burst of laughter startled Verity, and she turned to
see a blond girl sidle up to a soldier. She was clad in cheap
dirty finery, and the neck of her thin gown was cut so low

Verity blushed to see it. She walked unsteadily, as if she had imbibed deeply of gin. Verity recoiled as she noticed the expression on the soldier's face. It was similar to that of the man who had accosted her as she slept in her box at Vauxhall Gardens.

She quickly looked away from the amorous pair, wishing that the coach would arrive, and then, as a sudden realization struck her, she grimaced. If it had not been for the unwelcome attentions of that rogue at Vauxhall, she would not be standing here in this crowded, noisy innyard, surrounded by individuals whom, until very recently, she had viewed only from a coach window.

Of course, she, too, was to blame. Yet, she thought, as she exhaled a long breath, she was free of Derek's endless questions, recriminations, and terrifying outbursts of anger. She could smile at Alan and not be taken to task. She could stroll with him over the hills and down fascinating little cul-de-sacs and still count on returning to a peaceful chamber. The crowds, the noise, the thieves, the prospect of a hot uncomfortable journey, any and all of these were preferable to that which she had left behind in her storied castles and marble mansions. And, above all, she could write when she chose without fear of discovery. This, she knew, was real happiness!

Several times during the next few weeks, Verity remembered that transcendent moment in the courtyard of the Swan with Two Necks. and wished she might recapture the feeling—or, more specifically, wished she had a reason to emulate it. Unfortunately, she could not, and to look back was a sad waste of time, particularly when looming in the nearing future was her deadline for the novel. The date was October 1, and it rang like a funeral knell in the back of her mind. It had started tolling shortly after her return from London. More specifically, it had begun on that very day when, on settling down with her outline, she found that a rereading did not bring back any of the lines she had inscribed on her lost pages.

The "Dear and Beloved Friend" to whom she addressed her missives went unenlightened while at her small writing desk she sat, sometimes for hours, the ink drying on her quill, plagued by fugitive images which had very little to do with the problems of the girl she had called *The Canadian Cousin* flitted through her head. Practically anything could distract her—a walk with Alan, a romance borrowed from the local circulating library, which did not inspire her, but kept her reading (critically) on into the night. Then there was a change in the weather and the realization that none of the clothes Kitty had packed were suitable for the coming fall and winter. Rueful memories of the garments she had left behind helped her not at all. She would have to see Miss Catley and order some warmer and more serviceable gowns and a cloak or coat.

She visited Miss Catley, a soft-spoken little woman, greatly different in manner and appearance from Miss Micklestane. Where her former dressmaker had been shriveled of countenance and tart of tongue, Miss Catley was round and rosy and had a gentle, ingratiating manner. In fact, she was so very pleasant that almost without knowing it, Verity had agreed to have both a blue and a lavender merino dress made. She had also commissioned a dark blue wool cloak lined with beaver. These three costumes were, to her mind, amazingly inexpensive. Their total cost was only nineteen guineas! She had, she remembered, paid as much for a single cashmere shawl.

Naturally, she had to have several fittings on each garment, and that, too, cut into her writing time, and meanwhile the days slid by, and on a morning in late August, Verity, frowning at a paragraph that had pleased her the previous afternoon, realized that there were only nine days left to the month. Equally startling was the fact that she had already been living in the village for seven weeks. A further calculation was more terrifying than startling. In five weeks it would be the first of October! There was a pounding at the base of her throat. She had never dreamed that working to meet a deadline could be so intimidating or so stultifying to the creative spirit. Her resentment at what she was beginning to term "slavery" was close to boiling over into complaints that could be directed only at Kitty. Pride kept her from sharing her woes with Alan, and besides, he, too, was in the throes of composition. At least that was the reason he had given her for curtailing his visits.

Until her own deadline began to loom so large on her

horizon, she had half suspected that having seen her settled and, supposedly, hard at work, he was spending his leisure hours with others of his acquaintance. She did not doubt that he must have a large circle of friends in the village. He had lived here several years, and with his undeniable personal attractions, it would be surprising if he did not grace many a banquet table and ballroom. There were a number of fine houses in the district, and from the way he had described some of them on their walks, she guessed that their interiors were as familiar to him as their facades. Inadvertently, she had learned that he was lodged on Windmill Hill. During one of their early rambles, he had brought her up to its summit to show her some of the charming cottages that had been built there during the last century. Near a pleasant villa, with a large garden in front, she had seen a little boy rolling a hoop, and he, catching sight of them, ran up to Alan, excitedly thanking him for that same hoop.

Rather diffidently and, she thought, a shade reluctantly, Alan had introduced the youngster as Master Ridley, identifying him as the son of his landlady. Had he really been reluctant to impart that information to her, she had wondered at the time, or was she becoming oversuspicious because he had told her so very little about himself? She was turning that matter over in her mind on an afternoon when she was supposed to be working on her book. However, she had a particular reason not to concentrate—tonight she was finally going to a poetry reading at the home of Mr. and Mrs. Charles Dilke, the couple Alan had often mentioned but whom she had yet to meet. She had not met any of his friends—but of course they had both been busy. Her eyes gleamed—tonight she would meet John Keats!

She *had* seen him three nights ago when he returned from his travels. She would not soon forget that moment, and, not for the first time, she was glad that having grown weary of her rooms and her inability to work, she had come outside for a breath of fresh air. She had reached the garden just in time to see a small young man, not more than her height or maybe less, come trudging up the road. Much to her subsequent dismay, she had mistaken him for a vagrant. He had been most peculiarly dressed, she thought defensively. His shoes were broken, his jacket torn, and hanging over it had been a dusty, dingy plaid obviously made for a man twice his size. Though it was a very warm evening, he had also been wearing a battered fur hat! Yet his strange attire had been forogtten once she looked into his eyes and met a gaze so bright and compelling that it seemed to streak through her like a bolt of lightning. It was at that moment a woman called, "John, dear. Ah, at last you are back from Scotland! Oh, thank God. Your brother . . ."

She had heard him interrupt wearily, sadly, and hoarsely, "Yes, I know about Tom. I've come to care for him."

That had been when Verity identified him and, at the same time, wished she might give him a word of comfort concerning his poor brother. Even if she had had the courage to approach a stranger, who was also a poet of growing renown, there would have been very little in the way of comfort to offer. Mrs. Staples had told her that the lad was so weak he could scarcely leave his bed. "An' Mrs. Bently, she says it's a caution to hear him cough. She tries to keep her boys as quiet as possible, but 'tisn't easy with them so full of life and him . . . poor, poor lad . . . no more'n twenty-one." She had turned away, shaking her head and wiping her eyes.

Verity felt a constriction in her own throat as she thought of John Keats, whose mother had died from consumption. There seemed to be no question but that his brother would soon follow her.

Poor John Keats, whose sensitivity and vulnerability were there on his face, even though there was strength as well— and firmness in the set of his mouth. It was a pity for him to come home to such misery, and truthfully, he did not look or sound very well himself. She stiffened, remembering that Alan had told her John Keats had had a sore throat when he left for Scotland. Judging from the roughness of his tone, he still had it. Was it possible . . . ? She did not want to dwell on the fear that was winging through her mind lest she retain some vestige of it when they were introduced tonight.

She cast a look at the clock and winced. It was time and past time to dismiss the unhappy brothers Keats from her mind. The hands indicated that it was ten past the hour of two, and she had not put down a single sentence. With a sigh, she settled down to the tedious task of trying to recreate lines that were seeming more and more elusive as well as a plot which, given the changes in her own life, seemed patently false. That was the crux of the problem, she realized with a thrill of fear. She could no longer believe in the plot twists she had invented for her heroine. They were only the reworking of old themes she had heard before, recast in prose that had been sprightly—that she remembered. In her present mood, sprightliness was proving very difficult to achieve. She must make the effort—must, must. In addition to the necessity that ought to be the mother of invention—since there would come a day when she would earn her livelihood by her writing—she had to justify Alan Parry's faith in her ability. It was with something of a shock that she realized his good opinion meant even more to her than that of Mr. Newman.

Because she remembered that he had said he liked her in blue, Verity donned her turquoise silk and a matching turban, stitched with the same gold pattern that edged her hem. She had not expected that Kitty would burst into tears immediately after slipping the last hook into its embroidered eye.

"My dear!" Verity turned toward her. "What's amiss?"

"I . . . I remember when you first wore that, milady. 'Twas at the . . .''

Verity held up a warning hand. "No memories tonight, my dear Kitty. And what have I told you about calling me 'milady'?"

"It shouldn't ought to be," Kitty muttered under her breath but quite audibly enough to be heard.

"I beg you'll not repine," Verity said. "We might not be as comfortable as we were before—but there are compensations."

Meeting the abigail's tearful gaze in the mirror, Verity wondered if she missed more than the act of dressing her for the balls and routs she had just begun to attend in London. The girl did look singularly downcast, and, indeed, it must have been hard for her to be so summarily uprooted. No one of her class ever thought of her servants' needs or desires, she mused regretfully. In most establishments, "followers" were discouraged, quite as if these young women had no right to the love and affection their so-called "betters" craved.

She would sound Kitty out on her situation when she had more time. It was a pity the subject could not be approached at his very moment, but Betty was tapping on the door and it was time to join Alan. With a parting injunction not to wait up for her, which she feared Kitty would ignore, Verity hurried out.

Rather than being in the parlor, Alan stood in the hall at the bottom of the stairs, his eyes bright with the admiration that coated his tone as he said, "My dear Cousin Verity, you are a poem in yourself. If I were a poet, I would need to look no further for inspiration!"

She flushed with pleasure, and not knowing quite how to answer, she took refuge in teasing, "I fear you are waxing rather fulsome, Cousin Alan."

"Not at all," he insisted as she joined him. Bringing her hand to his lips, he said, as he released it, "May I be struck by lightning if I am not telling the truth!"

Glancing past him through the open door at a sky only faintly marked with wispy clouds, she said, "A safe wish, but I thank you anyway." She could return his compliments, she thought. Tonight, clad in a plum-colored coat she had never seen, his cravat elaborately tied and in gray Wellington trousers that outlined his shapely legs, he looked particularly attractive, and she guessed from the cut of the garments that he had recently patronized a London tailor. That, she thought with some satisfaction, was as it should be, given his burgeoning success. "You are quite the man of fashion, yourself, sir," she said appreciatively.

To her surprise, a strange moody look passed over his face and a frown flickered in his eyes. "I pray you'll not tell me that. I have the utmost loathing for the breed."

Lightly but conciliatingly, she replied, "I did not suggest that you were a dandy, sir."

"I know you did not." He was smiling again. "I should have accepted your remark as 'twas meant and will do so immediately. Thank you, Cousin Verity."

As she took his proffered arm, she wondered at the effect of her compliment. What had occasioned his dislike for the so-called "man of fashion"? She longed to probe more deeply into this mystery, but that, of course, was impossible. She did not know him well enough. Surprise shot through her. There were, she realized, times when she felt she had never known anyone half so well. Or was she confusing knowing with liking? It was a conundrum she preferred not to consider. Consequently, she dismissed it, saying as they strolled down the street, "I am so looking forward to this evening."

"And the Dilkes are looking forward to meeting you," he assured her.

She was conscious of a tiny flicker of fear. It was the first time she had been in a large gathering since leaving London, and she could not help feeling that she was there under false pretenses. How would they have received her had they known that she had been divorced?

The divorce must have been granted by now—but on second thought, why need she be concerned about that? Only Alan knew her true identity, and it was highly unlikely that any of those present would be acquainted with members of the so-called "exalted circle" of the Marquess of Unger. Men of Derek's estate might patronize poets, but they seldom fraternized with them, and certainly not with a Hunt or a Keats, whom they would not hesitate to describe as lowly "cits." Even Lord Byron and Percy Shelley, both of gentle birth, were not welcome in the drawing rooms of the old nobility, and that, she thought angrily, was its loss.

Was not the elevated mind preferable to the crested escutcheon? Nobility, after all, was only an accident of birth—better far the aristocracy of achievement! She stifled a giggle. If Derek had been party to her thoughts, he would have been appalled at opinions he must have categorized as dangerously liberal. But he was not present, and she was able to entertain ideas which might not even have occurred to her had nothing happened to separate them. When she was with him, she had been too confused and unhappy to engage in the luxury of abstract thought. Amazingly enough, her disgrace had brought her a freedom that, under ordinary circumstances, she might never have known. She chuckled at that particular irony—in falling, she had risen.

Stopping in midstride, Alan looked down at her. "What has amused you?" he asked curiously.

"The . . . specifics of freedom," she said slowly.

"That's a rather enigmatic answer."

"Do you think so?" She produced a provocative smile.

"No," he said slowly. "Actually I think I do know what

you mean, and I hope I am correct in assuming you've begun to appreciate that freedom."

"I have," she said fervently. "It is such a luxurious state of mind."

"Luxurious . . . yes, you're right. Freedom is a luxury, especially for those . . . who are not born to it."

She had the feeling he had intended to say something else but had decided against it. Why? Best not concentrate on any of her unanswered questions concerning her companion. It was far better to anticipate the delights awaiting her upon Olympus, or, rather, Parnassus.

"It's a pity," Alan said, breaking a small silence that had fallen between them as they turned a corner, "that I cannot take you to Hunt's place. I cannot count the number of times he's moved since I have become acquainted with him. Still, he will be present tonight, and Charles Dilke is a very good sort of fellow, as is Brown."

"I know I shall like them," she said shyly. "But I hope they will not think I am out of place, since I cannot qualify as a poet and I would just as soon not mention my romances."

"Keats will not think the less of you for that. He has no love for bluestockings."

"Then I'd best sit with my skirts over my shoes." She shot him a mischievous look. "Though I must say that his prejudice does not elevate him in my eyes."

"I'll warrant he's never met a bluestocking such as yourself. His prejudice was formed, I believe, by a meeting with our esteemed playwright and poetess Miss Joanna Baillie, who, though she has a reputation for sweetness of character, was a mite condescending to him."

"Miss Baillie . . . oh, yes, Mrs. Staples told me she lives here. There was a copy of her play *De Montfort* in my papa's library. I didn't like it; it was far too verbose. I trust she's not been invited tonight?"

"I think not. Nor would she come if she had been. She is very grand."

"Oh, dear, how tedious."

"Quite. . . . Ah, here we are at Wentworth Place."

Wentworth Place had, Verity learned, been built by two of the people who would be present that night, Charles Armitage Brown and Charles Wentworth Dilke. It was a pair of semide-

tached houses with a common garden. The houses, each with
its own entrance and tall casement window, were, she
discovered, not very large. They would have fitted easily
enough into any of the homes she had occupied during her
lifetime, but the sort of laughter that reached her from the
open door of the house on her left had never been heard in
any of those monumental piles. As they started up the path
leading to the front door, she glimpsed several gentlemen
inside talking to the tall, pleasant-faced young woman whom
she had seen with Keats two nights earlier.

Coming inside, she learned that the lady was Mrs. Dilke.
She had a charming manner, Verity thought, as Alan introduced them.

"Oh, yes." Mrs. Dilke surveyed Verity with frank interest.
"Alan's mentioned you to me quite often. I am so sorry
about your husband, my dear."

For a split second, Verity was both shocked and frightened,
then memory rescued her. "Thank you," she said feelingly.
" 'Twas a sad loss."

"And you so young," Mrs. Dilke said commiseratingly.

"Yes." Verity allowed a sigh to escape and prayed that
she looked suitably downcast. She was, however, considerably relieved when Alan saved her from dwelling any further
on her late "husband" by propelling her forward to meet her
host, a youngish man with a high intellectual forehead and
bright intelligent eyes.

She regarded Mr. Dilke with considerable respect, having
learned that he had edited no less than six volumes of old
English plays, which monumental undertaking he had finished in a matter of only two years. However, what really
endeared him to her and to Alan as well was his respect and
support for young Keats. She liked him on sight and listened
interestedly as both gentlemen spoke about Shelley, who,
somewhat to Mr. Dilke's disappointment, had moved his
rackety household to Italy. Keats had not yet arrived, and she
learned that another latecomer was expected, a patron of the
arts, she heard Dilke say, one Lord Glendacre, who had been
introduced to the circle by his good friend Bysshe Shelley.

Verity wished it were Shelley who was coming and smiled
to think how disapproving her grandmother had been at his
fall from grace. Lady Harcliffe had been acquainted with his

parents, and they had filled her ears with lamentations over
Bysshe's wild ways. Though he had been writing peotry since
a mere child, they had regarded it as a youthful fancy which
he would outgrow. That he had failed to do so surprised and
alarmed them. Still, if she admired Shelley's poetry—and
who could not—she had not admired the way he had deserted
his poor little wife, Harriet, who had drowned herself in the
Serpentine two years ago.

"And this, Verity, is Mr. Hunt," Alan said, rousing her
out of her thoughts. "Leigh, my cousin, Mrs. Farwell."

She blinked up at a man some thirty-nine or forty years of
age, with compelling dark eyes set in a handsome face. If she
had know nothing about him, still she would have been
impressed by that almost mesmerizing gaze. His smile was
charming, his look admiring. "I am delighted to make your
acquaintance, Mrs. Farwell."

"And I yours, sir," she replied. "My cousin has told . . ."

Whatever else she would have said was interrupted by Mrs.
Dilke's pleased cry of "John, my dear, at last!"

"I pray you'll excuse me, Mrs. Farwell." Hunt sketched a
quick bow and moved swiftly forward as the youthful poet
entered.

He looked considerably better rested than when Verity had
first glimpsed him. His face, however, was drawn and his
large brown eyes melancholy, becoming more so when Mrs.
Dilke mentioned his brother's illness. The hoarseness which
had been evident in his speech that first night remained.
However, Verity could see that once he was among his
friends, he looked much happier and considerably more at
ease. He seemed pleased to see Alan, who, with Hunt, had
hurried to greet him. She saw Keats glance in her direction
and smile, and a moment later, accompanied by Alan, he was
at her side. Subsequent to their introduction, he said cordially,
"I am told we're neighbors."

"Yes," she answered breathlessly, wondering if he would
think her dreadfully gauche were she to praise his poetry. She
could mention that she had met his brother, but she had seen
the adverse effect Mrs. Dilke's comments had had on his
spirits. Summoning up her courage, she said softly, "I have
read and reread your book, sir. I cannot tell you how your
verses have moved me."

"You have read . . . and reread my book?" he repeated in some surprise.

"And she's learned many of your lines by heart. I can vouch for that," Alan said.

The poet's glowing eyes were on her face. "I am quite amazed."

"I cannot imagine why you should be, sir," Verity said.

"I can tell you quite truthfully, Mrs. Farwell, that if it were not for you and a few others, mostly friends, I would think that my book would have been devoured mainly by rats reveling in its paste content."

"Oh!" Verity cried indignantly. "I cannot bear false modesty! I . . . oh, gracious." Her hand flew to her mouth, and not daring to look either at Alan or the slandered poet, she kept her eyes on the floor. "I am sorry," she muttered, and was surprised to hear Keats laugh.

" 'Tis not false modesty, I assure you, ma'am. I am fully cognizant of my worth . . . too much so, some say. My observation was based on sales figures alone."

"Oh." Well aware that she was blushing, she dared to look at him again and read a frank appreciation in his gaze that startled her. "You . . . have my apologies, sir."

"They are not needful, ma'am. I admire honesty above all things."

"John, dear." Mrs. Dilke joined them. "Lord Glendacre's come at last."

"And is being momentarily monopolized by Leigh, I see," Keats said, glancing toward the door and turning back to Verity. "Might I ask which of my poems you preferred, Mrs. Farwell?"

"How might one make a choice?" she demanded.

"Most of my friends have."

His eyes were mesmerizing, she thought, realizing at the same time that, as she had suspected, she and Keats were very much of a height. That must please him, she thought, for he, in common with herself, must be constantly needing to look up. And was he including her in his circle of friends? she wondered.

"My dear John." Hunt joined them again. "Here is Lord Glendacre come to welcome you back from the Highlands."

"And to hope that you've returned to us with a sheaf of verses, John, my friend."

Verity, looking at the new arrival, turned cold. The room seemed to whirl around her, but a voice in the back of her head was warning her not to betray by look or tone, by movement or gesture, that she had seen him before. It was possible though hardly probable that he would not recogize her as the frightened and disheveled young woman to whom he had given "assistance" that night in Vauxhall Gardens.

As if from a great distance, she heard Keats acknowledging Lord Glendacre's greeting, heard his lordship speaking to Alan, who, in turn, was introducing him to his "cousin."

He turned a face empty of recognition to her. "Mrs. Farwell," he said punctiliously, as he bowed over her hand. "I am delighted to meet you."

"And I, you, my lord," she murmured through stiff lips, recalling for some odd reason the name of Samuel Taylor Coleridge—no, she knew why she remembered it. *He* had mentioned it and had told her he often attended poetry readings. She felt a pressing need to be out of a room grown suddenly suffocating, but unless she fainted or pleaded sickness, she could not leave, and if he had not recognized her, such a move might jog his memory. She would have to remain. There was no help for it, none at all.

The evening passed. She did not know how. Keats was prevailed upon to read his poetry. She scarcely heard it as, surreptitiously, beneath the curtain of her long lashes, she surveyed the face of Lord Glendacre. He, in turn, seemed totally concentrated on Keats's reading of a poem called "Meg Merrilles" after a character in Scott's novel *Guy Mannering*. Occasionally a word would reach her and become lost amid her churning thoughts. Pain and regret chased themselves through her brain. Her disappearance must have been a topic of conversation and conjecture in many circles. It had not been mentioned in the *Morning Post*, Alan had told her. He had volunteered the opinion that her husband must have paid to keep it out. Consequently, Lord Glendacre might not know that she had disappeared. Furthermore, on the night they met, she had been so frightened, and her hair had been hanging in elf locks about her face. She remembered regretfully that she had tried to comb it and had not succeeded very

well. She also recalled bitterly that she had left her reticule in
his chamber and he had given it back to Derek—but all that
had taken place close on two months ago. Tonight, most of
her hair was bundled inside her turban. She had been introduced to him as Mrs. Farwell. He had glanced at her only
once or twice after the reading started. He had also looked at
Mrs. Dilke, had smiled at Hunt and Alan—but for the most
part, young Mr. Keats had his attention.

Finally, the reading was at an end. Lord Glendacre did not
linger. There would be no whispered confidences for her host
and hostess, for Leigh Hunt or Mr. Keats. Instead, the poet
accompanied herself and her "cousin" back to Well Walk,
receiving their congratulations, their sympathies, and their
best wishes for Tom and disappearing into the gray house
next door.

Alan did not show any disposition to remain, either, which
surprised Verity. She had been anticipating that he would
want to talk about Keats's verse, and to her all-abiding regret,
she could remember only the first line, which went "Old
Meg she was a gypsy . . ."

All through the walk, she had been trying to decide whether
she should or should not reveal the identity of Lord Glendacre.
However, she remembered Alan's fury at the man who had
played her such a dastardly trick. There was more than a
chance that he would call him out, and the idea of exposing
Alan to needless danger horrified her.

Yet, what was she going to do? If Glendacre had recognized
her, would she need to go away? Unfortunately, there was
but one answer to that question—and where would she go?

The thought of leaving Hampstead Village filled her with
regret. Before Glendacre had arrived, she had really been
enjoying herself. It had been exhilarating to be among young
and youngish people who were not concerned with the next
rout or what was the latest *on dit* around town or whose
reputation they could wreck or the disgraceful actions of the
Regent's fat unhappy wife. Scandals and personalities did not
interest the Dilkes and their friends. Poetry, art, and the
theater did. Their conversation was stimulating to the spirit.
Tears stung her eyes. She did not want to leave, but if she
stayed and he saw her again, he would surely recognize her,
and he would not scruple to make trouble. Then there was

every chance that Alan would call him out, and even if he did not, her own secrets would be revealed. Perhaps Glendacre did not know she was Derek's *wife*—so he would not be aware that she had disappeared. That hardly mattered. Derek *had* acknowledged that she was his mistress, a stigma even more damning than divorce. In any case, by now Glendacre would almost certainly have heard enough gossip to know she was indeed the former Lady Unger.

She went slowly up the stairs, and as she entered her chamber, Kitty rose from the sofa and followed her into the bedroom to help her undress.

"Kitty, dear," Verity protested. "You should have gone to bed!"

Kitty said stubbornly and with a toss of her brown locks, "I 'aven't never left you to do for youself, an' I'm not startin' now."

As Kitty unhooked her gown, Verity toyed with the notion of telling her what had happened, but meeting her eyes in the glass, she thought the girl looked very weary. It would be wrong to burden her with the news that they might soon have to leave. Yet, as she lay in bed, she wished she might have confided in someone. Unfortunately, she had not made any friends here. Alan had been too involved with his writing to introduce her to some of the people she might find compatible, he had explained, and she had told him that she was equally involved. Actually, used as she was to spending most of her days alone with Derek, she had not even noticed the lack. She had been completely happy just seeing Alan, and it was to him she longed to turn for advice—but she was glad she had not sought it. Sleep was long in coming and upon arriving brought with it uneasy dreams of Vauxhall Gardens. Interspersed with these were visions of Derek's angry face, and, for some reason, Alan, too, frowned at her from behind a hedge.

She awakened with his name on her lips, thinking that he had been strangely aloof and moody the previous evening. However, it was not of Alan she must think, but of Lord Glendacre of Cheyne Walk, Chelsea, who had done her so terrible a disservice and who stood ready to repeat his offense. She was gloomily positive of that!

Kitty, coming in with a cup of steaming hot chocolate for

her, regarded her out of heavy eyes as if she, too, had been bothered by nightmares. Verity regarded her concernedly.

"You are looking very tired, Kitty."

"Oh, milady," Kitty sighed. "I couldn't sleep for thinkin' about that poor young gentleman who lies so sick next door."

"Tom Keats?" Verity questioned in surprise.

"Yes, milady, I 'ope you don't mind. 'Tisn't much for me to do 'ere, an' 'e's so unhappy . . . so I've been stoppin' by to sit wi' 'im a bit."

"Of course I don't mind, Kitty. I'm sure he must be very glad of your company!"

" 'E did perk up a bit last night," she admitted. "Told me 'ow 'is brother George 'n' his wife is way off in America 'n' 'ow 'e 'oped 'e'd see 'em again." Kitty sobbed. "Only 'e won't. 'E do remind me o' my brother Charles wot went the same way. 'Twasn't more'n a matter o' a month or two 'n' we laid 'im in the churchyard."

"Oh, Kitty." Verity regarded her with dismay. "When did that happen?"

" 'Twas just afore we left the country, milady."

"And you never told me anything."

"Shouldn't've told you now, only 'twas that poor boy made me think o' Charlie."

Verity put a hand on the girl's arm. "Oh, Kitty, I am sorry. I hope you have other brothers and sisters."

"There was eleven o' us, milady, but Charlie, 'e were next besides me. We was real close-like."

"You're the eldest of eleven children!"

Kitty nodded. " 'Twere thirteen, only two died when they was no more'n a day old. They was the last."

"And the others?"

"They be all right, milady. Rosie, she's in service, and so's Jane. An' it looks like Jamie'll be a sojer like Dad. Dad was in the Tenth Foot, been all over, fightin' them Frenchies, 'n' never scratch on 'im until 'e lost 'is leg at Waterloo." Kitty suddenly looked very self-conscious. "Listen to me goin' on like this . . . I'd better fetch the water cans for you, milady." She whisked herself out of the room.

Verity ran her hands through her hair. She and Kitty were very much of an age, and thinking of all the abigail had told her, her own troubles seemed vastly diminished. She wished she might do something for that beleaguered family, but it was too late. If only Kitty had said something before, but probably the housekeeper and her parents, as well, had cautioned her against confiding anything to her so-called betters. She wished she had spoken to the girl about her family, but it had never occurred to her to do so. She was just as much at fault as everyone in her situation—or what had been her situation. Just for the moment, she wished she were back in it. She could have helped Kitty, but . . . she smiled sadly. She still would have known nothing.

She was thinking about Kitty when bathed and dressed she started up Well Walk, bound for the Heath. She had found her room too stuffy and the table with her papers strewn on it an unwelcome reminder of how much she had not written. Certainly she was in no mood to write this morning! As she reached the summit, she heard hurried footsteps behind her and frowned. In her present unhappy frame of mind she craved solitude. She cast a glance over her shoulder and froze as she saw Lord Glendacre approaching her. Amazingly, she had forgotten him in her concern over Kitty, but now all of her fears came tumbling back into her brain, and uppermost among them was the sure knowledge that he had recognized her.

"I have been waiting for you," he said as he joined her. "I would have sent a message, but I feared you'd not answer it. And so I have been in the Green Man at the window on the chance I would see you."

"And why would you want to see me?" she asked coldly. "To assure yourself that you were not wrong in your assumptions concerning my identity?"

"I knew you once," he said in a low voice. "I wanted to speak to you last night—but there was no opportunity."

There was a somber air about him and a grim twist to his mouth. Was she mistaken in imagining that there was also a shamed look in his eyes? It hardly mattered. "I cannot think that we have much to say to each other, my lord," she commented, and was glad there was no tremor in her speech.

"But we have!" he burst out. "I pray you'll listen to me. 'Twas out of spleen I spoke to Unger—but as God is my witness, I believed that you were his mistress. One does not expect to find a gently bred young matron alone . . ." He paused, and then with a mixture of anger and pain, he continued. " 'Twas madness for you to be in Vauxhall Gardens, unaccompanied. Whatever possessed you . . ."

"I was *not* unaccompanied!" she responded hotly. "My friend—rather, the woman who begged me to . . . to chaperon her so that she could see for the last time a man she loved—she, they promised to return quickly, and . . . oh, what can it matter now?"

"It matters to me," he said roughly. "And I expect that your . . . friend was craven and would not admit . . ."

"She admitted nothing," Verity acknowledged bitterly. "I expect she was frightened."

"And together, we have made a shambles of your life." He sighed deeply. "I was furious at being played such a trick by one whom I thought . . . as I told you, I did believe nearly everything I told your husband, and then I heard the gossip concerning his divorce—the gossip, the lampoons and the cartoons. I saw one of those scurrilous cartoons in a window, and it was like enough to you to set me wondering. I spoke with a friend who had seen you presented at court, and he gave me a description, too. I have wanted to seek you out and beg your pardon. I tried to reach Unger. I sent him a letter asking him to meet me, but following his action, he went up North. His mother, it seems, is very ill. Oh, my poor girl, I am so sorry. . . ."

Looking into his anguished face, she could not doubt that he was telling the truth, but she felt curiously detached, as if he were speaking about something that had happened to someone else, whom she barely knew. She said slowly, "I thank you for your efforts and for your apology, my lord, but it has ceased to matter to me whether or not my husband believes me."

"But 'tis all my fault," he cried. "I cannot bear to know that you are living in obscurity, cut off from all you knew, and I to blame for it. It has weighed heavily, heavily upon my conscience. I have prayed I might find you. I am glad that it has happened so soon. Lady Unger . . ."

She drew herself up. "My lord, I pray you not address me by a name I can no longer claim."

He bowed his head. "As you choose. But you must let me help you!"

"I do not need . . ." she began.

"Please, listen to me. I am not known to be overscrupulous in my dealings with women. But those with whom I have dallied are not respectable young matrons, either. And of late, I have grown weary of the chase. I have wanted to settle down. Lady Unger, please let me care for you—and give you my name in the place of the one you lost because of me. I beg you'll not refuse me."

She regarded him in utter amazement. It was a moment before she could say, "I . . . do thank you for your offer, my lord. 'Tis quite overwhelming, but I could never accept such a sacrifice."

" 'Tis no sacrifice," he said emphatically. "Watching you last night, I knew what you were thinking. I knew you were fearful I might betray you to your friends. You were in torment, and so was I, knowing that I and I alone am responsible for your so-called disgrace. And you are vulnerable. Someday, someone will recognize you and speak. I want to save you from that misery. It's not only out of chivalry that I make this offer. I would feel honored to claim you as my bride."

" 'Tis kind of you to tell me so, my lord, but . . ."

"It is not kindness," he protested. "It's the truth."

"I do not doubt you, my lord, but I cannot accept your offer. You must not imagine that I am unhappy."

"You are singularly courageous, but do you not realize that your life is ruined, and through no fault of your own? I am to blame."

"You are not entirely to blame, my lord. You only fanned a flame that was already kindled. You have been uncommonly generous, and I thank you." She stretched out her hand.

He took it, kissing it, and still grasping it, said unhappily, "I know you cannot love me, and nor do I love you, but I do admire you. You are not only beautiful, you have a generous nature. And while most women put in your position would have collapsed completely, it appears to me that adversity has only strengthened you. I am sure we would be compatible. Our backgrounds are similar, we have a mutual love of poetry, and were we together, I know we would achieve felicity. I want to make you happy . . . Lady Verity."

"Oddly enough, my lord, I am happier now than I have ever been," she said gently.

"I cannot believe that!"

"I assure you that I am," she insisted.

He regarded her in silence for a moment. "There is," he said slowly, "a serenity about you. One would not think that in your position . . ." He frowned and sighed. "After all, I find that I can believe you." He paused and then added, "Is there no way I can make amends?"

"You have made them already, my lord."

"I am not satisfied that that is true."

"You have my word on it."

Another sigh escaped him. "It seems I must bid you farewell, then."

"Farewell, my lord, and thank you."

"I pray you'll not thank me," he said gratingly. "May God be with you, my dear." He kissed her hand a second time, and turning on his heel, he went swiftly down the hill.

Watching him, Verity felt very near to tears. His offer had amazed and touched her. She could not doubt his sincerity. Yet if she had been Derek's mistress, would he have given a second thought to an incident that must surely have robbed her of her protector? She was being most ungenerous, she decided. He had honestly tried to atone for his betrayal. More than that, he had even been willing to brave society with a wife dishonored in its eyes—and that did take considerable courage!

"Verity!"

Turning, she saw Alan striding toward her across the Heath. She smiled and waved. She was delighted to see him. Now she need not be concerned over any friction between himself and Lord Glendacre. She could tell Alan about his offer, and no doubt he would be as surprised as she herself at so unexpected a turn of events. She could also confide her earlier fears concerning the possible betrayal of her true identity, and she was sure that Alan would agree that she had had a most fortunate escape. Happiness flooded through her; she would not need to leave Hampstead now.

As Alan came up to her, she favored him with a warm smile. "Good morning," she said liltingly. "I wonder if I thanked you enough for last night. 'Twas most enjoyable."

He gave her a thoughtful look. "I am glad you found it so. It seemed to me that you were rather abstracted."

"Well, I was a bit," she admitted, realizing that she should have guessed Alan would be attuned to her mood. "But I do feel much better this morning. You see . . ."

"Verity," he interrupted brusquely, "you did not tell me you know Lord Glendacre."

"I do not really know him . . ." she began.

"You were on uncommonly friendly terms with him this morning, especially for two people who professed to be meeting as strangers last night."

"We . . ." she began and paused, struck by his phrasing and by the look of accusation she read in his eyes. "Just what are you suggesting?" she inquired.

"I am not suggesting anything," he retorted. "I want to know why you found it necessary to practice this elaborate deception upon me!"

"My deception, as you are pleased to term it, was not directed at you, but . . ."

"But what?" he rasped.

His tone of voice had an all too familiar ring, and there was a look in his eyes that was equally familiar. Verity lifted her chin. "I am not obliged to explain my conduct to you, Alan," she said tensely.

"On the contrary, I think I do deserve an explanation! I think it high time that I be informed as to the exact nature of your . . . your connection with Lord Glendacre!"

"My connection?" she repeated in ascending accents. "Are you possibly suggesting that . . ."

He caught her arm, holding it in a painful grip. "What is Lord Glendacre to you?"

"Take your hand from my arm, please," she snapped. "You are hurting me."

He did not release her. Instead, his grasp actually tightened, as he repeated, "Why didn't you tell me that you knew him?"

"Because I did not choose to do so!" she said freezingly. "Now will you release me, please?"

He dropped his hand but said sharply, "That's no answer."

If she were to close her eyes, she could imagine it was Derek confronting her rather than Alan. Her bosom heaved.

"It is all the answer such a question requires. You are neither my husband nor my lover, Alan. And as my friend there are boundaries beyond which you have no right to pass."

Fury leaped into his eyes. "I do not want to be your friend. I love you. I have loved you ever since the first day I saw you."

She favored him with a withering stare. "I am very sorry for that, Alan. I do not love you!"

"I disagree. I do not believe you know your own mind. But perhaps I may clarify matters." Catching her in his arms, he pressed a passionate invading kiss upon her mouth.

Raising both her little hands and knotting them into fists, she beat against his chest until he finally released her. "Oh," she cried accusingly, bring her hand to her mouth. "How could you? I t-trusted you, and . . . and you are just like all the others . . . b-biding your time until . . ."

"Verity." He had grown very pale. "You . . . you must understand. I . . ."

"I do understand that you have made a most grievous error. I . . . I labored under the m-misapprehension that you were my friend. I needed a f-friend. I do not want a lover! I thank you for all your h-help, but I . . . I do not want to see you again—not ever!"

He grew even paler. "You cannot mean that," he said huskily.

"I do mean it."

"Verity," he said in a shaken tone, "I am sorry. I did not mean to overpower you. I am by nature . . . hot-blooded." His mouth twisted. "My damnable heritage. I am part Italian, and we . . . no matter. Oh, God, God, God, Verity, you cannot mean that you do not want to see me more!"

"I do mean it, Alan," she said icily. "And if you are telling me that your Italian blood has made you jealous, that is not necessary. I see that it has. As for your question concerning Lord Glendacre . . ."

He took a step toward her and stopped. "It does not matter!" he cried.

"I rather think it matters a great deal to you, Alan. I wish it didn't. However, I will tell you that there is nothing between Lord Glendacre and myself. You may believe me or you may not. It makes no difference now. Jealousy is something I have grown to loathe!'' Turning from him, she walked down the hill. She did not look back, and in her present state of anger, she was only pleased to discover that when she finally reached her door, he had not followed her.

Part Four

One

Verity had trudged up the hill to the Heath to pick blackberries, now ripening on bushes scattered through the autumn-touched shrubbery. She had a pail of them—enough for herself, Kitty, and the Stapleses, man and wife, not that Mr. Staples would appreciate them unless they were fermented and turned into wine. She made a little face, not liking him much, having been told by Kitty that he beat his poor wife. He looked as if he could. He was a dark-browed morose individual who spent most of his time at the Green Man, appearing only when it was time to collect the rents. She glanced at the sky and forgot all about Mr. Staples. The sun was very close to the western horizon. Night would soon be upon them, and in a few hours more, it would be Monday morning, October 8, 1818! And that was the day she and Kitty would take the stagecoach into London as they had the previous Monday— only this time she would not be presenting her completed manuscript, she would be hearing what the publisher had to say about it.

She dreaded the meeting. Though she had completed it, she was sure he would not find the work to his liking. If it had been a cake instead of sheets of foolscap, it would have been heavy, lumpish, and ill-shaped. Anyone eating it would find it indigestible. If Alan were here, he would have advised her not to take it in.

Thinking of him, she had an immediate vision of the last time she had seen him—here on the Heath six weeks earlier. Throughout the first week following their encounter, she had been fearful he would seek her out. She had no desire to see him. He had both infuriated and disappointed her. There had

163

been moments when she had paced up and down her bedchamber alternately reviling him and jeering at herself for having believed him different from the general breed of men.

Eventually she had calmed down. Eventually she began to wonder why, after his passionate declaration of love, he had not even troubled to see her—not that she wanted to see *him*, but she did think he would try to apologize again. However, when Kitty spoke about seeing him walking with Keats, she had begged the girl not to mention him anymore.

Of course, she was still angry at insinuations as ridiculous as any made by her husband. "How could he?" she muttered. "Knowing what he knew, to practically accuse me of . . . of . . . merely because he saw me talking . . ." But, as she had already decided a week or so ago, Alan did have something on his side, not that she would ever excuse his action! However, when they were at the reading she had given absolutely no indication of having ever met Lord Glendacre, and his lordship's attitude had been the same. Consequently, Alan had a right to be surprised when he saw them conversing on the Heath. Still, he did not need to leap to conclusions as if, indeed, all the horrid gossip were true and she were the abandoned creature characterized in the lampoons and the cartoons, which she was heartily glad she had not seen! And why was she wasting her time dwelling on *him*? It was getting darker now. The sun was only half visible over the hills, and there was a cool wind blowing.

She was about to start down the path that would bring her to the top of Well Walk, and as she did, she saw a man coming toward her. Her heart suddenly started pounding in the vicinity of her throat. He was of medium height. She could not distinguish his features, but he was hatless and his hair was dark. Alan? She would not wait to find out. She started down the path, then halted and turned back. He was closer now. She could see his face, and, of course, it was not Alan. How could it be, when he was in Italy and had been since the middle of September, according to Kitty, who had heard it from Tom. He had gone to gather material for another book and also visit with friends, among them the Shelleys, and, perhaps, he had relatives there, too—judging from what he had told her about his hot Italian blood! She also knew the identity of that solitary walker. He was Mr.

Entwistle, the curate from the Church of St. John in the village. They usually exchanged a few words every Sunday after service.

"Mrs. Farwell, good afternoon," he said. Without giving her a chance to reply, he added, "Is it not late for you to be upon the Heath?"

"It is," she agreed, pointing to her pail. "I've been gathering blackberries and am on my way home."

"I will walk with you, if you do not mind," he said punctiliously. "There are vagrants lurking about, you know, especially as the hours lengthen into evening."

"I'd not come here after dark," she assured him. "Not with the ghosts of Dick Turpin and Sixteen-String Jack to gallop over the ground."

"I hope you do not believe in ghosts," he said seriously.

"No, I was only joking." She stifled a sigh. Alan would have fallen in with her fantasy and, very likely, enlarged upon it. He had a wonderfully vivid imagination. She doubted if this nice young man had any imagination at all. It was amazing that she had even thought for an instant that he could be Alan. They were nothing like. Alan's hair was darker, and with a curl to it. His shoulders were broader, his waist more slender, his legs of a better shape, and he was taller, too. She blinked and was annoyed to find moisture in her eyes. The wind was stronger. It was blowing against her face and sending her hair flying out behind her. It was the buffeting of the wind that had irritated her eyes, she decided defiantly— nothing more.

Everything about the trip into London depressed Verity. The sky was overcast and a cool breeze was blowing. The stagecoach had been late, and it lumbered through traffic very slowly, tipping from side to side in a way that threatened bodily harm to the outside passengers and elicited groans and curses from those inside. Kitty, moreover, had contracted a cold, and looked ill. She had insisted upon accompanying Verity into the city. Scanning her flushed face and hearing her wracking cough, Verity was worried about her. Last week, she had been caught in a pelting rainstorm, and without drying herself off completely she had gone to sit with poor Tom Keats, insisting that she had promised to relieve his brother for an hour. Despite her worsening state of health, she had still been spending quite a bit of time administering to the sick boy. Verity, protesting her continued presence in the sickroom, found Kitty mulishly determined to remain by his side as long as she was needed. "It won't be much longer, milady," she had said dolefully. "Even though 'e's lastin' better'n Charlie, 'e won't see the New Year come in."

Verity reluctantly agreed with her. The news from the Bently house was bad. Twice she had seen Mrs. Dilke emerge from there in tears. She had not spoken with her. She had studiously avoided all those she had met at the Dilkes' house the night she had gone there with Alan. Not only had she been occupied with her book and weary after a long day's work, she did not want to chance a possible meeting with Lord Glendacre. She had glimpsed him through the parlor window one day last week, talking with John Keats. His expression had been somber. Keats was not looking well, either. He seldom left his brother's bedside, and Kitty had told her his sore throat persisted.

Verity's depression deepened. It was impossible not to connect Keats with her first and last evening at the Dilkes' cheery home. She had been so happy until the advent of Lord Glendacre. Being among people with whom she shared a common interest had been marvelously exhilarating. Or had her exhilaration stemmed from Alan's presence? She did wish he had not gone away. There was no use pretending that she did not regret the anger that had caused her to rebuff his declaration of love. The memory of his untoward embrace, even his jealousy, no longer infuriated her. If only she had been able to provide the explanation he had demanded . . . but he should not have *demanded* it. If he had been reasonable rather than accusing, suspicious, *jealous*. It had been Derek all over again! No, not quite. His actions had called Derek to mind—but Derek would not have let her go off without even following her, or if not following her, at least making an effort to see her again. Of course, she would have refused to see him . . . but he might have made the effort.

A loud and grating cough interrupted her ruminations. She looked at Kitty with considerable concern. "My dear, 'tis a cold day. You never should have come with me."

"Couldn't let you go alone, milady," Kitty croaked.

"Are you warm enough?"

"Quite warm. I've me shawl," Kitty said staunchly. "You don't need to worry none about me."

By the time they had reached Leadenhall Street, Verity was even more concerned. What had been a cool breeze when they left the village was now a chill wind with a smell of rain in it, tearing at them as they hurried into the offices of the Minerva Press. Though there was a fire crackling on the hearth, it was surprisingly cold in the anteroom. A thick wool shawl was folded over the clerk's shoulders.

He clambered off his stool as they came in, saying, "I'll tell Mr. Newman you're here, Mrs. Farwell."

"Thank you." Verity turned back to Kitty and pointed at a chair facing the hearth. "Sit here, dear," she ordered, and looking about her, she added, "You'd not think 'twould be so cold, but 'tis an old building with many crannies. Keep your shawl about you, do."

"I am warm enough, milady," Kitty insisted. " 'Tis not right you should concern yourself about me."

"But I am concerned, child," Verity said.

" 'Child,' " Kitty laughed weakly. "An' me 'oo could give you seven months."

"Seven months does not put you in a class with Methuselah, my dear Kitty."

Kitty's giggle turned into a paroxysm of coughing that frightened Kitty and at the same time rendered her even more regretful that she had allowed the girl to come with her. "You ought to be home and in bed," she said unhappily.

"I be all right, milady," Kitty rasped. "Wouldn't want you to go alone . . . wot's never . . ." She began to cough again.

"Shhhhh, don't talk," Verity commanded. "Lean your head back against the chair."

"Mrs. Farwell, Mr. Newman will see you now," the clerk said.

Verity was aware of an unpleasant pounding in her throat. It was the first time Mr. Newman had not come out to greet her. Feeling once more as if she were treading a path that must end at the scaffold, she walked slowly into the inner office. The publisher was standing near the door. Looking at him, Verity knew she had divined his mood correctly. He appeared sober and regretful. Indicating a chair by his desk, he said, "Please sit down, my dear."

She obeyed, but as he, too, sat down, she said, "You do not need to tell me what I knew when I gave you the manuscript."

He sighed. "It's a pity that your original chapters were so wantonly destroyed. It must have been a great shock."

"It was unfortunate," she admitted. "But even with their inclusion, much remained to be written. And when I perused the outline again, I found the material no longer appealed to me."

"But it is quite in line with your other two books." He frowned.

She paused, trying to collect her thoughts. "Since I began that novel, my life has undergone great changes. I find I am no longer attuned to the characters. The heroine seems too frivolous to me . . . too childish. Her problems are solved so neatly. That does not always happen. Consequently, she . . . none of the people in the story seem to live. And I have not been able to imbue them with life."

He looked at her solemnly, but there was a note of respect in his tone as he answered, "You have left me with very little to say, Mrs. Farwell, save that I must regretfully agree with you. I am, however, willing to take the manuscript on our original terms. I could let someone else work on it."

"No," she said quickly. "It is very good of you, but I could not accept such an offer. I would prefer to try again on another subject that interests me more."

The publisher sighed deeply. "That is a wise decision, Mrs. Farwell. And you may be assured that I will be delighted to read any material you choose to submit. Do you wish to take your manuscript back with you?"

"No, it will be too heavy to carry. You may put it on your fire." Verity rose.

"As you choose." He also got to his feet. "Please, I pray you'll not be discouraged, my dear. Most writers have shared your experience, except that they have had many novels rejected before one was taken. You have been singularly fortunate in having your first books published. And as your initial chapters of *The Canadian Cousin* indicated, you have every chance of repeating your earlier successes once you've found a subject more to your liking. Above all, I pray you'll not be discouraged by this slight setback."

"I assure you I am not," she said staunchly.

Coming back to Kitty, Verity was glad that the interview had passed so quickly. Though the girl was sitting close to the fire, she was shivering violently, and the clerk was bending over her.

He said sharply, accusingly, "This young woman never should have been allowed to come out. She's extremely ill."

The implication that she had forced her abigail to come with her filled Verity with righteous indignation. Her chin went up and she was about to give the man a cold reprimand, but now, she realized, was no time to defend her actions. Kitty came first. "Could you please get me a hackney? I'll take her directly back to Hampstead."

"An 'ackney, all the way to 'ampstead," Kitty protested. "You mustn't, milady. 'Tis too dear."

"I will take care of that." Mr. Newman had come into the anteroom.

"There's no need," Verity said quickly. "I have sufficient funds with me."

"As you choose, my dear. Aloysius," he said to the clerk, "find a hackney, at once."

"Thank you, sir." Verity bent over Kitty again. "We'll be home soon," she said softly. "And you'll feel better, you'll see."

Mr. Mortimer, the physician recommended by Mrs. Staples, was a tall heavyset man with a pompous air and cold gray eyes. Meeting him four days earlier, Verity had disliked him on sight. He had seemed actually affronted when told that his patient was a servant. Standing in the parlor with Verity, his gaze was still cool and unconcerned. "No need to be overanxious regarding your . . . abigail. She'll be on the mend soon enough. These women are hardier than you might think. Peasant stock, my dear lady."

Verity opened her mouth on a protest but reluctantly swallowed the words. She said, "Her brother died . . ."

"Yes, yes, I understand," he interrupted. "But she's not contracted consumption. 'Tis no more than a quinsy. If she does not improve within the next day or two, I'll bleed her again—and a second purging might also be in order.''

Verity said concernedly, ''Are you sure that this treatment has helped her? She looks so very pale.''

''My dear lady.'' The physician favored her with a lofty and affronted stare. ''It is necessary to draw out all the impurities. I assure you that her fever must soon abate. She'll be up and around in no time. If she is not, you may send for me again, but I trust that will not be necessary.''

''I hope you are right,'' Verity said doubtfully. Ignoring his indignant glance, she counted out his fee and hurried back to Kitty. Much to the combined disapproval of Mr. Mortimer and the girl herself, she had insisted that Staples bring Kitty down from her chilly little cubbyhole under the eaves to her own bed. Staples had also disapproved. ''You ought to keep 'em in their place, Mrs. Farwell,'' he had warned. ''Don't do to let a girl get above 'erself.''

His attitude, an unpleasant combination of the servile and the familiar, the latter sentiment expressed in the admiring glance he visited on her person, had infuriated her. In a manner closely resembling that of her grandmother when reproving an underling, she had said coldly, ''I think you must let me be the best judge of that, Staples. Thank you for bringing her down. You may go now.''

Anger had glinted in his eyes, and it had been with an exaggerated bow that he had said, ''Yes, milady,'' before lumbering out of the room. The incident had been unpleasant. It had also left her with the wish that she had not been so hasty with her reprimand. For some reason she was thinking about that as she came to sit by the bed. No, she was not being entirely accurate. She had a very good reason for thinking about Staples. It would soon be the third of November and the week's rent due. She did not have enough to cover it, and furthermore she was already in arrears, having been able to give Staples only half of the necessary amount in the last fortnight. He had not protested as much as she had feared. He had accepted her excuse that she was a trifle short but that she was expecting money from home. She had even less money now, and she would have to buy more medicine for the sick girl.

''Mark,'' Kitty mumbled. ''I 'ave to go wi' 'er ladyship,

couldn't stay be'ind. Yes, I do, I do. . . .'' She held out her arms. "Oh, Mark . . .'' Her arms fell to her sides and her speech grew unintelligible, but Verity knew she was talking to the young groom she had left to follow her mistress into her self-determined exile. Putting a hand to the girl's brow, she winced. The fever still raged, and the bleeding had left her very weak. Rising, she dipped a cloth in the basin on top of the night-table and sponged Kitty's face and neck.

Sitting down near the bed again, Verity was pleased to find that the invalid had fallen asleep again. She looked at her regretfully. If only Kitty had told her about Mark, she would not have brought her here. She would have pensioned her off—but she doubted Kitty would have agreed to that. She would have believed, and rightly, at least at that time, that Verity could not manage without her, who had waited on her hand and foot ever since her fifteenth birthday.

The last four days had been a revelation to her. She had found she could manage amazingly well without a maid, could button buttons, could slip hooks into their proper place, could adjust her stockings, brush her hair, and even arrange it quite becomingly. Every day, these tasks seemed easier. In addition she was caring for Kitty, performing all the duties necessary in a sickroom. If she had not been so sore beset by financial worries, she would have been extremely pleased with the way she was managing, managing with everything except money, and soon she would have to lay out another sixpence paying Betty to sit with Kitty this afternoon while she went to London to meet her sister Caroline.

She shivered. She had sent the letter by penny post, the day before yesterday. Caroline should have had it by now. She hoped that she would be able to bring her the money she had requested. If not . . . Verity groaned, wondering how she had so easily gone through the money her grandmother had given her. She could not account for her diminished resources. Five pounds had gone to Kitty—and that was a year's salary! She had received fifty pounds. It should have lasted her for at least two years, and she had been away from her former home for only five months and a little over. Of course, she had sent ten pounds to Miss Marshall, and, she had spent eighteen pounds on the garments purchased from Miss Catley—not pounds, guineas, which made it a trifle more, but not much.

And where had the rest gone? She ran her hands through her hair. She could not remember! Rent, food, books, paper, pens, trifles she had seen and wanted in the village stores, and, oh, yes, shoes, a stout pair of walking shoes. Fresh fruit for Kitty to give Tom. . . . It was fortunate she had seen a notice in the *Morning Post* to the effect that the Ladies Caroline and Eva Stratton were residing with their grandmother, the Dowager Marchioness of Harcliffe.

She prayed that Caroline had received her letter. She had asked that they meet at Hatchard's Bookstore, located on Piccadilly not far from her grandmother's house. Though it was tempting fate to be seen in a spot much frequented by the *ton*, she would wear her bonnet with the drawstring veil and hope that she would not be recognized. She had another worry. It was very possible that her sister might not be able to meet her. However, she had chosen a time when their grandmother was generally napping. She could only hope for the best.

Refusing the assistance of several polite clerks and protesting that she merely wished to browse, Verity stood near the front part of Hatchard's Bookstore, an eye cocked at one of its front windows. In the last half hour, she had noted among those passing the store several young ladies with their abigails in close attendance. None of them bore any resemblance to Caroline. Her earlier fears had returned. Her letter might not have reached its destination, or, more specifically, it might not have reached the one for whom it was intended. She did not like to contemplate what her grandmother must have said had the missive fallen into her hands. Lady Harcliffe's rages were not pretty to witness or to hear. Doubtless she would have treated the letter much as Derek had treated her chapters. Verity swallowed a small groan. It was a great pity her pride had not allowed her to accept the money offered by Mr. Newman. Had she anticipated that Kitty's illness would become so much worse, she might not have been so quick to refuse him. Given her financial condition even at that time, she should never have refused him. She had not been thinking, or if she had been thinking, she had harkened back to the old days when she could afford to be proud.

She moved restively, wishing there were some place to sit

down. It had been a long walk from the Swam with Two Necks—and if Caroline could not help her, she faced an even longer walk back to Hampstead. She dared not spend any more money on what she was beginning to fear was a fruitless journey.

"Verity," someone mouthed, directly behind her.

Turning swiftly, Verity found her sister, garbed in a long cloak and with a hood over her head. In the shadow of that hood, Caroline's eyes were wide and accusing. Still, she had come. As Verity stepped forward, Caroline, beckoning her to follow, walked hurriedly out of the store.

She had come alone. Verity was pleased at that. Not all abigails were as trustworthy as Kitty. Catching up with Caroline, she said, "I do thank you."

Caroline gave her a brief nod. "We'll go to St. James's Church and stand in the back by the font. You needn't walk with me," she hissed.

Her sister's chill manner confused and angered Verity. Caroline was conventional-minded, she knew. She knew, too, that it must have been a grave disappointment being sent back to the country last summer, but her exile had not been of long duration. Furthermore, Caroline had tried to cover for her in the face of Derek's questioning. Consequently, she was hard put to understand her present attitude, particularly when she *had* come.

Her heart was beating unpleasantly fast by the time she entered the church, a few paces behind her sister. As she joined her, Caroline murmured, "I think we'd best sit in a pew. Then the curate will not come and converse with us."

Nodding, Verity followed her into a pew halfway down the aisle on the far side. Taking a second cue from Caroline, she knelt beside her and bowed her head on her arms.

Opening her reticule, Caroline took out two pound notes and seven shillings. "This is all I can spare," she muttered. "If it was known I had come to meet you, I should be sent back to the country!"

"I . . . I would not have tried to get in touch with you if I had not been in such sore straits. I do thank you for coming."

"I almost didn't come." Caroline frowned at her. "But I wanted to know why you tried to place the blame on Cassie

. . . she's stopped speaking to me, and so has Rob." She choked back a sob. "I always thought that R-Rob . . . "

"Caroline," Verity said in a voice she strove to keep from trembling, "he is not worth your consideration. He must have known Cassie was lying, and she *was* lying. She did ask me to chaperon her. And Reggie met us, and then they disappeared and left me all alone!"

"All alone!" Caroline inadvertently repeated.

"They said they would be back in a half hour . . . but what's the use of telling you what you probably know."

Caroline said almost reluctantly, "Cassie always did like Reggie above half. I never did."

"Nor did I," Verity agreed. "And he looks dreadful—all puffy and yellow."

"So I have heard," Caroline agreed.

"Then . . ." Verity broke off as measured footsteps caused her to glance quickly to one side. She glimpsed the dark garments of a curate and fell silent, burying her face in her arms. Out of the corner her eye, she saw Caroline do the same. It was only after several minutes that she dared to lift her head. Caroline was facing her again, and the angry look was back in her eyes.

"What happened to your lover?" she asked.

"I never had a lover!" Verity retorted.

"You were seen getting out of a hackney and into another helped by a gentleman—on the day you disappeared from London!" Caroline said accusingly. "The lady who saw you is a dear friend of Grandmother's and close-mouthed, thank God, else we should have had even more to bear. Grandmother was in a rare taking, I can tell you. She wrote us absolutely blistering letters and said that she would never let us come back from the country, and . . ." She broke off. "Who was he? Are you still with him?"

"Caroline!" Verity cried, caught between shock and, surprisingly enough, amusement at her sister's evident curiosity. "The gentleman she saw was a friend, not a lover, believe me."

"Truly?" Caroline questioned disappointedly.

"Truly. You know I am not in the habit of lying." She paused and added bitterly, "You did help me lie to Derek, did you not—so I expect you don't believe anything I tell you."

"Oh, Verity, do not look that way." Caroline put her arms around her. "I . . . I have been told I must forget I had a sister. Grandmother was so angry. You see, she did believe everything you told her, and she was willing to send you to the country, where . . . you would have been perfectly miserable. We were. We were watched so closely. It's a little better now, though I did have to wait until Grandmother fell asleep. I was reading to her, as usual, and I didn't think she ever would. I was also terrified that Maggie, that horrid elderly maid of hers, would catch me sneaking out of the side door, but she didn't. And I am so sorry that I cannot be of more help, but we are given very little pocket money . . . but, oh, I have thought of you so often and missed you so much, and so has Eva. We both love you."

"Oh, Carrie, thank you. I love you, and I miss you and Eva. I know it's been difficult for you, and . . ."

"I want you to know something else," Caroline interrupted. "I never liked Derek. I thought he was perfectly horrid!"

"Oh, my dearest," Verity said happily. "How kind of you to say so!"

"I am not being kind," Caroline emphasized. "I dislike him even more now. He did his best to vilify me. He told Grandmother that we were two of a kind." Caroline's eyes brightened. "And Grandmother gave him a strong set-down and said that while she held no brief for you, she would not receive him in her house again!"

"Oh, lovely." Verity clapped her hands softly. "I am glad you told me."

Caroline stared at her. "You seem much thinner," she commented anxiously. "Are you well?"

"Yes, I am in very good health, thank you, but poor Kitty's ill."

"Kitty?"

"My abigail."

"Oh, yes, I liked her. I hope she gets better soon. Where are you living?"

"I do not think I had better tell you, my dear. If by some mischance Grandmother were to learn that you left the house this afternoon and . . ."

Caroline held up her hand. "Say no more. I do understand.
But I wish I could help you. Do you have nothing you can
pawn?"

"Pawn?" Verity repeated. "I left all my jewels with Derek,
but there are a few trinkets. Perhaps I might . . ."

"Oh, my poor Verity," Caroline cried. "I will try to save
some money for you. Send me a note later. Perhaps we can
meet again. I do not want you to be in such sore straits!"

Verity clasped her sister's hand. "I pray you'll not fret.
The fact that you've been so kind means more to me than
anything. I thought at first that you must hate me, too."

"I could never hate you. I was angry with you because of
Rob, but I think I've always known that Cassie lied—just as I
know you to be as honest as your name, Verity. Now I'd best
go, my dear."

"Yes, you must. I'll remain here a moment longer."

"Perhaps that would be best. Farewell, Verity. God be
with you." Caroline kissed her cheek.

"And with you, Caroline."

Verity listened to her sister's soft footsteps on the marble
floor until she could hear them no longer, until the church
was briefly brightened by the opening and closing of the outer
door. Then, wiping away tears she had not been able to
restrain, she, too, rose and went out.

Verity closed her portmanteau and regarded it thoughtfully,
hoping that she had included the garments that would fetch
the best price from the pawnbroker. Inside was her white
satin evening dress covered with sarsenet, a pelisse of merino
cloth, and a walking dress of green washing silk. She had
reluctantly included her purple poplin round gown, which she
had never worn, and her newest mantle, fashioned of dark
purple satin, also never worn. Smaller items included a bonnet with a love of an ostrich plume in sapphire blue, a
Wellington hat, several pairs of kid gloves, and two pairs of
Morocco leather slippers, also new. She had little in the
way of trinkets and she could not bring herself to part with
her cameo set—but in her reticule reposed the small pearl
necklace given her by her late godfather.

The gowns had been made by the finest dressmakers and it
was with considerable regret that she was relinquishing them,

but they would fetch money in a pawnshop, of that she was certain. She was not precisely sure if all these places were situated in Covent Garden. She would have preferred not to go there, especially alone. Miss Marshall had told her that it was a particularly unpleasant district, much frequented by thieves. She hoped someone on board the coach might know of another location. Perhaps the coachman himself might be able to provide that information. She released a long quavering breath. The idea of going to such a place was daunting, but even more daunting was the fact that she had not yet paid her rent and stood in danger of being turned out on the street. No one had said anything as yet—but Staples had given her a long, hard look yesterday, one she had no trouble interpreting.

In the last fortnight, she had skimped on food, too, buying writing materials instead. She had hoped to begin a novel which would meet with Mr. Newman's approval. Unfortunately, inspiration still lagged. It was difficult to concentrate on light romances with so much else preying on her mind, and it was only this week that Kitty's health had begun to improve. Yesterday she had insisted on returning to her attic quarters, and Verity, with her errand in mind, had not protested. If Kitty had known what she intended to do, there would have been an argument, and the girl might have taken a turn for the worse.

The portmanteau proved unexpectedly heavy, and as she dragged it down the stairs, Verity prayed that she would not meet Staples. He might very well think that she was trying to flee. She did not meet him, but as she came out into the chill of a November day and started up the street, she glimpsed John Keats standing outside the Bently house, staring morosely into space. She had not seen him lately, and it was with considerable regret that she noted he had lost weight. His features, no longer sun-browned, were white and pinched. He looked ill, too ill to be burdened with the care of poor dying Tom. She thought of inquiring after his brother and decided against it. Such a question, however well meant, must only cause him pain. In that moment, he turned and walked slowly back inside. Verity went on her way. Against her will, she was remembering the long-ago evening she had spent at Wentworth Place. More specifically, she was thinking about Alan.

Was he still in Italy? The anger his name had once evoked was completely gone. All that remained was a futile wish that she had not acted in so arbitrary a manner. Furthermore, she had been cruel—repulsing his love in so vehement a manner. If she had to do it again . . . but there was no sense dwelling on that folly. She was depressed enough already.

As usual, the coach was full, and Verity, sitting between a heavyset man and a woman who had squeezed in at the last moment, was unable to keep from falling against one or the other at every lurch of the vehicle. "I am very sorry," she gasped for the fourth time.

"Ye don't need to keep beggin' my pardon," the woman told her with a gap-toothed smile. " 'Tisn't yer fault . . . 'tis the fault o' these 'ere roads. I'll be glad to be back in London, I will. Visitin' my sister up north I was. Cold as a dog's nose it were."

"Yes, the North can be cold at this time of year," Verity agreed. "Do you live in London?"

"That I do," was the ready answer. "Born'n raised to the sound o' Bow Bells."

"I expect you must know the city quite well, then?"

"That I do."

"I wonder . . . would you know of a reputable pawnshop?" Verity inquired, thinking that her companion might very well have such information. She was clad in a shabby, much-mended gray cloak, and her gown looked equally shabby. Her hair, a foxy red, was barely concealed by a battered old bonnet.

"A reputable . . ." The woman chuckled. " 'Tisn't many o' those. Skinflints the lot o' 'em, I knows, I can tell ye. You 'aven't got to go to the Jews, 'ave ye?"

"I find I must," Verity said reluctantly.

"Well, 'as it 'appens, I do know of a place. 'Tis in Leicester Square."

"Oh, that's good. I thought they were mainly in Convent Garden."

"No, no, ye'd not want to go there. 'Tisn't nothing but stews about 'n' they'd skin you alive, little thing like you. Down on yer luck, eh?"

A withering retort trembled on Verity's lips, but she did

not utter it. The woman was only offering her sympathy and no matter how she resented it, pride was too costly an emotion at present. "A little," she admitted reluctantly.

The woman regarded her out of narrow eyes set in a sharp-featured face. Verity guessed her to be in her late thirties or early forties. There was, she thought suddenly, something she did not like about her. She could not have said exactly what—but she did wish they had not started to converse. Her regret on that count increased as the woman said, "Can't see through that veil yer wearin', but you 'ave a nice voice, 'n' yer young. Might be to your advantage to work in a drapery shop. I knows a lady wot 'as one in Charlotte Street. She's always on the lookout for genteel girls like yerself. You can do well for yerself in a drapery shop . . . if yer out front. All the gentry goes there."

Verity longed to give her a set-down she wouldn't soon forget but managed to say politely, "I do thank you for your suggestion, but I fear it would not do. Could you tell me the name of the pawnshop you mentioned?"

"It's called Lawton's, 'n' they won't cheat you. I 'appen to be goin' in that direction myself. I could show it to you if you like."

Verity shook her head quickly. "That's very kind of you, but I know that part of London quite well, and I wouldn't think of putting you to the trouble."

" 'Twouldn't be no trouble." The woman displayed her gap-toothed smile again.

"Still, I know that I can find it," Verity told her firmly.

"As you choose," she said shortly and lapsed into silence.

Once at the Swam with Two Necks, Verity, waiting impatiently for her portmanteau to be thrown down from the roof, was glad the woman had not approached her again. She had been one of the first to receive her luggage, and she had hurried away without another word. Watching her, Verity was considerably relieved. She knew it was silly to imagine her fellow passenger might follow her, and it was equally silly to have formed so quick a dislike for one who was, after all, trying to be helpful. However, the implication that she might want to join the coterie of damsels who labored in drapery shops until their youth and beauty brought them a rich protector rankled. Moreover, it was possible that she was one of those dragons who were ever on the prowl for innocent young girls they might decoy into a house of prostitution. She chuckled over this second theory; not only did it sound too lurid to be anything save her novelist's imagination, but procuresses would have to be considerably better dressed and more respectable-looking.

Save for the three golden balls that hung over its main entrance, Lawton's could have been any ordinary business office. A clerk sat at a high desk in the anteroom, and behind a gate stretched a hallway with small curtained cubicles on either side. There were several chairs in the anteroom, and these were occupied by surprisingly well-dressed men and a scattering of women. For the most part they were young and seemingly without the look of anxiety one would expect to find in such an establishment.

Verity shyly gave her name to the clerk and was politely told that she must wait her turn. As she started to stand against the wall, one of the young men proffered his chair. She managed a smile for him and, thanking him, sat down, folding her hands in her lap, trying not to clasp them too tightly. Bits of conversation drifted toward her. Most of the talk, she discovered, concerned betting on horses or the high stakes at Watier's or White's. Nearly all of them spoke of having used a system which had failed, but which had usually been infalliable and would be again once they had more of the ready. The sums mentioned ran into the tens of thousands. Seemingly those who had parted with them were positive that luck was still waiting for them at the turn of a card, the rattle of dice, or the hoof that first crossed the finish line. Verity glanced nervously at her portmanteau, wondering if she had been misdirected. A place that was in the habit of loaning so much money would hardly be interested in her few bits of clothing. It might have been better if, after all, she had gone to Convent Garden. She was trying to make up her mind about that when she heard her name called. Rising, she came timorously forward and was politely shown into one of the curtained cubicles. It contained two chairs with a table between them.

She was joined by a nattily dressed young man, who eyed her portmanteau without the disdain she had anticipated.

"Might I be of help?" he asked politely. There was a hesitancy about his H's, but if his accent smacked of the cockney, his manner was extremely genteel.

"I have some . . . garments to pawn," Verity said, trying not to sound too anxious.

"Very well, let's see them." He pointed to the table.

It was with considerable pain that she watched him examine each garment, closely, with a sharp, suspicious look which contrasted greatly with the politeness of his address. "Give you ten pounds for the lot," he said finally.

"Ten . . . pounds!" she repeated in horror. "But they were very expensive. They . . ."

"We are not buying them, madame, we are loaning you money on them. That is all we are prepared to offer," he said crisply.

There was no help for it. She would have to take it. Ten pounds would pay her rent and food for the next two months. She was wearing her fur-lined cloak, and she toyed with the idea of giving him that as well—but thought better of it. "Very well," she sighed. Reluctantly, she produced the pearl necklace. "Would it be possible for you to tell me how much I might realize on this?"

"Oh—and where had you that?" he inquired with an abruptness that angered her.

With some difficulty she kept her tone even as she said, "It was a present from my godfather."

"If you will excuse me, I must speak to Mr. Lawton." Before she could answer, he had taken the necklace and hurried out of the room. It seemed a very long time before he returned. Verity's fears increased. The sum she had received would not take her very far. She had expected at least three times as much on garments which had cost hundreds of pounds. What could she do after that money ran out? Possibly she could go out to be a governess. Yes, why could she not? She had always been an apt pupil, and she had had the benefit of Miss Marshall's teaching. She spoke French and Italian fluently. She could embroider and draw. She could also play the pianoforte and the harp. She ought to have thought of that before—but she could not have left Kitty. Now . . .

The clerk returned. "Two pounds," he said.

"Two pounds?" she echoed indignantly. "No, I'll not

accept so meager a sum." She stretched out her hand for the necklace.

He did not reutrn it. "Two and six."

"No, I find I would prefer not to pawn it."

"Three pounds."

She regarded him ruefully, realizing that she should have bargained with him on the garments. Thirteen pounds would give her a breathing space. Meanwhile she would look for work. "Three pounds and five," she said.

"Three and three."

She could see from his expression he would go no further. "Three pounds and three," she capitulated.

Coming outside, Verity's optimism increased. It had been singularly exhilarating to watch the clerk count out the money. She started down the street and had gone about half a block when she felt a hand clasp her arm. She turned and was startled to find the woman from the coach at her side.

"Almost missed ye, I did," she said. " 'Ow did you do, lovey?" She smiled down at Verity, who realized now that they were standing that her companion was at least a head taller than she.

Her heart was beginning to pound. "Reasonably well, thank you," she said, trying to speak calmly. Her earlier fears had returned in full. "I must go now," she said, staring about her and wishing the sidewalk were not so crowded.

"I'll walk along wi' ye. Got to worryin' about ye after we parted. That's why I came to find ye. Little thing like you oughtn't to be walkin' down 'ere all by 'erself. 'Tis not a good part o' town for a woman alone. Ye ought to 'ave yer abilgail wi' ye."

"I am sure you mean well, and I am grateful," Verity said coldly, "but I am perfectly capable of looking after myself. I have no need for such protection as you might offer—and please let go of my arm."

"I only wants to 'elp ye." The woman tightened her grasp on Verity's arm, giving it a hurtful twist, and, bringing up her knee, she delivered a heavy blow to her stomach.

Pain such as Verity had never experienced shot through her. With a moan she sank to her knees, and in that same moment, her tormentor bent over and wrenched the reticule from her arm, then dodged through the crowds and vanished around the corner.

"Stop . . . stop her . . ." Verity mouthed, but could not speak, nor could she move. She could only lie gasping for breath and sobbing while a crowd of people gathered around her. It was a good five minutes before she could tell them what had happened.

A half hour later, she gave a second explanation to the Bow Street Runner someone had fetched. He looked knowing as she described the woman.

"Aye, Sal's 'er name. Sociable Sal, we calls 'er. Rides the coaches lookin' for such tender young pigeons as you to pluck. Shouldn't get chummy wi' strangers, my girl." He had a sympathetic look for Verity. "I'll gi' you the money to get 'ome, but you don't 'ave a chance o' retrievin' yer blunt. 'Tis a pity."

"Yes," Verity said stonily.

" 'Ere, I'll take ye to yer coach."

As she walked beside him, Verity wondered which of the men had been assigned to follow her, all those months ago. She stopped wondering. Other more pertinent and frightening speculations were filling her mind. She had not paid her rent. Would Mrs. Staples, hearing what had happened to her, be understanding? It was then that she belatedly remembered that it was not Mrs. Staples whom she must confront.

Two

Sitting next to the window of the old, battered, badly sprung post chaise bearing herself and three other people across London Bridge to St. George's Fields in Southwark, site of, among others, the King's Bench Prison, Verity stared out at a gray sky that looked the grayer because of her veil. The vista was also blurry, and that was due to the tears she could no longer quell. She had not wept when she had left Hampstead. At least she could pride herself on her admirable calm in the face of Staples's odious grin and triumphant stare when she opened her chamber door to his peremptory knock. Once more she envisioned the scene.

" 'E's 'ere,'' he said with great satisfaction. "An' you'd better look sharp, else 'e'll be comin' up to fetch you. 'E's got other stops to make 'n' 'e don't like to be kept waitin'.''

"You may tell him that I will be down directly," Verity replied coolly.

Behind her, Kitty, who had been weeping as she packed Verity's few belongings, burst out sobbing afresh, and a moment after Staples clumped down the stairs, Mrs. Staples hurried into the chamber looking quite as upset as the abigail.

"I did my best to argue wi' 'im yesterday when 'e told me wot 'e were goin' to do. I said you'd 'ave no trouble gettin' work as a governess if 'e'd give you a little more time, but 'e'd not listen. 'E 'as someone as wants the room." She slipped a half crown into Verity's hand. "Ere, lovey."

"I can't take this, Mrs. Staples," she had protested.

"You 'ave to take it, my dear. You'll need money there, 'n' this is not near enough, but 'tis all I can spare. I'll try to get you more. I 'ave a friend can bring it to you. 'E's an 'ard man is Staples, but don't you worry about Kitty. 'E'll not put her in the work'ouse like 'e threatened. She can 'elp me.''

"I want to come wi' ye," Kitty sobbed, standing beside Verity.

"No, child," Verity told her gently. "You're not well enough. You've only been on your feet for a week. You do not know what conditions you'll find there."

"Or you," Kitty moaned. " 'Tis no place for you." She stared resentfully at the landlady. " 'Tis cruel after all that 'appened to 'er in London."

"I agree." Mrs. Staples sighed deeply. "Is there no one could 'elp you, Mrs. Farwell?"

"There is . . ." Kitty began.

"No one." Verity gave her a repressive glance. Kitty meant her grandmother, of course. The abigail did not know that Verity, swallowing her pride, had finally written to her—explaining her plight and asking for her help. The letter had been sent three days ago. There had been no answer. "I am quite alone in the world, Mrs. Staples," she stressed. "And I have been foolishly wasteful." She paused, swallowing a threatening obstruction in her throat. "I must suffer the consequences."

"If only your cousin were 'ere." Mrs. Staples sighed. "You wouldn't be alone, then."

"He's out of the country and not likely to return soon," Verity said, hoping the ladlady had not noticed her slip concerning her lack of kin.

"Oh, that 'e should 'ave to be away now." Mrs. Staples' deep, regretful sigh was reassuring to Verity. Her reputation would, at least, remain intact.

And now they were going over the bridge. It was so noisy. She heard the clatter of a battalion of wheels bumping over the stones. There were loud shouts and curses mingling with the creaking of wagons, the neighs and whinnies of horses driven beyond their endurance. As the old coach edged near to the side of the bridge, she could see the river cluttered with boats of all sizes. There seemed to be three times the amount of noise she had heard on the night she and Cassie Dilhorne had traveled to Vauxhall Gardens, five months earlier. Had it been only five months? It seemed as if five centuries had

passed since she embarked upon the fateful journey that
spelled the end of all that had been secure in her life—and
what would happen now?

Prison.

The idea was horrifying to her, and the way the baliff had
addressed her was equally terrible. His manner was sullen,
his eyes cold. He had made no effort to help her into the
coach. It was natural that, as they jounced over the stones,
she should think of another embattled lady—Queen Marie
Antoinette on her way to the guillotine, a tragedy much
mourned by her grandmother, who had been presented to the
King and Queen of France some thirty years ago.

Her grandmother. If there had been a way to send her a
note the previous night, she would have done so—but she
could not afford the cost of a messenger, and upon mature
reflection, she was glad of that. In her present state of mind,
Lady Harcliffe would probably have done nothing above
saying that Verity was getting her just deserts. Caroline could
not tell her that her sister had not fled with a lover—because
that would suggest they had been in communication.

What was she to do?

She had heard that debtors spent years behind those walls,
and there was no one to bail her out. Her debt amounted to
ten pounds. She had spent more than that on a pair of satin
slippers and thrown them out two days later because they had
been ruined in the rain! If she had them now, if she had
anything worth selling—but she had parted with the best of
her wardrobe. All that remained was her new blue merino and
that other foolish purchase, her fur-lined cloak. It was keeping her warm now, but at what a price! Her freedom! She
turned her gaze away from the depressing view of that wintery
sky and glanced at her companions in misery. There were
three of them.

Facing her was a small thin individual who looked as if he
was a clerk. Beside him sat a tiny woman, clinging to his arm
and occasionally patting his hand as if to comfort him. She
had a homely scrap of a face dominated by big hazel eyes.
Her nose and mouth were both small, and since her features
were almost duplicated in the countenance of the man with
her, it was obvious that she was sister rather than wife. The
other occupant of the hackney was seated beside Verity. He

was a fair, handsome young man whom she guessed to be about twenty-eight. He was dressed in the height of fashion, and now, as she gave him a brief side glance, he winked at her.

"Your first time, is it?" he inquired politely.

Before she could answer, the woman moaned, "Ah, it is, and 'tis unfair that my brother 'oo only 'elped someone wot didn't repay 'im should be forced into the terrible place."

"There, there, Fanny," the thin man muttered.

" 'Tis not so terrible as you'd believe," the sprig of fashion replied calmly. "If you're a sportsman or a gambler, you'll not want for entertainment. Or you can stroll about the streets or watch the lads play tennis."

"Tennis?" The other man regarded him incredulously.

"Aye, tennis, that's the game. Great recreation. Of course, 'tis better in summer, but if it don't snow, you'll see a number of us in the courtyard, hard at it."

"They are allowed to play *tennis*?" Verity questioned amazedly. "I thought . . ."

"You thought 'twas a place of thumbscrews and manacles, racks and wheels?" He laughed merrily and called, "Bailiff, tell the ladies that durance is not as vile as they imagine."

As the bailiff, who was sitting with the driver, did not turn his head, he continued, "Chap's in a fit of the sullens. He's not allowed on the courts, do you see. Has to ferry lost souls across the Styx every day. Rum business, especially with the road being what it is. Shouldn't be surprised if his insides're all topsy-turvy. 'Twould account for his dyspeptic expression, shouldn't you think. Unless, perhaps, he dines on green apples."

Verity, who had been convinced that she would never laugh again, laughed. "You do talk a deal of nonsense," she observed.

"Of course," he responded. "For are we not, all of us, in the most nonsensical of positions?"

"Nonsensical, sir?" The thin man frowned.

"Extremely nonsensical," was the light response. " 'Tis not as if we'd waylaid some unfortunate traveler on the road and lifted his gold or murdered a fellow citizen or blown up the Houses of Parliament. We have become financially embarrassed. Would it not be easier to be outside and in a position to earn or win back all that we have lost so we might repay our sniveling creditors? I am sure none of you will disagree with me on that count. But instead, we're clapped into the dungeon where we can do naught but . . . play tennis."

"That does make remarkably good sense," Verity approved.

"I am glad you agree. But you seem an intelligent young woman—at least I believe you must be young under that veil." He bent a quizzical eye upon her. "Looks can be deceiving, but voices rarely, Miss—er, Mrs.—"

"Farwell, sir," she said. "Mrs. Farwell, and you are . . ."

"Gerald Sutcliffe."

She was no longer weeping, and so she drew her veil aside, and heard a gasp from the other woman. She quailed inside, wondering if she had been recognized, but said calmly enough, "We've not learned the identities of our fellow passengers . . . save that I know your given name's Fanny."

" 'Tis F-Fanny Gibbs, and this is my brother Thomas," the little woman said, her wondering eyes still fixed on Verity's face. She added tremulously, "But you're so young and b-beautiful. You shouldn't be in such a position. Do you not agree, Tom?"

"I am sure we must all agree," Mr. Sutcliffe observed somewhat breathlessly.

Some of Verity's tension departed. "I do thank you, but I rather think appearance has little to do with penury."

"Is there no Mr. Farwell?" Mr. Sutcliffe demanded almost angrily.

She shook her head. "He died from his wounds at Waterloo, sir."

"I was at Waterloo," he returned. "What regiment was your husband in?"

"The Eighteenth Hussars." Verity breathed a prayer that Mr. Sutcliffe had not been in that particular corps.

"Ah, then I did not know him. I myself was in the Royal Horse Guards."

"And you sustained no wounds, sir," Miss Gibbs said shyly. "How fortunate."

"Yes, very." Mr. Sutcliffe's face had grown grim. He suddenly looked much older.

Watching him, Verity felt totally ashamed of herself. She wished heartily she had never agreed to pose as the widow of one who had died in that terrible conflict. It seemed almost criminal to accept the commiseration of her companions, especially in regards to Mr. Sutcliffe. In escaping with his life, he could not have escaped the horror of watching men he knew, and with whom he might even have attended the Duchess of Richmond's famous ball on the preceding night, go forth into battle and be blown to bits on the field. It came almost as a relief when little Miss Gibbs said tensely, "We're slowing down. I think we must be near our destination."

Verity had expected bars and thick walls, and though she assured herself she was being ridiculous, she carried in her mind a vivid image of the dungeons at Unger Castle. These Derek had reluctantly and at her insistence shown her. Located in the bowels of the castle, damp from the nearness of the sea, they had been horridly small cubicles with barred windows set high in the wall. In the floor, there had been an oubliette, so named because anyone placed in there was forgotten by all save their jailers. Debtors, she knew, did not suffer such dread punishments, but she was very vague as to what accommodations the King's Bench Prison did offer.

Consequently, upon descending from the hackney, she was not surprised to see high walls and an office where a turnkey sat. Her heart was beating fast as she approached this place. She had drawn her veil across her face again, and with a mixture of resentment and fear she obeyed the turnkey's curt command to pull it back. However, she was pleased that her voice did not quaver when at another command she gave him her name, direction, and reason for confinement.

Much to her surprise, she was asked if she had the price of a room. And upon explaining that she did not know she was expected to pay for a chamber, derisive smiles were exchanged. Her heart sank when she learned it would be a shilling per week for a room and another shilling for furniture. "Women can be put in the infirmary when there's nothing available, but the infirmary is crowded," the turnkey explained.

"I do not . . ." she began.

"I believe that my friend Jasper Lithcombe is still here?" Mr. Sutcliffe spoke over Verity's shoulder.

The turnkey raised a bushy eyebrow over a small, twinkling blue eye and grinned widely. "Well, Sir Gerald," he drawled. "I thought as 'ow we'd seen the last o' you."

"So did I, Mr. Joliffe," Sir Gerald responded blithely, "but it appears we were both mistaken."

" 'Orses or dogs?" inquired the turnkey with an even wider grin.

"Add cards and you'll have the worst streak of luck that ever plagued a deserving member of the human race." Sir Gerald heaved a long sigh.

"I am sure Mr. Lithcombe will be delighted to see you again," the turnkey observed.

"I hope so. I also hope you'll let me show this young lady where she might bed down. She's the widow of a fellow officer."

"Oh, indeed." Mr. Joliffe eyed Verity. "You 'ave my permission. Only . . ."

"I know what you're going to say, my dear fellow," Sir Gerald said. "And I can only assure you that you need have no fears, and nor must she." He glanced at Verity.

"I'll 'old you to that." Mr. Joliffe winked.

"Mrs. Farwell," Sir Gerald said gently, "I hope you'll let me introduce you to this charming establishment."

She regarded him thoughtfully. Though he was certainly a rakish young man, there was something very likable about him and, she thought, kind. She also trusted him, but, she remembered, she had trusted Lord Glendacre, too. That was a different situation and a different time; she was no longer a terrified and naive young woman. She said, "I would appreciate that, sir."

"Come, then." He took her arm, adding, "Be not afraid, fair maid. Tigers do abound, but not upon this holy ground."

"I do not recognize the source of that quotation." She smiled.

" 'Tis extempore from my mother wit."

"I recognize that one . . . 'tis from the *Taming of the Shrew*."

"Bravo. You know your Shakespeare."

"Some of him, but . . . oh!" Verity halted, staring at a stretch of garden that lay within the walls. Though it was largely winter-stripped, there were yet some firs and some late-blooming flowers. "I did not expect . . ."

"This is tended mainly by the prisoners," he explained. "Many combine light fingers with a green thumb."

"It must be very pleasant in summer. I thought . . ." she began, and paused, staring at a long crowded street with merchant's stalls on either side and strolling vendors crying their wares. The whole looked as if it had been plucked from the center of London and replanted. "But this . . ." she began, only to be interrupted.

"Yes, save for the presence of the keeper of the gates and his holy minions, we are well situated. The breeze from the river floats over yon walls, and though I can say with Marlowe's Mephistophilis, 'Why this is hell nor am I out of it,' it is a mighty comfortable hell, once you know your way among the ashes. Furthermore, I assure you that you'll not have to slip shillings into their pockets in order to have a comfortable and reasonably well-furnished room. I know that I can speak for my friend Jasper as well as for myself when I tell you, you may occupy our suite for the length of your stay, without, I might add, any obligation on your part."

"But I cannot accept . . ." she began.

"Of course you can . . . are you not the relict of a fallen comrade? It little matters that I knew him not; we were all comrades at Waterloo."

The truth trembled on Verity's lips and vanished into the cavity of her throat. To reveal her deception would rob her of a needed friend, and besides, there was nothing with which she could replace the lie other than that truth she would not, must not mention. "You are kind," she said in a small voice.

He came to a stop and looked down at her. "I have a feeling you are still timorous. Well, 'tis not pleasant to be a debtor, but sooner or later, you'll be freed. If it does not come through a friend of your, one of mine will do the honors. There are several that I know who are rusticating or traveling . . . but will be back. And when I fly, you'll take wing, too."

"I could not . . ."

He said merrily, "Do not make any rash decisions at this moment. 'Tis not necessary. For the moment, we are here and must partake of such pleasures as await us. And if he is not wielding a racquet, the first among these will be my old friend Jasper.''

The building to which Sir Gerald led Verity was large and, he explained, contained twelve good-sized rooms fitted up with elderly but serviceable furniture. Across the street from this domicile was another humbler abode which much resembled a military barracks and was for those prisoners ''who had not two pennies to rub together,'' Sir Gerald informed her.

"But how do they exist?'' Verity asked in some distress.

''Oh, there are always good souls who go about with baskets on their arm, just as they do outside. The King's Bench is a microcosm of the world beyond these walls. There are pauper princes and princely paupers. And before I wax more philosophical, I pray you'll mount these stairs, holding fast to the balustrade, for I cannot think they have mended the treads since last I was here.''

As she walked up a narrow flight of stairs, which were, she saw, badly broken in places, she was startled to hear a voice going up and down the scales. It was a pretty light soprano, the sort she could imagine in *The Beggar's Opera* or a similar work.

''Ah hah, we can expect a musical evening, I see,'' Sir Gerald remaked. ''But oh, for a tragic muse. I am a devotee of the theater, and we have entertained some notable thespians here . . . or rather they have entertained us!''

''Have you met writers as well?'' Verity asked shyly.

''Writers, scribblers, my dear lady, enough to fill a library— and of all persuasions from poets to pamphleteers—or perhaps I should have turned that phrase around. Never put the ridiculous before the sublime . . . except at present, when I must rouse dear Jasper from his possible slumbers.'' Approaching a door hard by the top of the stairs, he doubled his hand into a fist and produced a knock so thunderous that Verity was afraid the scarred and battered portal must fall in.

'' 'Here's a knocking indeed. If a man were porter of hell-gate he should have old turning the key,' '' growled a rich baritone voice. The door was jerked open and a young man, bare to the waist and with a tangled mass of black hair on head and chest, stood framed in the doorway, glowering at

ir Gerald out of dark bloodshot eyes, which opened wider as
e stared at his visitor. "Zounds, Gerry." He flung his arms
round Sir Gerald's neck. "Hast come to free me, varlet?"

"Nay, nay, proud porter, leave that to Shakespeare, whom
tou hast just cribbed. I've come to lay my weary bones
mong you all, and where's your shirt, man? We've a damsel
ere to whom thou and I must needs give sanctuary."

"A d-damsel, didst thou say?"

"Aye, a fair flower from a golden garden," acknowledged
ir Gerald. "And . . ." He paused as the door was suddenly
lammed. "Never fear," he continued. "Jasper will appear
gain when he is properly habited. He . . ." He paused as the
oor was flung back and Jasper, wearing a wrinkled but clean
nen shirt over black stockingette trousers, emerged with a
lare for his friend, which swiftly vanished as he caught sight
f Verity. "Ah, what light through yonder window breaks? A
)aniel has come to judgment."

"That, too, but what say you, my liege lord, if Cordelia,
ere, has our chamber for the time being?"

"I say . . . clear out the buried ancestors and let her have
ne crypt."

Sir Gerald turned to Verity and executed a deep bow.
"Friar Lawrence has spoken. The cell is yours . . . unoccu-
ied by all save the rats, mice, cockroaches, and fleas with
vhich the good Lord has seen fit to populate the earth. But I
hink that I must introduce you. Mrs. Farwell, Mr. Jasper
.ithcombe, late of the Temple, disciple of the Tempter, who
as yet to release his minion."

"I am delighted to meet you." Mr. Lithcombe bowed. He
estured at the door. "All that I have is yours . . . and, of
ourse, this esteemed establishment's proprietors'."

"But I cannot take your room," Verity protested.

"Of course you can take it," Mr. Lithcombe responded.
" 'Tis not the Carlton House, nor is it Windsor Palace . . .
ut you'll find 'twill suffice as soon as we have produced
lean sheets to cover thy couch, which is not so hard as a
ock, but . . ."

"I pray you!" Verity flung out her hands. "You must not
. . I mean, where will you go?"

"Westward ho, to far Cathay!" Sir Gerald cried.

"Cathay," Mr. Lithcombe corrected, "is eastward ho."

"But what will you do?" Verity demanded.

"As we have done before," Sir Gerald told her. "I beg you'll not fret. We have ways and means."

"Means?" Mr. Lithcombe's dark eyes gleamed. "Dos that indicate, fair knight, that thou art not entirely in the basket?"

"Not entirely. 'Tis only that I yearned for your mos excellent company. Also at thy command, I didst see the fai Phoebe, nymph in her orisons . . ."

Mr. Lithcombe's smile suddenly vanished, and a yearning look crept into his eyes. "Did you?" he demanded earnestly "And what had she to tell you?"

"Her message was for you. . . . She said, 'Forever.' "

"Ah!" Mr. Lithcombe's smile returned. "And that wa all?"

"There was more; 'twill be unburdened at a later hour Now . . ." Sir Gerald fixed his eyes on Verity. "I beg you' sit in here whilst we fall to and clean this bower."

"But . . ."

"Not another word," he interrupted firmly. "Jasper and have much to discuss, and your procrastinations are wearying him, are they not, foul varlet?"

"To the limits of my patiences," Mr. Lithcombe groaned "I have half a mind to carry her inside."

"I pray, refrain, fair sirs." Verity laughed and walked into the room. It was not large, but it was furnished with a wide bed, a night table, a chair, another table, and an armoire There were two candleholders adorned with half-melted candles and a worn rug on the floor. Though the furniture was ancien and battered, the bed was unmade, and a tangle of Mr Lithcombe's garments lay on the floor, it was a place to stay and since her new companions were insistent that she accep their hospitality, she decided to abandon argument. Though there was no key in the door, Verity had no fear that her new companions would attempt an invasion once she was settled Honesty and goodwill radiated from their countenances. I she had any fears it was that her deception would be revealed That, however, was highly unlikely, since she could no imagine that any of her husband's friends would be incarcer ated here. And for once she could bless the fact that she had remained at Unger Castle for so much of her married life

hus precluding a wide acquaintance among the *ton*. A grim
ittle smiled play about her lips as she pondered the irony of
being notorious and, at the same time, unknown.

> "Go naughty man, I can't abide you,
>   And then your vows so soon forgot?
> Ah! now I see if I had tried you,
>   What would have been my hopeful lot.
>
> But here I charge you—make them happy;
>   Bless the fond pair, and crown their bliss:
> Come, be a dear, good natur'd pappy,
>   And I'll reward you with a kiss."

Verity, who had been in a state of euphoria coupled with
amazement ever since she had been set beyond the gates of
the King's Bench Prison that afternoon, clapped loudly for
pretty blond Miss Elsie Duggan, late of Drury Lane, as,
finishing the air from *Love in a Village,* she curtsied and went
to sit down next to Randal Gresham, also of the theater. Mr.
Gresham's soliloquy from *Hamlet* had been received with
rather less enthusiasm by the assembled company, but he was
generous in his admiration for Miss Duggan.

Earlier in the evening, Percy Clive, a would-be poet, had
read his latest effusion, which was full of nymphs, shepherds,
and Arcadian glades, but did not scan very well. However,
he, too, had been roundly applauded by a group which con-
sisted of herself, Mr. Lithcombe, Sir Gerald, the aforemen-
tioned actors and poet, an elderly woman called Lady Greer,
who had also been in the theater, a Mr. Howell, who was
vague about his calling, and a Mr. Morpeth, who was not,
frankly admitting that he worked in a pawnshop.

Verity, ensconced on a ragged quilt, next to the "temporarily
embarrassed" Miss Duggan, who was waiting for her dear
friend Mr. Porter to come back from Birmingham, where he
was playing the Second Gravedigger in a production of *Hamlet*
starring that eminent tragedian Charles Mayne Young. "Once
Arnold finds what a fix I'm in, 'e'll come through wi' the
ready, you'll see," Miss Duggan had confided confidently.
"I 'opes you 'ave a fellow'll do the same for you."

Verity was about to answer in the negative when Sir Gerald, who had evidently overheard this exchange, said, "You must remember, Mrs. Farwell, when I go, you'll go."

"And you can believe him," Mr. Lithcombe averred.

"I do," Verity surprised herself by answering. Her optimism had returned, and, astonishingly enough, she was enjoying herself more than she had at any other time in recent years, save for the night she and Alan Parry had spent at Charles Dilke's home, and that had been cut short by Lord Glendacre's ill-timed entrance.

Indeed, the present company was not unlike that she had encountered at Wentworth Place. They were, most of them, young, and while they could have been called companions in misery, none seemed in the least miserable. In fact, they were amazingly optimistic. It occurred to her that she would like to write about them—about the place itself—but the subject would not make an entire book. However, a novel with one episode taking place in debtors' prison and other scenes . . . she would have to think about it, when she was alone and able to concentrate more completely.

She usually thought better in the morning, and she did have some writing material in her portmanteau. She felt a surge of enthusiasm, the like of which she had not experienced in months. She recalled there had been a time when she could hardly wait for the morning to come. In the last few months, however, she had been so anxious, so disturbed, so full of regrets and self-blame, that the days had taken on a gray sameness, with morning hardly distinguishable from afternoon or afternoon from evening. It seemed particularly strange to her that she should feel so liberated when, in fact, she was in prison! Yet, in a sense, she was free, free from all the worries that had been consuming her of late. The worst had happened, and it remained for her to make the best of it.

The following morning, Verity found that not only did her hosts' generosity extend to their room but there was water brought for ablutions as well as a rasher of bacon, tea, and toast. She wanted to refuse this largesse, but they would not hear of it, only begging her to watch them play tennis at twelve noon, which was the only time they could procure a court.

"We've laid a bet as to whether or not my game, which was always more skillful than Jasper's here, will have faltered for lack of practice," Sir Gerald explained, wincing at a far from gentle tap from his friend's racquet.

"My companion's exalted opinion of his prowess is seldom borne out in performance," Mr. Lithcombe assured her.

"Mrs. Farwell will be the best judge of that," Sir Gerald countered. "Might we expect you at twelve . . . and afterwards we will have some light refreshment?"

She promised with alacrity. "I have only a bit of writing to do."

"Letters?" Sir Gerald inquired.

She shook her head, saying diffidently, "I have written novels."

"Novels?" Mr. Lithcombe exclaimed. "You are an authoress!"

"In a small way," she admitted.

"Have you been published?" Sir Gerald asked.

"Yes, by the Minerva Press," she said with a touch of defiance.

"Hear, hear." The two young men gazed at her delightedly and applauded. "Did I not tell you she was a goddess—an Athena come among us?" Mr. Lithcombe said.

"I would call her a heroine, rather," Sir Gerald responded thoughtfully. "She is beautiful, brave, and in trouble. My sister frequents circulating libraries and I have whiled away several hours reading some of the scores of books she brings home, or brought home whilst I was living there. As far as I could gather, all the heroines were beautiful, brave, and in trouble, from which they were eventually extricated by the hero. I think you must write about yourself this time, Mrs. Farwell, even without the requisite hero. I am sure he will turn up sooner or later. Unless you've already chosen a subject."

"I will consider your suggestion, sir," she responded.

"Very well . . . and may you be visited by Inspiration!" He bowed and left the room, followed by Mr. Lithcombe.

"Why not?" Verity muttered. "And again"—her eyes lighted—"why not?"

Initially, it had been her intention merely to set down some

of the impressions she had received the previous day. Sir
Gerald's suggestion had given another shape to her thoughts,
and faced with an empty sheet of foolscap, an inkwell, and
quill, it was with actual glee that she wrote at the top of the
page: *The Divorce: Being the Vicissitues and Eventual Triumph
of Lady Portia Pennington.*

She could never have anticipated the pleasure it gave her to
write about her heroine's forced marriage to a mother-ridden
peer, who, in appearance, closely resembled Derek. The pen
seemed to fly across the paper, impelled by an invisible
force, as she happily described Lady Portia's secret connection with the theater and the success of her first play. Her
writing of a second play and her visits to the playhouse would
proceed along the lines of her own forays to Leadenhall
Street. She intended to leave the episode with Cassie virtually
intact. What she imagined must be a saturnine smile curled
her lips as she recalled that one of her reasons for acceding to
Cassie's request was that she might see the Gardens and
perhaps use them as a setting for one of her novels.

Meanwhile, she was having considerable enjoyment in setting down her opinions of Lady Unger and that moldering
castle on the Scottish border. She had just painted a vivid
word picture of the drafty hall with its frayed banners from
many a forgotten conflict descending from the splintering
railing of the gallery and the rusty suits of armor below when
there was a thunderous pounding on her door.

The sound startled and confused her. Staring vaguely about
her, she blinked and blinked again, wondering what had
happened to the ceiling-high shelves of books, the leather-
backed chairs, and the marble busts of Aristotle and Socrates
glowering from the mantelshelf. A second later, she was
jolted back to realty and to a fear that after all she might be
dragged to some dungeon.

She rose swiftly and timorously opened the door to find Sir
Gerald and Mr. Lithcombe regarding her with considerable
hauteur. They were, she noted with some compunction, carrying tennis racquets.

"Oh, dear, I shall come right away," she said apologetically.

"There is no need now, ma'am," Mr. Lithcombe informed
her lugubriously.

"No." Sir Gerald's tone was reproving. "Our game is at an end."

"But . . . how could it be?" she demanded. "You told me you'd not play until noon."

"And so we did," Sir Gerald pointed out. "And now nightfall is nigh—and soon it will be time to escort you to supper rather than dinner."

"It . . . it could not be near nightfall," she protested.

"What does thine own vision reveal, fair scribe?" inquired Mr. Lithcombe.

She turned toward the windows and found the sky painted with the orange of sunset. Incredulity was blended with regret and a touch of joy. Occasionally when Derek was away she had written for hours on end—but of late, creation had come only in fits and starts. "Oh, dear, I am sorry. I was so immersed in my writing that I did not realize how much time had passed."

"Well." Sir Gerald turned surprised eyes upon Mr. Lithcombe. "That is what I call an energetic muse."

"I must agree, and in those circumstances, we must forgive her. Was it not in debtors' prison that Cervantes penned *Don Quixote*?"

"I think you may be correct," Sir Gerald agreed.

" 'Stone walls do not a prison make nor iron bars a cage,' " Mr. Lithcombe quoted soulfully. He bowed low. "And you can always watch us tomorrow."

"I will . . . tomorrow," she promised.

She had meant what she said—but fortunately, she awakened to a drizzle that soon changed to a pelting rain. Secure in knowing that her friends would not be able to have their game, she settled down to write, and again the pen seemed to fly across the paper without her guidance. Much to her amazement, she found herself laughing as she wrote. Seen from a perspective of months, the whole situation seemed almost as ridiculous as the impromptu farce that Miss Duggan and Mr. Gresham had staged for the edification of them all the previous night. Even her meeting with Lord Glendacre had its comic aspects. And the woman in the coach, the pawnshop, and Staples consigning her to prison. She paused in her work, thinking of the triumph written large upon his unprepossessing features as he told her what he had done.

"But you didn't imprison me, Staples, you freed me," she murmured. It was true. She had never been so free as in these last two days and nights, mixing with her fellow "prisoners," and none to chaperon her, none to reprimand her for "putting herself forward," nor to look daggers when she engaged in friendly conversations with Sir Gerald or Mr. Lithcombe. Even doing without Kitty was, in a sense, a pleasure. To awaken alone in the mornings without the need of the sort of small talk one exchanged with servants, however friendly, was a boon in itself. She could go immediately to her desk and write. If she was to be honest, the world, *her* world, at least, had actually been more confining than the one in which she was currently moving.

Standing by the tennis courts watching Mr. Lithcombe being badly trounced by a more agile Sir Gerald, Verity shifted her gaze toward the sky, cerulean blue and centered by a distant sun. It had turned very cold, and the idea of returning to her room was not pleasant. The euphoria of the past fortnight had vanished; she knew exactly when it had gone: with the arrival of Kitty, who had come to visit, bringing with her a few more coins from the regretful and sympathetic Mrs. Staples and the news that Tom Keats was sinking fast.

This gloomy intelligence had left Verity with a plethora of "ifs" revolving in her mind. *If* she had been wealthy, she could have purchased a number of creature comforts for the poor lad, could have supplied servants to relieve his brother of the nursing chores that were wearing him down. Kitty had confided that the poet was far from well. The ominous observation. " 'Tis a long for 'im to 'ave a sore throat, milady" still resounded in Verity's head. And there were other ifs. Kitty's health had improved, and she spoke about the kindness of Mrs. Staples in letting her work in the house, but her eyes were red-rimmed and her expression in repose was woebegone. Verity recalled the name she had cried out in her delirium. *If* she could have afforded it . . . but when would she ever be able to afford *anything* again?

With that in mind, she had sat through another evening of merriment. Two more actors had arrived to swell the little group, enough to do a rousing if cut version of *The Beggar's Opera,* a singularly apt selection, considering their surroundings. Still, it seemed to her that everyone present had added an extra ingredient to the performance—pretense. They were trying to convince themselves and each other that they were not fearful, that they did not hate the idea of spending Christmas at the King's Bench, that they wondered how many other holidays they would pass there. Yesterday, she had seen the timorous sister and brother who had traveled up from London with Sir Gerald and herself. That they were not enjoying the "freedom" of the Bench was only too obvious. They seemed to have dwindled in size, and she noted that they were going in the direction of the building Sir Gerald described as little more than a barracks.

"If . . ." Verity murmured bitterly and went slowly back to her chamber. The chill yellow-white sunlight brought out every chink in the wall, every scratch on the furniture. The ceiling was stained, the plaster broken, the floor splintery. Settling wearily down at the table, she took up her quill and put it down again. But she dared not abandon Lady Portia Pennington, not when she might hold the key to her prison. With a sharp little sigh, she dipped her quill into the ink and starting writing.

A chill wind rattled the windowpanes, and when she had last glanced outside, Verity had found the ground covered with a light snow. However, she was no longer sunk in the dismals. Her feelings of despondency had departed in the matter of a day, and in the last fortnight, she had been able to spend most of her time writing. She had expected to finish her first draft this morning, but she had just run into a snag. Her characters were refusing to follow her outline!

In vain she argued with Lady Portia, Lord Lucius (her name for Derek), and Orlando Curwen (Alan Parry). Portia was refusing love-in-a-cottage with Orlando, and the grieving Lord Lucius was determined that his wife return to him. Unfortunately, Lady Portia was demonstrating a strong disposition to go!

Of course, it was all her fault. In an effort to disguise her characters if not the plot, she had made Derek far more appealing than she had originally intended, while Alan Parry seemed enigmatic and almost sinister. It was too late to go back and change his character, and besides, Alan *had* been mysterious and enigmatic. Still, mysterious, enigmatic, and even sinsister heroes strode across the pages of many a popular romance, and heroines regularly swooned into their arms. And no heroine in her right mind ought to be willing to take back her jealous, suspicious husband. Lady Portia, however, was willing to forgive the Lord Lucius her creator had inadvertently painted.

"What can I do?" she muttered.

Something Mr. Newman had said regarding *Elvira* popped into her head. "You have that sixth sense which is invaluable for any novelist. You know what your readers want and you give to them."

And what would her readers want? A happy ending, of course!

Verity groaned.

Her readers would want a chastened Lord Lucius to come and beg his former wife's pardon and bear her off to the marble halls. As for Orlando Curwen, he would depart on a voyage to Greece or Turkey or Egypt or he would travel to Rome and visit his equally mysterious relations—perhaps he was related to those who were hoping to overthrow the Austrians. And, of course, Lady Portia, cleared by an abject Kathie Dearbourne and secure in her husband's undying love, would take her place in society and become one of its great hostesses (an idea which made her cringe).

"Uggghh," Verity said, producing something between a groan and a growl, and she settled down to write this last and obligatory chapter.

Much to her pained surprise, her pen went on toward this miserable ending as rapidly as it had through most of the book. It did give her considerable pleasure to describe Lord Lucius's remorseful countenance and her (or rather Lady Portia's) chill reception of apologies as numerous as they were abject. She did manage to resist a scene which had him groveling upon the floor. That was not in character, or, rather, it was not in the character of the man she had created—who had very little to do with the real Derek, except in the first part of the novel. She had just reached the difficult part—when she, or rather Lady Portia, would have to recognize the fact that her husband was, indeed, sincerely remorseful. This most fictitious of all fictions would be, she knew, very hard to frame. It would require the utmost concentration. For what could Lady Portia say? That in spite of everything, his jealousy, his spying, his accusations, and his wanton destruction of the manuscript of her latest play, she loved him? Had always loved him?

Taking a deep breath, she dipped her pen in the inkwell and wrote, "Lord Lucius . . . " Or would it be, "My lord . . ." Or . . .

She paused as a strong knock on her door scattered all her thoughts. The pen fell from her hand, and ink splattered on the paper, though fortunately not on the written part. Her visitor could only be Sir Gerald or Mr. Lithcombe, but in the days when it was cool they usually played piquet—endlessly until it was time for lunch or supper. Or had the weather cleared? She glanced over her shoulder. No, it was still dismal. In that moment, the knock was repeated, even more strongly than before.

Rising, she ran to the door and said crossly as she opened it, "What is it you want? I am writing."

"So I was told. I could not credit such bravery!"

She froze, staring unbelievingly at the man who stood in the semidarkness of that dingy hall. "Alan?" she said uncertainly.

"Yes, my dear cousin." He strode into the room and, looking about him, shuddered, saying huskily, "I could scarce believe my ears when Kitty told me what had happened. You here and I all unknowing."

Her heart was beating in her throat. She wanted to fling herself into his arms or, rather, she wanted him to fling his arms around her—instead of standing the length of an arm or perhaps two arms away from her, the while his angry gaze moved from her to the room, dim now in the shadows of a winter afternoon. He did reach out to her, taking her hand and kissing it, releasing it all too quickly. He was looking well and prosperous. His clothes were beautifully cut. She felt very shabby beside him. But he had said something. Yes, she remembered it now. "How might you know I was here when you were in Italy?" she asked reasonably. She added, "Oh, it is good to see you."

"It is passing painful for me to see you here in these surroundings," he said heavily. "Why did you not get in touch with Tony? Surely . . ."

"Tony?" she interrupted. "Oh, you mean Mr. Newman."

"Yes. He would have advanced you monies."

"On what? I was not writing, and we agreed that my last book was not worth printing." Her eyes gleamed. "But my next will be. Can you imagine, Alan, I am nearly through with it! I am on my last chapter! And it is true to life, or very nearly. And . . ."

"Verity," he interrupted. "Was there none who'd come to your aid? Your grandmother?"

"I wrote to my grandmother," she said with a touch of bitterness. "I received no answer. And Staples . . ."

"That damned brute!" Alan interrupted furiously. "Kitty told me the whole of it. I'd have come that very day, but I did not arrive until late, and as luck would have it, I reached home to find messages that demanded my appearance in the country. It was imperative that I go, and believe me, I resented every moment I could not come here and fetch you."

"But I owe . . ."

"That petty debt has been discharged," he said.

"By you?" she asked in a small voice.

"By me, of course."

"You should not say 'of course,' " she cried. "You have helped me in so many ways . . . I do not want . . ."

"Hush, my dear, are we not cousins?"

She raised tearful eyes to his face. "I do not deserve to be your cousin, Alan, not after all the horrid things I said."

"My dear," he countered gently, "that is water under many bridges. And you must continue to call me cousin, else I would be hard put to answer to Gerry and Jasper—both have told me they are your protectors."

"Oh," Verity squeaked. "Do you know them?"

"Yes, we were at Eton together. Gerry and I were in the same form and Jasper a term behind us."

"Oh, that is a coincidence!"

"There are many such coincidences in debtors' prisons." He grimaced. He added with a frown, "You've been fortunate indeed to have Gerry and Jasper to shield you. When I think of what might have happened . . ."

"I know I've been uncommonly fortunate," she agreed.

"Oh, Verity, Verity." He put his arms around her holding her against him. "If only I'd been here." He released her quickly. "But I am here, and it's growing late. You must not spend another night under this roof. Where's your portmanteau? Do you have much to pack? Kitty told me that many of your garments were lost when . . . oh, God, that abandoned creature!" He frowned at her. "How could you have trusted a stranger met in a stagecoach?"

"I didn't trust her," she flared. "Far from it. I only asked a direction."

"Of a pawnshop," he finished. "Did you not know that she would immediately guess your purpose? But what choice had you, poor girl, with nowhere to turn? I cannot believe that your grandmother would be so adamant. It is very possible that she was not at home."

"I do not suppose anything of the sort," Verity responded. "She wanted me to go to the country, and I did not go. She was also informed that I eloped"—Verity flushed—"with you. Someone she knows saw me getting into your hackney. Fortunately, she didn't know your identity. Anyhow, had Grandmother helped me I would have been exchanging one prison for another. And actually, I've enjoyed myself here. I've felt so free."

"Free!" he exploded.

"Well, 'tis true," she insisted. "But I shall be glad to leave," she hastened to assure him, not wanting him to believe her ungrateful. Actually, she realized, she was utterly delighted to be leaving, even though she was not sure where they would be going. She could not return to the Staples menage, surely. And nor did she want to be dependent upon Alan, but she could not raise that question now. Her mind, wrested from her story, was in a turmoil, and the more she tried to concentrate, the more involved her thoughts became. Dominating them was, of course, *Alan*, looking so handsome in his new garments, and there was so much she wanted to say to him—so much she wanted to hear him tell her about his travels. She had not realized she had missed him so much. It had been wonderful to feel his arms around her—but why had he released her so quickly? Once he had told her that he loved her, but obviously he had taken her rejection much to heart.

Her whirling thoughts were interrupted by the loud knocks on the door that she had grown to associate with Sir Gerald and Mr. Lithcombe, who did not wait for her response, but came striding into the room to stare at Alan, who smiled back at them.

"I see you found her," Mr. Lithcombe observed.

"I did, thank you."

"And no doubt she has agreed to leave with you?" Sir Gerald inquired.

"She has not raised any objection to my plan," Alan responded.

"Oh, dear, I wish you were going with us." Verity held out both hands and had them rapturously kissed by her two protectors.

"They will be gone from here as soon as I can arrange it," Alan assured her.

Sir Gerald stared at him and then cleared his throat. "Lord, man, that's carrying the old school spirit a bit far. I cannot repay such generosity quickly."

"Nor I," Mr. Lithcombe agreed, blinking his eyelids very fast.

"You will pay me when you can," Alan said and shrugged.

"That might take a—reasonably long time," Mr. Lithcombe said gruffly.

"I can wait," Alan assured him. He added, "While I would dearly like to remain here and . . ."

"No, you wouldn't, old man," Mr. Lithcombe interrupted. "And will you remember . . ."

"To speak to Miss Renard? Yes, but 'twill hardly be necessary. You will be seeing her on the morrow."

"Heigh-ho for the old school spirit!" Mr. Lithcombe said throatily, and there was no concealing the tears that began to roll down his cheeks. Then, before Verity knew it, she was hugged by both gentlemen, who released her hastily, apologizing practically in unison for having taken such liberties.

There were tears in her own eyes as she hugged each of them in turn.

A short time later, Verity, with Alan carrying her portmanteau and exclaiming angrily over its lightness, came down the stairs, walking hastily through the snowy twilight toward the prison gates.

Three

"For oft, when on my couch I lie
In vacant or in pensive mood,
They flash upon that inward eye,
Which is the bliss of solitude;
And then my heart with pleasure fills,
And dances with the daffodils."

Staring at the daffodils fluttering in a breeze which must be much akin to that which had set Wordsworth's famous "crowd of golden daffodils" in motion, Verity found moody pleasure in his words. Though he was no longer in fashion and was much denigrated by younger poets such as Byron, she disagreed with them. Wordsworth still enchanted her.

Sinking down upon the tall spring grass sprouting on the Heath, Verity wished she could find her present solitude as blissful as had the poet or that she could draw some inspiration from the myriads of wild flowers that had seemingly sprung up overnight. Keats would have had no difficulty. She envied him for his detachment, though he was not to be envied, surely, with his brother dead and himself ill, though not gravely, she prayed. She did not want to think of that but of the fact that he had met a girl called Fanny Brawne and had fallen deeply in love. Think of the fact that he had left his lodgings in Well Walk and was now dwelling with Charles Amitage Brown in Wentworth Place and, the Dilkes having moved out, was a wall away from Fanny, her mother and sister, who had rented the other half of the cottage. She did wish the best for Keats—wanted to see him sharing the entire cottage with Fanny Brawne, such a pretty girl, so bright and gay.

She frowned. It seemed so unfair that Keats should live under the threat of consumption when scribblers like herself were so healthy, though Alan had told her that in meeting Sir Gerald, she had been granted more than a room.

"Had you been put in the infirmary, you might have contracted jail fever." He had actually shuddered.

She had been singularly fortunate, she knew. Lying back on the grass, she actually glared at that vivid spring sky.

She had no right to be in so contrary a frame of mind, and would not be if she had resisted what she had imagined to be the enchantment of a May morning on Hampstead Heath. In a sense it was enchanting, and if she were a poet, she would have written about warbling birds and buzzing insects, sprouting grasses, but not daffodils; she would have chosen another flower, certainly. She might also have thrown in squirrels and badgers, though she hadn't seen many. One did not really *see* badgers, did one? They burrowed in the ground—and she wouldn't have seen one had it sat on her hand. She was too intent on her inner visions and more specifically that of Lord Glendacre striding across this same Heath. No, not Glendacre. She could be much more specific than that. She could remember Alan, who had been jealous and herself angry. He had said he loved her and she had furiously rejected his love.

Had she been furious?

She had been extremely furious, had told him she never wanted to see him again . . . damn him! She smote the ground with her fist. Why had he not asked her a second time? And what had happened in Rome? Recently he had spoken of wanting to go back there. She sniffed, blinked, and frowned. Of what use were sniffles and tears? It was too late to weep over Alan. And besides, if she had lost him as a lover, at least he had remained her friend. He had been unswervingly helpful in these last few months.

He had found out through some grapevine or other that her grandmother and sisters were visiting in Devon, which is why she had not heard from her. He had paid her debts. He had insisted on finding and paying for new lodgings in the Vale of Health, not far from Leigh Hunt's old villa and far enough away from Well Walk so that she need not be reminded of her unfortunate experiences there. When she had protested his generosity, insisting that she could not accept money from him, he had responded that he expected to be paid back from the proceeds of her book.

"But you've not read it," she had protested.

"I do not need to read it. I read your face when you spoke of your writing and I knew you believed in it. Consequently, I must perforce believe in it, also."

"You must read it!"

"I shall be delighted to read it," he responded eagerly.

The frown she had not known she retained until she felt it lowering her eyebrows grew even deeper. He had read it in a night and returned it to her early in the morning. He had told her she had tapped a gold mine. She remembered his words— "There have been books that have sold out at first printing simply on the reputation of the author. You will have such a reputation once this book is released. That is what I prophesy, Cousin Verity." He had kissed her hand.

Though she was sure he meant what he had told her, she had sensed a certain inexplicable withdrawal in him—a formality that had not been present before he read the book. She hoped it was her imagination. It was not her imagination. At first, she had feared his disapproving of the autobiographical character of the novel. Yet, when she questioned him about that, he had assured her that she was following the lead of nearly every author who had penned a book. "Each of us puts part of himself into his work. Nothing is ever plucked whole from the realms of fantasy."

"But you've not been in Egypt or Greece," she had argued.

"I cannot think people differ so greatly from era to era or from country to country. Religions might change, governments, too—but not human nature," he had responded. "I have never known an Italian to complain about Shakespeare's *Othello*, which is set partially in Venice. Nor do I think a Dane would find Hamlet's motives out of the ordinary." He had gone on to mention a good many other works, eventually waxing quite philosophical on the subject of writing. Yet the feeling of estrangement had remained and still troubled her.

If she could not blame it on the book, what had occasioned it?

Maybe it was her imagination—for certainly he had continued to visit her, and also he had taken her book to Mr. Newman, who had subsequently told her it had been Alan's enthusiasm for the work that had prompted him to read it overnight, something he rarely did.

Consequently, she could credit Alan with its almost instant publication, for once Mr. Newman read it, he had changed his schedules and placed *The Divorce, or: The Fall and Rise of Lady Portia Pennington*, as it was now entitled, at the top of his lists. It had come out in April, and now, though it was only the middle of May, a second edition had sold out and a third had just appeared.

Alan had rejoiced with her, had brought her to Hunt's house in Kentish Town, where she had been praised by the great man himself, who, though he had admitted he read few romances, said he had found this surprisingly readable. He also admired her bravery in describing a situation he, himself, found most reprehensible, saying, "Jealousy is the most deadly of all the seven sins—or perhaps I should call it the eighth sin, since envy is not quite the same thing."

Hunt had also assured her that though he knew her identity, he would never reveal it, and he went on to say that Alan had told him her writing was more than a cut above those authors whose effusions usually appeared in the shelves of circulating libraries. He had cocked an eye at her and added, "My dear, I not only found that Alan was quite correct about your writing ability, I also found that I could not put it down." He had added, "I can quite understand why it has caused such a stir."

That had confused her. "Such a stir?" she questioned.

"It has sold out twice and extremely rapidly; a third edition is planned. Would you not call that a stir?" Alan had inquired.

She could have sworn that he was annoyed, but since there could be only one reason for this and she dared not even think of professional jealousy in connection with him, she decided that once more she was letting her imagination roam too freely. No, something *was* wrong, she was sure of it, and once she would have asked him—but that was a long time ago, before she had so curtly rejected his love.

"Ohhhh." She turned over on her stomach, face down in the grass with some of its blades tickling her cheeks and all sorts of little sounds reaching her ears—sounds that she could

not identify, sounds that might belong to the insect world.
Miss Marshall had studied insects. She could easily have told
her what they were.

Miss Marshall.

Verity sat up and hugged her knees, wondering about her
governess and chiding herself for not having thought about
her recently. She did miss her, had missed her and had not
even realized that she missed her. Miss Marshall had been her
one confidante—more than that, her dear friend, who was so
very wise—and how was she faring? She could send money
to her now—she had money to spare and had repaid her debt
to Alan. He had not wanted to take it, but she had insisted.
She would discuss the matter of Miss Marshall with Alan.
Perhaps they could even go to see her. Where was Clavering
from here? Alan would know. Her eyes gleamed. He would
be here this afternoon. He had promised to bring her the first
volume of the third edition.

He was so kind.

She did not want him to be kind! She wanted him to be
bold and aggressive—to seize her in his arms as had Uni, his
Egyptian slave hero, after capturing the haughty Princess
Seneb-nek-tet. There had been a similarly exciting moment in
his Grecian novel when Theo, his charioteer hero, had rescued the beautiful priestess of Delphi, Aphrodite. Oh, she
was being nonsensical, and worse yet, childish. If the last
months had taught her anything, they had taught her the utter
futility of yearning for the impossible. Realistically speaking,
she had Alan's friendship and must needs be satisfied with
that. He was a proud man, she knew. She had not only
rejected him, she had done it so cruelly, cruelly, cruelly!
Tears moistened her eyes. She had wounded him, and
consequently, while he was abroad in Italy, he had found
someone to assuage his hurts.

Alan was handsome, charming, courteous, and, she was
positive, beginning to be well-to-do. There were plenty of
women who would be only too happy if he glanced in their
direction.

Whom had he seen who pleased him? she wondered fiercely.
A Roman girl? A Venetian? A Florentine?

If only Miss Marshall had been here to advise her all those
months ago!

"If, if, if," she muttered resentfully. Rising, she went down the hill toward her lodgings. She would rest, bathe, and perhaps do a little writing before Alan appeared. She had an idea for another book, but it was quite amorphous at present. She would be perfectly composed when he arrived, perfectly friendly when she greeted him, because that was all he seemed to want.

Three hours later, Verity was wearing her latest muslin gown, finished only yesterday by the talented Miss Catley. As usual, it was surprisingly stylish, and with the new fuller body, something she hoped Alan would notice. She moved up and down her bedroom impatiently. Alan was late, which was unusual for him. Though she knew she was being ridiculous, her punishing mind kept presenting her with horrid visions of his horse stumbling and throwing him into a ditch or, worse yet, in the path of a curricle or stagecoach. Such accidents had happened, were always happening. She read about them every day in the London *Times*.

"Milady!" A door slammed.

Verity turned to find Kitty dashing toward her. She tensed. To have just pictured Alan lying pale and bloodied under the hooves of four horses and to see Kitty, wide-eyed and breathless, was extremely jolting. "My dear, what has happened?" she cried.

"Oh, milady, it's 'im and M-Mark. An' 'e's been promoted to 'ead coachman and looks as smart as anything, milady. An' . . . an' I never thought it would 'appen."

"What?" Verity hurried to Kitty's side and caught her by the shoulders. To her horror, tears were coursing down the abigail's cheeks. "What has happened?" she cried. "An accident?"

"Oh, no, milady. 'E wants to see you, 'n' Mark, 'e still remembers me. I didn't think 'e would 'n' 'e said 'e'd missed me somethin' dreadful all these months. Oh, milady!" Kitty grew even paler. "Listen to me . . . I beg yer pardon. I shouldn't 'ave gone on about it, only 'twas so unexpected-like. An' 'e's waitin' outside. 'E says 'e must see you." Kitty burst into great sobs.

"Kitty." Verity put an arm around her. "My dear, what is the matter?"

'' 'E . . . 'is lordship wishes to see you, milady.'' Kitty actually wrung her hands. '' 'E's in the downstairs parlor.''

"His lordship?" Verity repeated, wonderingly.

'' 'E's downstairs, milady.'' Kitty wiped her eyes with the back of her hand.

"His lordship," Verity said a second time. "You'd not be meaning . . . my . . . Lord Unger?"

She did not need Kitty's whispered corroboration. Panic went through her. Derek had come to see her, and in a moment Alan would be arriving, and Derek would be positive that his worst suspicions had been fully born out. But perhaps it was not too late to head him off. Her first frantic idea had been to order Kitty to tell his lordship she was not at home. However, her second and better idea was to tell the abigail that she would see his lordship in her own parlor and that she must join Mark to await Alan's arrival—and explain that she had agreed to see her ex-husband and that she would speak to him later. Having issued this directive, she had a moment of pleasure in seeing the way Kitty's eyes lighted. Then, moving into her little parlor, she steeled herself to see Derek.

She had no doubt as to what had brought him here. He must have read the book! That was amazing, for he was not a novel reader, particularly of such novels as rolled off the Minerva Press. Someone of his or her acquaintance must have recognized the story and out of sheer malice presented it to him. Had her grandmother also received a book . . . and Caroline? Whether they had read it or not was hardly important. How had Derek managed to find her—that was important. She could think of only one way, and it hardly seemed feasible. Mr. Newman never revealed either the real names of his authors or their locations. Mail that came for them was always forwarded to them from his office. Or was it possible that Lord Unger had met Sir Gerald? But Sir Gerald knew her only as Mrs. Farwell, and her pen name was Maiden. How had he found out?

"Milady." Kitty appeared in the doorway. "Lord Unger."

Verity managed to quell a sudden wild wish to inform Kitty she did not wish to see him. Then, with a calmness that amazed her, she said, "Please admit his lordship, Kitty."

"Yes, milady." Kitty's tones held a slight quaver. They sounded the way she was beginning to feel, but need *not* feel, because he had no claim on her, none at all! He could not drag her back to his chill castle and chain her in one of the towers as an enterprising ancestor had done to the woman of his choice. She was no longer the woman of Derek's choice. They were legally parted at his wish.

Her cogitations came to an abrupt end when he appeared in the doorway. She smothered a small cry. Was it because he was all in black that he looked so thin? No, his face, too, was thin. His cheekbones were more pronounced and his eyes were sunk in cavernous hollows. She had not known what she would say to him, but looking at him now, she could only ask, "You've been ill, my lord?"

"No, I am quite well, thank you. You are looking very well."

Had she caught a touch of surprise in his tone? She was not sure. "I thank you, my lord," she said, trying to ascertain his mood and not succeeding. Save for his wasted frame, he seemed much as he always seemed. Self-assured—and did she read condescension in his manner? Again, she was not sure.

"Verity." He smiled now. "What a time this has been. All this needless suffering, and for what? If, in the beginning, you had trusted me as a woman is supposed to trust her husband and let me know you were a published author, none of this confusion and folly would have taken place. Your comings and goings would not have been conducted under a shroud of secrecy. But no matter, I have read your book."

"I did not know you were fond of romances, my lord," she said caustically.

He paused, and then he said with some asperity, "Did you imagine I would not read this volume when it is the talk of the town?"

"The talk of the town?" she repeated incredulously.

"Sure that cannot surprise you," he burst out, and for the first time, his eyes blazed with the white-hot fury she remembered so well. "I am glad that my poor mother . . ." He paused in midsentence. "No matter," he said in a calmer voice. "As I told you, I have read your book. And I have found your explanation entirely satisfactory."

She did not care for his manner. The condescension she

had suspected was very much in evidence now. She said,
"That is what you have come to tell me, my lord?"

"Not entirely. I also wish you to know that I went to see
Cassandra Dilhorne just before she was sent to the country.
The servants attempted to deny me access, but I did manage
to see her. She has confessed the whole imposture, she and
Glendacre, too, though it was he who came to see me."

"Glendacre!" Verity exclaimed. "He told you where to
find me?"

"No, no, that man Mr. Hunter, whom I met when I was
attempting to persuade your publisher to give me your direction.
He very kindly told me where I might find you."

"He did!" she exclaimed incredulously.

"Yes, yes," he said impatiently. "But what can it matter
who told me, Verity? I am here. I know the truth, and I have
reached the conclusion that I acted very hastily. You, of
course, were partially to blame. If, as I have mentioned, you
had been frank with me . . . but I will not dwell upon the
past. I will freely admit that an injustice has been done. I
was, as I have said, hasty in my assumptions—but what man
would not have been confounded by your falsehoods, your
stratagems, and your most unconvincing explanations? Quite
naturally, I suspected a liaison. I am very pleased to have
been proved wrong. I wish you to know that I do believe the
account contained in your novel is largely accurate."

Verity's teeth came together with a click. She was beginning to breathe deeply. Her fingers were curled against her
palms, the nails biting into her flesh. Words piled upon her
tongue, words about his odious and *extremely* apparent
condescension! His attitude reminded her strongly of a judge
pardoning one who, suspected of criminal activities, has been
exonerated but, at the same time, gently denigrating him for
his arrant stupidity. Her range was two-pronged, part of it
directed at Alan, who had told her husband where to find her.
How could he have betrayed her, he who knew how much
she had suffered because of Derek's untoward behavior? Why
had he done it? Why, why? The question beat against her
brain, but she could not try to fathom the workings of his
mind at this moment, not with Derek standing here munifi-
cently forgiving her—forgiving *her!* With deceptive sweetness,

she said softly, "It's kind of you to tell me that, my lord. I can imagine the effort it must have cost you."

"No." He smiled at her now. "It was no effort at all, my dear. I deemed it necessary to let you know that I have been partially in error."

"I see," she said, wishing he would leave, needing to find Alan, longing to tell him exactly what she thought of him.

"Verity, I have something else I wish to say to you."

She stifled a groan. Evidently she was not to be rid of Derek so soon, unless she ordered him out. She could not do that, but she would try to cut short his visit. She said dismissively, "I do not think you have to tell me anything more, my lord."

"You do not understand the main purpose of my visit." He hesitated and swallowed. "This has been a trying . . . a very difficult winter for me—and for you, too, I gather. And . . ."

"I have survived, my lord," she interjected coldly.

"Please." He held up a hand. "I pray you'll let me continue. My mother's dead." He paused, but before she could offer condolences, he hurried on. "I have been very lonely without you. I want you to know that I have decided that we should resume our marriage."

There was a roaring in her ears. She felt as if she must be dreaming. "I . . . do not know what to say. . . ." She faltered.

"I understand. I know you must be surprised, because I am a man who rarely changes his mind. But I have changed my mind. Your book pointed the way. It was very well expressed. And certain of my friends who have a bent for literature have praised it, all unknowing that I had any connection with the author. In your book, you wrote of Lord Lucius's dislike of romances. However, I would not frown on your continuing with your work. In her younger years, my mother enjoyed painting with water colors. There are some examples of them at Unger Castle."

"I have seen them," Verity said through her teeth, her fury rising again at his daring to compare those ghastly daubs with her writing.

"Yes, they are unexceptionable, are they not? As I was saying, however, I want you to take your place beside me as my wife again. I will publish a retraction of all my claims in the divorce. I will send it to the *Times* and to the *Morning Post*. We will go through another marriage ceremony, private, of course. I should like to arrange it as soon as possible. Within the week. Are you in agreement with me, Verity?''

"No, my lord, I am not," she said in a small constricted voice. Her fury had swelled to immense proportions. Again, she was decrying her lack of inches. She would have given a great deal to meet him eye to eye.

"Perhaps a week is a little early," he continued. "A fortnight?"

"I do not wish to resume our marriage, my lord."

He regarded her amazedly. "But you do. 'Tis why I came!"

"And who provided you with that information, my lord? Mr. Hunter, perhaps?"

"Mr. Hunter, no! 'Twas in your book!"

"My book?" she echoed incredulously. "What can you mean?"

He seized her by the shoulders. "Do not tell me you do not understand me. Oh, God, do not continue to punish me in this cruel way, Verity. I know I have been unreasonable, and perhaps you still fear the jealousy you described, the jealousy that left you alone and unprotected. Oh, Verity, to think of you in such terrible straits, in a debtors' prison. 'Twas all my fault. I never should have mistrusted you. It was only that I love you so much, and my mother . . . No, I blame myself for all that happened. I have been in torment. Oh, Verity, why are you so silent? Please tell me that I haven't lost you. Tell me that you'll come back to me. I feel only half alive without you. Lady Portia forgave Lord Lucius when he came to see her and said he was truly sorry. I am truly sorry, my dearest. Please say you forgive me." Amazingly, he fell on his knees. "See, I kneel at your feet. I want you. I need you. Come back with me, come back today. Oh, Verity, please forgive me." There were tears in his eyes.

Her book. She remembered now. Lady Portia had forgiven Lord Lucius, and Derek, reading *The Divorce*, had taken it literally. That was why he had come.

"Verity!" Derek rose and caught her hand. "Tell me that you have forgiven me."

Looking into his anguished eyes, she found them full of tears. She was thunderstruck. In the nearly two years of their marriage, she had often seen him angry, but seldom contrite. She had never seen him weep! Facing him, her anger melted away. She had not expected to pity him, but she did. As for forgiving him, she could do that, too. If it had not been for him, she might never have had experiences which had not only enriched her life but had given her insights into human nature she could never have gained had she continued living in the sheltered, circumscribed existence she had shared with Derek.

Because of her husband's irrational jealousy, she had been pushed out of that world and had become, she hoped, a wiser and better person, more attuned to the sufferings of others, attuned, also, to Derek's inner turmoil. She blamed much of that on his mother. She could not mourn the late marchioness. Something Reggie had said on that fatal night came back to her. He had called Derek the Hermit of Unger and also mentioned that his father had been a "merry old soul." And unfaithful as well, she guessed. The marchioness must have been very jealous, and had she transmitted some of those feelings to the son, whom she had ruled with so firm a hand? She was to blame for much of Derek's notions. She had filled him with vainglorious pride and never allowed the better, the more tender part of his nature to expand—and he could be tender, she recalled. He had been a tender lover. It was very possible that his mother had fanned his suspicions of herself in the hopes that he would put her aside and marry again to provide the estate with a bride who in turn could produce an heir. She pushed these memories away, saying gently, "Yes, I do forgive you, Derek."

"Oh, my dearest, thank God. If you only knew how much I have missed you! I have been in agony. Please, please, say you will come back to me!"

Listening to him, Verity felt very sorry for this man who had been her husband, but, at the same time, her impatience was increasing. She wanted to see Alan, who had inadvertently forced this uncomfortable scene upon her. Yet if she were to give Derek an outright refusal, there would be an argument and more anguished protestations of his love. She did not think she could bear that.

She said carefully, "I cannot give you an answer at this moment, Derek. I must think about it."

"Think about it?" he repeated incredulously and with a trace of his old irascibility.

"Yes, I must think about it," she repeated, wishing he would leave, willing him to go.

"No." He seized her hands in a convulsive and hurtful grip. "You need not think, nor need you fear that in returning you'll be ostricized. As I have said, I will make them take you back. Your grandmother will stand behind you. I have seen her and your sisters. They miss you, too. Verity, you do not belong in this backwater. You belong with *me*. I want you to come now, at this moment. Have your abigail pack your things. No, I will buy you all you need. Come with me now, be with me." He released her hands only to fling his arms around her, kissing her passionately.

Any pity she might have entertained for him was replaced by anger at this untoward but typical behavior. Despite all he had said, he had learned nothing. He had never considered her feelings, and he never would. Since she was not strong enough to push him away, she waited passively until he finally lifted his head, and then she slapped him hard across the cheek. "How dare you treat me in so disrespectful a manner, my lord!" she demanded coldly.

"Disrespectful?" he echoed angrily. "You are my wife!"

"We are no longer wed, my lord."

"We are in the sight of God!" he exclaimed.

"But not in the sight of the magistrate's court," she responded hotly. "Now I must ask you to leave, please."

"I will not leave until you come with me." He moved toward her purposefully.

She looked him directly in the eyes. "My lord, you have no right to intimidate me. Now, please, I beg you will go."

His whole body seemed to sag. He released a long quavering sigh that ended in a moan. "Oh, Verity, I am sorry. I have acted as I promised myself I would never act toward you again. It's just that I love you so desperately. My life is nothing without you beside me. In the months you have been gone, my mother pressed me to wed again, but I could not look at another woman. But I will go now and let you think on what I have said. Believe me, I have learned my lesson, and if you should do me the great honor of returning to me, I will spend my life proving to you that I *am* a changed man. Please tell me that you believe me.''

Alan, Alan, Alan. His name pounded through her brain. She wanted to dismiss Derek, longed to tell him that she did not believe him because in that one action he had negated all his promises, had proved he would never be able to contain his passions or control his jealousy. Once he had her back, it would be the same as it had always been. She had difficulty repressing a shudder. Total rejection trembled on her tongue, but she needed to get to Alan, quickly, quickly, she was not sure why, she only knew that it was imperative that she see him at once. As calmly and evenly as she might, she said, ''I will think about what you have told me, Derek, but I must ask you to leave me now, please.''

He seemed to actually tremble, and when he spoke again it was in low throbbing tones. ''When may I come to you again?''

Her patience was fast deserting her. She must, must, must get rid of him. ''Tomorrow!'' she said hastily.

He seized her hand, carrying it to his lips. ''When tomorrow?''

''In the afternoon.'' Would he never go!

''When in the afternoon?''

''Two!''

''Can it not be earlier? In the morning, please?''

Looking into his eager, pleading, anxious eyes, Verity's heart turned over. In her haste to see Alan, she was being wantonly cruel. She could not dismiss Derek with hope in his heart. He had suffered enough. She said gently, ''Derek, I am deeply sorry, but I cannot see you tomorrow or any other time.''

''You cannot . . .'' he repeated incredulously, the color draining from his face. ''But you said . . .''

''I know what I said, and I was wrong. I would only tell you tomorrow what I have tried to tell you today. I cannot be your wife again. Too much has happened. I would not fit into your world anymore.''

''That is madness,'' he cried desperately. ''It's your world, too.''

"No," she said gently. "No longer. I would not be received."

"You would, you will. I will stand behind you."

"No, Derek. Even were I to be pardoned for my . . . sins, I would not feel comfortable, knowing what I know now, about cruelty and injustice. I could not attend the theater without thinking what can happen to a young actress if she is not a Miss O'Neill or a Miss Mardyn, if, for instance, she is behind in her rent and without a part and must be thrown into debtors' prison. I could not patronize fancy mantua makers and know that there are poor girls pawning their garments for a crust of bread. I could not dance at Carlton House and see all those riches and remember that here in Hampstead Village, there is a poet who has more beauty crammed into his head than is in all of those marble staircases and those paintings, and this poor young man must live in poverty and perhaps die of it. I am only giving you a tiny fragment of what I have seen, and there is much more. You must understand why I am not able to return."

His brows had drawn together. "I think I do understand, madame."

She tensed. He had spoken in the tone of voice he had used that night. "I am glad," she said. "Now will you go? I do not think we have anything more to say to each other, my lord."

"Who is this poet?" he actually snarled. "No matter—I do not wish to know his name."

"And if you did, would you call him out?" she inquired contemptuously.

"Do not try my patience too far, madame." He caught her by the shoulders. "I should have known," he continued between gritted teeth. "I should have known that in all this time you'd not have wanted for companionship. Nor have you. Why do you not tell me the truth, wanton? Why do you not tell me that you and your lovers . . ."

"Let me go, Derek," she said icily.

"Very well, I will let you go, and good riddance. Stay here in your dung heap, madame. I am done with you." Shaking her, he threw her down, and turning on his heel, he rushed from the room.

Verity lay where she had fallen for no longer than the

second it took him to leave. Then she stood up slowly. Various parts of her body ached, but at the same time, she felt marvelously free. In his previously chastened mood, it had been difficult to dismiss Derek. Despite the fact that she no longer had any feeling for him, she would not have wanted to hurt the man he had supposedly become, but he had not changed. Only she had changed.

She went to the window, and looking down in the street she saw Derek's post chaise. Standing beside it were Kitty and Mark, his coachman. As she watched, she saw them smiling at each other. Then they broke apart quickly and Mark leaped to his seat while a footman hurried forward to open the door of the vehicle. Derek, coming into view, thrust the man aside, climbing into the post chaise, and leaned forward, obviously yelling a command. There was barely time for the footman to clamber to his perch before they were off and whirling out of sight in a cloud of dust.

Verity darted to the door and dashed down the stairs, barely missing Kitty, who was coming up.

"Where are you going, milady?" the girl cried.

"Nowhere—I'll be back," Verity answered.

"You'll need your cloak. 'Tis turning cool."

Verity did not answer. She only quickened her steps. It was not until she had climbed up Windmill Hill and was in sight of Alan's lodgings that she slowed down long enough to catch her breath. Reaching the door of the house she had seen such a long time ago, she remembered the little boy rolling his hoop, remembered, also, Alan's reluctance to identify him. Probably he would not approve her coming, but his approval or the lack of it did not concern her. She wanted to know, had to know, why he had deliberately told Derek where to find her. Reaching the door, she slammed the knocker against its plate.

A minute later, a heavyset woman, dressed in a neat blue-and-white gingham gown, opened the door. "Yes?" she asked in some surprise.

Verity, discerning a resemblance to that small boy, guessed she was Mrs. Ridley, Alan's landlady, and felt embarrassed. In her mad dash up the hill she had not considered how unconventional her visit must seem. It was too late to consider the conventions. Though she could not have explained why she felt as she did, she knew she must see him as soon as possible. Endeavoring to sound a good deal more dignified than she felt, she said, "I am a friend of Mr. Parry, your lodger. I must see him. I hope he is home."

The woman eyed her curiously. "He has his own entrance, miss. It's that green door at the side of the house—if he's still there. I think he might be. I didn't hear him ride away."

"He is leaving?"

"Yes." The landlady sounded regretful. "He tells me he plans to start traveling again, across the seas, perhaps. He did not know whether he would leave this afternoon or tomorrow morning. It's sorry I am to see him go. He is such a nice-mannered gentleman."

"Yes," Verity agreed, thinking bitterly that his manners were too nice—especially in regards to estranged husbands! "His lodgings are where?"

"To your right, miss. A green door."

"Thank you." Verity hurried down the path and around the side of the house. There was the green door with its bright brass knocker. She hurried up a pair of steps, lifted the knocker, and slammed it against its plate as loudly as she could. Had he gone? She strained to hear the sound of footsteps—but heard nothing. She lifted the knocker again and again slammed it down as hard as she could, and then did it again. He could not have gone, not yet, not yet, but perhaps he would have done her the courtesy of bidding her farewell—and here she was on the hill and he would ride away and she would never see him again and never under-stand the reasons behind his actions, never, never. She knocked a fourth time and would have done it a fifth had not the door been pulled open and sent crashing back against the wall.

Verity stepped back as she was confronted by an Alan she had never seen before. He was in shirt and trousers only. His feet were bare and his hair was tousled. His eyes, she noted, were bloodshot and angry. "Well, wha'sit?" he demanded in a strangely slurred voice.

"Alan!" she cried. "I must talk to you!"

He seemed to become aware of her for the first time. "Ver'ty, wha you doin' here?" He stared at her owlishly. "Oh, think I understan' . . . come in." He moved back.

She came into a small hall and thence into a roomy parlor,

with a large window to one side. It was lined with books, and
there were more volumes piled on the floor. There was a
large desk, several comfortable chairs, and a table. On the
table was a bottle of brandy and a goblet.

"Sit down . . . sit down . . ." Alan waved at a chair.
"Suppose you want to thank me . . . don' have to thank me,
though. Knew you wanted it . . . two lovin' hearts torn
asunder . . . reunited . . . jus' like the book said."

"You're drunk!" she accused.

"Yes." He gave her a lopsided bow, coupling it with a
mocking smile. "But I'm not so far gone tha' I cannot
understan' your expressions of gratitude—gentleman can always hold his liquor, tha's what my father said. Father a
gentleman. But why're you here? Should've thought that by
now, little Kitty'd packed an' you'd be on your way back to
London to your rightful place in society to live happily ever
after. Wasn't that how you had it in your novel?"

"My novel!"

"Yes, your novel . . . lil' Portia an' Lord Lucius . . . long
may they reign!" Moving to the table, he picked up the
bottle. "Think I'll toast the happy couple. Felicitations all
around."

"Oh, Alan!" She ran to him and took the bottle out of his
hand. "You fool!"

"Fool!" He glared at her. "Why're you calling me a
fool?"

"Because you are!" she cried hotly. "Oh, why are you
foxed? You won't be able to understand anything I would
very much like to tell you. How could you knowing what you
know . . . how could you dream that I would want to live
happily ever after with Derek?"

"Said as much in your book . . . said it, wrote it . . ." He
passed a hand over his brow. "And I read it."

"My book's a novel, damn you!"

"Not novel . . . true, all true, just clad in novel binding
. . . like sheep in wolf's clothing . . ."

"It was a novel, I tell you! At least part of it was. And for
you to give Derek my direction, when I never wanted to see
him again! Oh, it is outside of enough!" She stamped her
foot.

He stared at her for a long moment before he said confusedly but a trifle more clearly, "You seem to be angry."

"No," she retorted. "I am not angry, Alan, I am furious, do you understand? Oh, dear, how can you understand anything?"

He stared down at her. "I understand that you are furious. Why're you furious?"

"Because . . . I mean, how could you think that I loved Derek when I love you . . ." She paused, one hand creeping to her mouth. She had not meant to tell him that. "I mean . . ."

"What do you mean, Verity?" His eyes had grown much more intent. "My understanding's a bit clouded, but it seems to me you just said . . ."

Looking up at him, she found she could not retract anything she had said. "I love you, Alan. I do, my dearest. I have loved you for such a long, long time." Her voice broke.

He said slowly, half unbelievingly, "But you told me once . . ."

"I know. I remember. I have wanted to . . . I . . . a thousand times, I've wanted, but . . ." Her tongue was becoming hopelessly twisted. "I thought you didn't care for me because I'd hurt you so . . . but, oh, Alan, my darling, was it only that stupid book?"

"It seemed to me that you wanted to go back to him."

"Never! I wrote it that way because of my readers, who'd expect Portia to return to her c-castles. They couldn't understand why she wanted to be free or that she hadn't known what living was like until she'd fallen from grace. They'd not understand why she couldn't go back to constraint and fear and misery and jealousy, where she could not mention any man, look at any man, talk to any man without being accused of . . . but you know, you should understand. I told you what it was like." Her eyes filled with tears. "Alan, prisons without bars are more terrible than anyone can ever realize."

"I should know that," he said slowly. "I, too, have lived in such prisons." He stared at her. "You're weeping," he added huskily. "You shouldn't weep. My head's not clear enough, you know. Never could drink brandy . . . drank too much. After meeting your Lord Lucius and telling him how to reach you, I wanted oblivion. I was miserable. I thought I was the villain of the piece, do you see."

"Oh, no, oh, no, not you. Not you, my dearest, dearest Alan, I never thought that you would t-take it . . . personally." She began to cry in earnest.

He touched her hair and let his hand trail down her cheek, "Don't . . . mustn't cry, Verity. It hurts me. I love you. I love you so much."

"Still . . ." she whispered.

"Still, always and forever." He opened his arms and then let them fall to his side. "But you know nothing about me."

"I know all I want to know," she said tremulously.

"Not enough. . . . I want you to . . . meet my mother."

She felt a jolt of surprise. Somehow she had never connected Alan with a family—but everyone had a family. "I would love to meet your mother," she said warmly.

"Then you shall . . . you must. You'll have to come in here." He pointed to a door at the back of the parlor. "Bedchamber. You'll be safe. I'm a gentleman even in my cups."

"I know that," she said softly, keeping her arms pressed to her sides. He loved her. He still loved her and she loved him. She wanted to touch him, caress him, but now was not the time—and what could he mean about his mother?

His bedroom was small, furnished with a narrow bed, a chair, an armoire, and a night table. Hanging over the fireplace was a large portrait, depicting a ballerina clad in a long pink tutu. Her feet, encased in pink satin toe shoes, were crossed, and her long elegant hands were folded in her lap. A garland of ivy encircled her smooth dark hair. Her face was beautiful and familiar—the eyes, the dark eyes, were Alan's eyes! The shape of the face, the mouth, they too were duplicated in his features. "Oh, how lovely she is!" Verity breathed.

"Was," he corrected harshly.

"Oh, I am sorry."

"Do not be. I cannot think she was sorry to leave this world."

"She was a . . ."

"An opera dancer." His mocking smile reappeared. "Father saw her at Covent Garden. She'd come with an Italian company from Rome. He hastened backstage to meet her. He was just down from Oxford and he wanted to keep her. It was and is the thing to have at least one opera dancer as your mistress—but though my mother was attracted to him, she refused to bow to custom. She did not want to be his mistress. Her family was good, although poor. Her father was imprisoned in the Castel Sant'Angelo for his politics. Her dancing helped support her mother and younger brothers. Father fancied himself in love with her, and being wild to have her, he married her. His family was furious, but, you see, he was the only son. They had to stomach her even though they hated her."

"Oh, no," Verity whispered.

"Yes, it was difficult for her. But none of that mattered, because she loved my father and their marriage was blessed by a son. But my mother was frail. After my birth she became a semi-invalid, and that bored my father. He enjoyed London life, good company, pretty women—and when he was home, he loved the hunt. My mother was often ill, and he tired of her. She was miserable. I was miserable, too. Loved her, do you see."

"Oh, dear, how sad," Verity murmured.

"Yes," he agreed, adding bitterly, "She died when I was seven. Six months later, my father married a proper English lady of high degree, who loathed me, particularly after my half brother was born and she was forced to face the fact that he would inherit neither title nor estates."

"And your father?"

"He was of a similar persuasion. It embarrassed him that I was so dark, so un-English in appearance. They kept me out of sight whenever there were house parties. I spent a great deal of time in the library. That's where I started to write. Then I was sent to Eton, and after that my stepmother suggested I join the army. I was nothing loath. It meant being away from home. To them, it meant I might be killed and my brother could inherit."

"Oh, no," she moaned.

His mocking smile returned. "Unfortunately, the three fates are women and consequently capricious. I did not die. I survived, but was wounded at Vitoria and invalided home. I had lost a great many good comrades and I decided to sell out, and in order to forget the horrors I'd witnessed, I lived what is called a 'riotous existence.' I'll spare you the particulars—suffice it to say I got into debt and into the Marshalsea, not quite as comfortable a prison as the King's Bench. My father heard about it and paid my debts. 'Twas my stepmother suggested I sign my estates over to my brother, which I did and gladly.''

"Gladly?"

"Gladly." He smiled. "For by then I'd discovered I could write and support myself on the proceeds of my pen, which I have done, but as it happens, those fates have intervened again. My stepmother was killed in a hunting accident. My father is old, and very recently my half brother went boating on the lake that lies on our property and was drowned in a squall. So now I am called to come home and be a proper English gentleman. I had planned—cravenly, perhaps—to put as much space between myself and Somerset, where our holdings lie, as was possible. I had thought to journey, perhaps to America, but now . . ." He stared at her. "Perhaps I will make my peace with my father and take you to my home—where I shall try to be that proper English gentleman . . . if you can stomach my mother.''

"Oh," she cried indignantly. "You cannot know me if you ask me such a question. I wish only that she had not died . . . I should have liked to know her.''

"Oh, Verity . . ." He would have put his arms around her, but she moved away him.

"Alan, you must never be proper." She flushed. "I mean . . ."

His somber eyes suddenly glinted with laughter. "Yes, you must tell me what you mean.''

"I mean you must not go back to your home.''

He gave her a strange look. "You are speaking with your emotions, Verity. Home is a great estate . . . home is wealth and comfort . . . an earldom.''

"But you were never happy there.''

"They talk of duty. And now, it seems to me, I should assume those duties.''

"Damn them," she cried hotly. "They had a duty to you . . . and your mother. Your father sounds like a monster.''

"Not a monster, a peer of the realm, who loved unwisely and not well."

"Oh, no, then he was very wise," she said softly. "Your mother must have been a wonderful woman to have given birth to such a son."

"Verity," he said brokenly. "How is it possible to love you any more than I do already?"

"Alan." She held out her arms, crying passionately, "Take me . . . and show me how you love me."

"No, Verity." He shook his head. "You must go. Were I to touch you now, I'd not have the strength to let you go."

"I do not want you to let me go!"

"Only until tomorrow."

"Not tomorrow. I want to be with you now . . . let me stay, Alan. Please."

He shook his head. "I am my mother's son, my dearest. You can remain with me only if we are wed. And when we are wed, I will take you home with me. I could not continue living this hole-in-corner existence with you."

"Could you not?" She moved away from him and turned to face him. "Then, I beg you'll not marry me."

"Verity!" He looked at her in shock. "What can you mean?"

"I do not want you to be shackled!"

"Oh, my dearest angel." He crossed to her side. "I will love those chains!"

"I will not. I want to be here in Hampstead Village. I want a cottage. I want to write and I want you to write, or perhaps we may travel, but I have grown to love this place and everything about it. Oh, my darling, please stay . . . for my sake."

He stared down at her incredulously. "You really want to remain here, Verity?"

"With all my heart, Alan. Can you face me—can you look me in the eye and tell me that you do not want it, too?"

"No," he said slowly. "I cannot tell you that."

"Then, live with me here . . . where we both want to be. Will you . . . and find someone to manage your estates?"

"I could do that, could I not?"

"You could. You must."

"Yes, I must." His dark eyes gleamed. "My own darling

. . . my head is clear now . . . and I have reached two decisions.''

''Tell me what they are,'' she begged.

''One is . . . that we will stay, and the other . . . we must be wed tonight.''

''Tonight!'' she exclaimed. ''But we have to post banns . . . get a license . . .''

''My dearest love, I have never enjoyed my heritage until this moment.''

She regarded him confusedly. ''I do not understand. You are telling me that . . .''

''I am telling you that due to my family background and my own title, I have the connections to secure a special license.'' He smiled tenderly down at her. ''Which I shall do directly—but first . . .'' He pulled her into an embrace which, though postponed so long, proved to be entirely satisfactory in every respect.

Epilogue

The luggage, heaps of it, crammed the small hall, and seated on the lowest steps of the stairs going up to the first floor was a dark-haired little boy, crying loudly and inconsolably.

"Gracious!" exclaimed his harried mother, who was brushing the black curls of his four-year-old sister. "Where is Kitty?"

"With the baby, no doubt," said Lady Harcliffe, who was sitting on a high-backed chair in the sitting room adjoining the master bedroom of one of the larger villas on Windmill Hill. "Where is Miss Marshall? And my eldest grandson. I refuse to say great-grandson."

"They have gone into the city with Alan."

"Mama," the child complained. "You are pulling my hair."

"Sorry, Rosa, my love." Verity dropped a kiss on her daughter's head. "But I am finished with you. You may go and ask your brother what ails him."

"He wants to go to Wome, and so do I." Rosa looked at her mother out of accusing dark eyes.

"You will one day, my dearest."

"I want to go now."

" 'Tis too long a journey, my love. You will enjoy the country. Just think, you'll have your very own pony to ride, and you can play with Robbie, Uncle Jasper's little boy, and . . ."

"I like Wobbie." Rosa looked more cheerful. "Only he cannot wide as good as me."

"I thought Miss Marshall was teaching them grammar, not to mention pronunciation," Lady Harcliffe said tartly.

"Go along and comfort Alan." Verity cocked an ear. "But I do not think he is crying anymore."

"All wight. . . ." Rosa slipped out of the chair, curtsied to her great-grandmother, and dashed out of the room.

"You see, she does know her manners," Verity said defensively. "And you can hardly blame Miss Marshall because Rosa cannot pronounce her R's. It is possible that when you were four, you might have had trouble with them, too."

"I was never four," her ladyship said grandly. "And do not defend that woman to me. You know what I think of her."

"I think that you agree with me that she is a jewel," Verity teased.

"Well," Lady Harcliffe said grudgingly, "she is good with the children. Which is why you should not take her to Rome with you."

"I would not dream of leaving her behind. It is her life's ambition to see the Eternal City." She sighed. "And she has long wanted to visit poor John Keats's grave, and Shelley's, too."

"Poor Bysshe," Lady Harcliffe said soberly. "To drown like that. And young Keats . . . they were both so young."

Verity nodded. "And now they lie side by side in the Protestant cemetery." She shook her head and said, "Jasper will miss Miss Marshall, too. He cannot cope with our tenants as she does, and the school she's started will be in recess until she returns. And Phoebe will have to visit the debtors' prisons in her stead."

"Jasper," Lady Harcliffe mused. "I like that man. And his wife, too, though I did think it odd that you and Alan made him estate manager, when you met him in debtors' prison. I do not call that proper credentials for managing."

"I met Sir Gerald in debtors' prison, and now . . ."

"Please, my dear, do not bruit that about. Your sister Eva's extremely touchy on the subject, especially now that he's become a Member of Parliament."

"I do hope Eva's not turning into a snob." Verity frowned.

"Eva's more cognizant of her position than either you or Caroline. It's hard for her, poor child, with the two of you wed to earls and she the wife of a mere baronet."

"She disapproves of me greatly." Verity laughed.

"I do, too." Her grandmother smiled at her. "You have done nothing right. Imagine with that huge estate in Somerset—and you will live here, the two of you, and scribble your books."

"Alan's novel *A Garden in Babylon* was favorably mentioned by the *Edingburgh Review*," Verity reminded her.

"I did not say you haven't done well, but your poor children are not even aware of their positions in life."

"Their positions, Grandmother, are to be our children," Verity said crisply. "We do not choose to live in Somerset, and we aren't going to leave them to the tender mercies of servants or even to Jasper and Phoebe, who have their own three. And Miss Marshall has all she can do, caring for the tenants' children and administering the fund for 'deserving prisoners.' Our children are perfectly happy here."

"And will you not send the boys to school?"

"When they are of age, they'll go to Eton and, I hope, to Cambridge, but it will be a long time before we must needs turn our attention to that."

"I suppose," Lady Harcliffe said tartly, "that we cannot expect proper behavior from artists. But I am glad that you had the good sense not to take them to Rome with you."

"No, that would be difficult, but I shall miss them."

"You'll be back with them soon enough," Lady Harcliffe said unsympathetically. She rose stiffly. "Well, I must go. I have waited to say farewell to your scapegrace husband long enough, but you must say it for me, my dear."

"I shall." Verity kissed her grandmother's withered cheek and accompanied her out to her waiting coach. She stood waving until it started down the hill, and after it had gone, she still stood just beyond the gates. She cast a look at the sky. Though the weather had been fine all that week, it could turn gray and cloudy at a moment's notice and might be just contrary enough to do it on the morrow when they would be taking ship from the London docks. And though in her busy life she was not given to dwelling much on the past, her grandmother's words had brought it back to her. She thought of her harried climb up this very hill all those years ago when Derek had told her Alan had given him her direction. She had been afraid, she remembered, that he no longer loved her . . . and then even more afraid that he had gone away. . . .

Well, they were still dwelling here and Derek was wed again, but none had seen his bride, because they never left the gloomy fastness of Unger Castle. She was unwilling to think about that. Better to think of their twice-postponed journey to Rome—once because of Eva's wedding to Sir Gerald Sutcliffe, which they could not have missed, and last year because she had found she was with child. She smiled fondly, thinking of little Verity, who much resembled Alan— all her children did, though Rosa, named after his mother, bore a slight resemblance to her great-grandmother. John, their eldest, named after John Keats, looked a bit like her— but he, too, would be dark, like his father.

John Keats.

Again Derek was in her mind, or rather that last mad outburst, when she had mentioned the poet and he had demanded to know his name. Would he have challenged poor John to a duel? He would surely have killed him—but a greater enemy than Derek had snuffed out that young life. And poor Fanny in black like a widow and looking like a ghost of her former self. . . . Tears filled Verity's eyes as she thought of his lonely death in Rome, where he never should have gone, it having been far too late to halt the progress of the disease.

She and Alan would strew flowers on his grave, beneath the stone, marked, at the poet's request, "Here lies one whose name was writ in water"—such bitterness, such unhappiness, such a longing to live and love, but his name was not written in water but in that same script that kept William Shakespeare's name alive. . . .

Her thoughts were scattered as a post chaise came up the hill. Jasper, who was due to collect the children this afternoon? No, it was their own—with Mark driving at that breakneck pace he still enjoyed, even though he was a staid married man these past five years, and Kitty, the mother of three children, who were also to be sent to the country, since her abigail would not be denied a sight of Rome. Mark had hardly brought the horses to a standstill when John jumped out, followed by his father and Miss Marshall, who seized hold of him and marched him toward their front door. He must have been naughty, Verity thought, and was about to follow them inside when Alan came up to her.

"What's amiss?" she inquired, gazing into his frowning face.

"Your son went a-wandering. Miss Marshall was frantic. And so was I."

"Oh, dear, did he go far?"

"Far enough. I was afraid we'd have to send the Runners after him."

"But he came back, it seems."

"He came back." Alan sighed. "It's a burden being a father."

"And, alas, one you cannot put down."

"Nor would I." His frown vanished, and he slipped his arm around her waist. "Are you nearly ready?"

"I shall be by dawn tomorrow, my love. You missed Grandmother—she has just gone."

"A pity."

"I do not believe you mean that," she chided.

"I am in no mood for one of her lectures on the subject of my high estate and low life."

"She is very fond of you."

"I am flattered." He bent to kiss her ear. "You are looking very lovely."

"Come, come, sir, I fear you jest. I am a mother of four and I am nearing thirty."

"In two years' time . . . and have kept your figure, your beauty, and your equilibrium. And as a blonde, I shall be hard put to protect you in Rome, where the entire masculine population will form into a queue and follow you down the street!"

"Oh, such nonsense as you talk!" she chided. "I will be hard to put to keep the ladies from languishing for you. But it will be delightful . . . or rather wonderful to see the Eternal City. I can hardly wait!"

"You will have to wait . . . it's a long journey."

"I shan't mind . . . I know it will inspire me as well as you."

His arm tightened about her waist, and he bent to whisper, "As you ought to know without my telling you, my own beloved, I have long ceased to find my inspiration in foreign cities." He kissed her.

"Oh, that was lovely," she said when he finally lifted his

ad. "But you shouldn't really embrace me out here . . .
ink what Grandmother would say? She . . ."

Her words were muffled by a second kiss that was longer
d even more satisfying than the first. "It is late to talk of
nventions, is it not?" he inquired softly.

Verity nodded. "I expect it is," she agreed happily. Arm
arm with her husband, she walked up the flagstoned path
at stretched across their blooming garden.

About the Author

Ellen Fitzgerald is a pseudonym for a well-known romance writer. A graduate of the University of Southern California with a B.A. in English and an M.A. in Drama, Ms. Fitzgerald has also attended Yale University and has had numerous plays produced throughout the country. In her spare time, she designs and sells jewelry. Ms. Fitzgerald lives in New York City.

JOIN THE *REGENCY ROMANCE* READERS' PANEL

Help us bring you more of the books you like by filling out this survey and mailing it in today.

1. Book Title: _____

   Book #: _____

2. Using the scale below, how would you rate this book on the following features? Please write in one rating from 0-10 for each feature in the spaces provided.

POOR		NOT SO GOOD			O.K.			GOOD		EXCEL-LENT
0	1	2	3	4	5	6	7	8	9	10

RATING

Overall opinion of book .... _____

Plot/Story .... _____

Setting/Location .... _____

Writing Style .... _____

Character Development .... _____

Conclusion/Ending .... _____

Scene on Front Cover .... _____

3. About how many romance books do you buy for yourself each month? _____

4. How would you classify yourself as a reader of Regency romances?
   I am a ( ) light ( ) medium ( ) heavy reader.

5. What is your education?
   ( ) High School (or less) ( ) 4 yrs. college
   ( ) 2 yrs. college ( ) Post Graduate

6. Age _____ 7. Sex: ( ) Male ( ) Female

Please Print Name_____

Address_____

City _____ State _____ Zip _____

Phone # ( ) _____

Thank you. Please send to New American Library, Research Dept., 1633 Broadway, New York, NY 10019.

SIGNET Regency Romances You'll Enjoy